NANCY WILLIAMS

HELLBENDER BOOKS

an imprint of Sunbury Press, Inc.
Mechanicsburg, PA USA

an imprint of Sunbury Press, Inc.
Mechanicsburg, PA USA

For information about special discounts for bulk purchases, please contact Sunbury Press Orders Dept. at (855) 338-8359 or orders@sunburypress.com.

To request one of our authors for speaking engagements or book signings, please contact Sunbury Press Publicity Dept. at publicity@sunburypress.com.

ISBN: 978-1-62006-326-2 (Trade paperback)

Library of Congress Control Number: 2019951175

FIRST HELLBENDER BOOKS EDITION: September 2019

Product of the United States of America
0 1 1 2 3 5 8 13 21 34 55

Set in Bookman Old Style
Designed by Crystal Devine
Cover by Lawrence Knorr
Edited by Lawrence Knorr

Continue the Enlightenment!

For Chloe

1

HE MIGHT BE THE ONE.

She stole a glance at his profile, dimly lit by the dashboard lights, a profile only three hours old. She'd met him in a most convenient way, at a bar. The Firehouse, to be exact, this very night, and their conversation had been easy from the beginning, with none of the nervous halts and starts she'd come to know too well. He was handsome enough and laughed at her jokes. Most nights, that's all it took.

Now, bumping along the pock-marked road up Radio Tower Hill, the summer slipstream lifting her hair through the open window, she knew it was more than that. It *could* be more than that. The funny way he talked about his friends, his mother. His quirky cousin in New Jersey who painted western sunsets on broom handles and made a living at it. She felt in on his life. In on *him*.

"Where are we going?" she asked.

He gave her a sly look she liked. "You don't know?"

She did, of course. Everyone knew the breakaway atop Radio Tower Hill was a classic make-out spot. It overlooked the soft lights of town, surrounded by woods and cupped by stars. It was also known to be haunted.

"Ever been up here?" he asked.

She shook her head and looked out the window. "I never kiss and tell."

He laughed and took her hand. "Me either."

He turned the car onto a side road that was little more than a cow path. There *had* been cows up here at one time, or some kind of livestock. Farmers from some old country she cared little about. The only thing she cared about was what would happen next.

He parked and cut the engine. The cooling ticks gave way to a silence that loomed suddenly. Beyond the hood of the car lay a whole lot of open air: the road ended at a precipice with a two-hundred-foot drop, a scree slope that tumbled into an exhausted gravel pit. Around them arched the shadows of old-growth timber, some of whose roots drooped exposed by the crumbling fall, groping like petrified tentacles.

He turned to her. She'd never gone this quick before, always made them wait like a good girl. But when he leaned in to kiss her, she knew it was all right. His hands in her hair, his tongue, just enough. *You're beautiful,* she thought. This *is beautiful.*

He broke the kiss and looked at her. "Let's go for a walk."

She blinked. "What? A walk?"

"Yeah." That sly grin came again. "I want to show you something."

She shifted in her seat and then offered her own version of his smile. "I don't want to see anything I can't see from right here."

He laughed. "Seriously. Come on—it'll be fun."

She looked about uneasily. "I don't want to. You know what they say about it up here. About those *things.*"

He gave her a patronizing look. "Oh, for God's sake. That's an urban legend. Monsters to scare you around the campfire and at slumber parties when we were kids. Don't worry—I'll be the perfect gentleman. I'll even get the door for you."

He swung out of the car and disappeared. She shivered. She felt very alone and vulnerable, of a sudden. What was she doing up here in a place supposedly possessed by mad beasts with a man she barely knew? *I can't do this anymore,* she thought. *This is the last time.*

Minutes passed, stacking up like cordwood. Where had he gone? She pulled out her phone. Fifteen minutes. Then twenty. She looked out into the dark, but the dark told her nothing. Fear that had been sitting at the base of her spine like a red ball of mercury started inching upward, toward the flashing light of full-blown panic.

Something bumped the car. She uttered a small cry and craned her neck around. There was nothing to see but blackness. She called his name, her voice wobbling.

The bump came again, harder this time. Moaning, she fumbled at the door handle, her hair hanging in her face. God, where *was* he?

The passenger door flew open, squealing on its hinges. She screamed. Someone—some *thing*—grabbed her and flung her from the car. She landed on her side and rolled onto her back, her arms shielding her face.

A shadow loomed near, blocking out the stars. It extended a hand, and in the dark, terror driving out all rational thought, she saw a monstrosity: fingers curled into claws, the nails thick and yellowed. Eyes glowed an electric blue, suspended like phosphorescence in a black sea.

The shadow drew nearer, and she had only a moment to recognize it for what it was. Then it fell on her.

CARRIE SAT IN THE PARKING LOT of the Pickway Plaza, waiting for eight-thirty. The sun rose in a perfect red orb outside her driver's side window, promising to burn off the mist clinging to the low hills surrounding the town. Gulls squabbled over scraps of pizza crust and other offal; if she closed her eyes, she could almost imagine she was at the beach, albeit a shitty one.

She was waiting for Bro's Notary to open, and the start of her new job. It wasn't her first day—that had been two months ago—but it still felt foreign and stressful. Eight-thirty was when the first of her co-workers would arrive. She wouldn't get her own key until she'd passed her probationary period, which, she hoped, she would never see.

She'd been laid off from her real job: Volunteer Coordinator at the local battered women's shelter. An unfortunate budget shortfall at the state level; nothing to be done. The director, a woman Carrie had worked with for eight years, cried when she delivered the news, promising when things improved, Carrie's job would be reinstated. That had been a year ago. She continued to volunteer in the evenings a couple of times a week, helping in the shelter and on the crisis hotline, despite how awkward it felt. Then her unemployment had run out. The local economy being what it was, that is to say, in the shitter, she'd found nothing comparable to her old job.

Fortunately, Carrie's husband had a decent job working in the IT department at the local college, but it was not good enough that they could make it on one income. Ben had kindly told Carrie to take her time and look—something would give. Something had: her. And here she was.

An El Camino pulled up alongside her Honda, its muffler blatting and belching black smoke. The driver gunned the engine once before killing it and opened the door in her own cloud of smoke—blue instead of black. Roberta Bromeyer, all three hundred pounds of her, emerged, hefting a purse the size of a saddlebag in one hand and an insulated lunch sack in the other, a cigarette dangling from her mouth. She was loud, abrasive and swore like a sailor; somewhere, Carrie assumed, underneath the thick layer of fat and cynicism, beat the heart of a decent person, but she had yet to encounter it.

"Good morning, Bert," Carrie said, shutting her door.

"Nothing good about it so far," Bert said. "Old Bob took a big shit on the living room rug this morning. I near stepped in it."

"Is Old Bob one of your dogs?"

Bert gave her a dry look. "No, he's my husband."

She unlocked the door to the office and flipped on the light. The office itself was small: one big room with a counter running the length of it, a locked closet containing license plates, a small bathroom, and an even smaller breakroom.

"Best tell Lola to order some more passenger plates if she ever gets here," Bert said, setting her saddlebag on the counter with a grunt. "We're near out, last I looked."

The other woman who worked there was not named Lola but Jennifer. Bert called her Lola for reasons of her own. Jennifer was in her late forties and a little flaky by anyone's standards.

Bert looked over the morning paper while Carrie got the cash drawer out. "Looks like another girl went missing," she mused. "Emily Dawson, thirty-two, from Saegertown."

Carrie looked up. "That's the second one since March."

The door opened and Lola/Jennifer came in. "Sorry I'm late—hello everyone!"

Bert folded the paper and gave her a look. "Lucky for you this ain't corporate America. What's that stink?"

Lola/Jennifer carried her personals in a giant tote bag she'd gotten for free from one of the local funeral homes. From this, she withdrew her lunch which, by the smell, probably consisted of the usual tofu, seaweed and soba noodles in some pungent sauce, the ingredients of which she was reluctant to reveal, but insisted were the key to good health. This seemed unlikely since she called in sick a lot. Bert, who lived on her own admixture of light beer, cigarettes, and KFC, had never taken a sick day in her life.

Carrie didn't want to let the missing girls drop. "Are the police getting anywhere? Two missing women in a town this small is pretty excessive."

"More'n that," Bert said, pulling the string on the open sign. "This one makes eight or nine by now. This's been going on for fifteen years. Anyway, I thought runaways were your department."

"Battered women aren't all runaways, Bert." Carrie picked up the paper and scanned it. "Besides, this girl wasn't a runaway. She was last seen leaving a bar with some guy. Of course, no one can remember what he looked like. I bet the cops would love to get their hands on him."

Bert made no comment. Carrie went to the breakroom to put her own lunch, a very pedestrian P B and J, in the fridge. The dead girls wouldn't leave her—she didn't know if they were dead, of course, but it was a likely assumption. Whatever the police were doing, the town was on high alert. Women Carrie knew were avoiding going out at night alone—though this last case took the starch out of that strategy—and Meadville's few homeless men had been rounded up and questioned with no results.

Except for one: Reggie Spavine, a young street rat who'd been a straight-A student at Meadville High until he took a sharp turn off the grid about a year after he graduated, eight years before. He had become a bit of a fixture, buzzing through town on an old Schwinn bicycle, plastic wicker basket and all, and, most notably, with his cat Gravy Train, or GT to his most dedicated followers. Gravy Train would ride, regal and unaffected, draped over Reggie's shoulders, even as Reggie pedaled madly through traffic, rain or shine, snow or sun.

"It's the Pig People," Reggie had said when interviewed by the paper. "They are running out of women up on Round Top and they're coming into town. You can lock your doors, but if they want you, they will get you."

Needless to say, local law enforcement was unimpressed by this theory. The pig people story had been around for years; Carrie didn't give it any credence either, but a lot of Reggie's fans did. Propaganda-style posters went up around town depicting Porky Pig with horns and a pitchfork, a bloodied virgin slung over one shoulder with the caption, "Save our sisters—eat more bacon!" In a not so funny prank, someone left a gutted pig carcass on the courthouse lawn.

Carrie emerged from the back just as the front doorbell jangled. The guy who came through the door was late thirty-ish, decent-looking, and held the tell-tale manila envelope signaling title transfer in one hand. Bert was still reconciling the deposit and Lola/Jennifer was busy doing anything to avoid eye contact with their first customer. Carrie sighed.

"Can I help you?"

He stepped forward, a little awkwardly, she thought. "I hope so. I just moved back to Pennsylvania and I need to register my truck. I have my driver's license, insurance. I'm not sure what else you need."

Of course you don't. "Do you have the title?"

He opened his folder and showed it to her. She rummaged through a drawer and then handed him a form. "This is an MV-41. The state requires you get the VIN and the GVWR verified. Take it to an inspection mechanic along with the truck and he'll fill out the highlighted parts. Bring it back, along with your driver's license and insurance. Any questions?"

He shifted from one foot to the other, giving it a lot of thought, apparently. Carrie decided he was more than just decent-looking. He was tall with a pair of fine gray eyes that met hers with what seemed to be a bit of a troubled look. Haunted.

"You said you're moving back to PA," Carrie ventured. She looked at his newly minted license. "Andrew. Korn. Andy Korn?"

His blush was sudden and furious. "Yes. I was living in New York. Syracuse. But now I'm back. I grew up here."

"Oh." Carrie heard echoes of schoolyard taunts: *Candy Korn, Candy Andy, Kornhole Andy, haha!* "Well. Welcome back?"

"Maybe."

His gaze went from troubled to outright pained, so much so Carrie wished she'd kept her mouth shut. Even Lola/Jennifer paused in her busy work and studied the man with interest.

Carrie reached out and gave his hand an impulsive squeeze. "A fresh start. Tough, but it'll be good."

He caught her hand and held it, smoothing her fingers, thumbing her wedding band. She let him, watching the creases in his face deepen, some memory tracking across it like the shadows of clouds. Then he let go and gathered up his things.

"Thank you. I'll get this form filled out."

"What was that all about?" Bert said from the doorway of her office after he left.

"Something bad happened in New York," Carrie said, watching out the window as Andy got into his truck. "He wasn't wearing a wedding ring."

"He certainly was interested in yours," Lola/Jennifer said. "Weird."

"If anybody's an expert on weird, that'd be you, Lola," Bert said and disappeared into the office again.

Later that evening, after supper with Ben, Carrie left for the shelter to put in a six-hour stint. The regular volunteer had called off; normally Carrie wouldn't agree to such a long shift on a weeknight. She'd be beat tomorrow, but if the funding ever rolled back in, she didn't want anyone to be able to say that Carrie Owens didn't go the extra mile.

Carrie hit the buzzer and waited to be let in. The security system wasn't state of the art, but pretty good. Nina, the volunteer she was relieving, opened the door. "Hey. How's the notary business?"

"Fabulous," Carrie said, rolling her eyes. "How's things here?"

Nina gave her an apologetic look. "I'm leaving you with some new business. The cops just dropped off a pregnant girl they found wandering around over by Mill Run. She says she was raped. They had her checked out at the hospital and then she told them she wanted to come here."

"Is she a return customer?"

"I didn't get a chance to look. We've also got Tula Mae and her three kids back for round two. She's in the playroom trying to get them ready for bed with a bunch of video games and a half-gallon of Kool-Aid."

"Nice." Carrie followed Nina back to the shelter office, a small room with two phones, a desk, and a couple of chairs. A closed-circuit TV with a view of the front door hung on the wall above the desk. "Where is she?"

"Room three. Her name is Paula Davis. Sorry to leave you with this. Good luck."

Carrie arranged a water bottle, snacks and an old Stephen King paperback on the desk and then poked her head into the playroom. Tula Mae was a skinny young thing scared of her own shadow who hadn't been able to convince herself, despite all evidence to the contrary, the man she'd married was a monster.

"Hey, Tula. How's things?"

The girl shrugged. "Back again. Did Nina tell you about the cats?"

Carrie paused. "No. What cats?"

"I'm friends with a girl who works at the animal shelter and she said somebody broke in last night and stole, like, three. Creepy, huh? I hope they're all right. People do things to cats, you know? I had this neighbor—"

Carrie held up her hand. "Don't tell me. I'll have nightmares as it is. Maybe it was a cat lover. They're known to do crazy things."

Tula laughed. "Right."

Carrie went back to room three and rapped on the door. The girl sat on the bed like a limp marionette, wearing a filthy tank top that didn't come close to covering her protruding belly. The bloated cones of her breasts lolled atop it, her nipples commanding attention. Below this, hospital scrubs and socks with rubber grips on both sides. The smell hit Carrie like a wall. Evidently, the girl hadn't bathed in a long time.

"Hi," Carrie said, mustering warmth. "My name is Carrie. I'll be helping you get settled in tonight. Your name is Paula?"

The girl lifted her face and looked at Carrie. Her eyes were fierce and desperate; her hands and feet came to life as if someone had engaged a set of invisible strings. She gripped the edge of the bed.

"I need to have an abortion."

Carrie felt a chill, but not from shock or horror at the request. Something in the woman's face, worse than despair at her situation or the myriad other things she might be feeling. It was terror.

Carrie held out her hand. "Come on, Paula. Let's go talk about it."

She got the young woman a sweatshirt and a cup of tea. Out in the hall, Tula Mae walked back and forth, ostensibly to get her one-year-old to sleep, all the while sizing up the new inmate. Irritated, Carrie got up and closed the office door.

"Where were you staying before the police found you?"

Paula uttered a high-pitched jittery laugh. "Staying? Up on Round Top."

"Were you being held against your will?" Carrie asked. Paula nodded. "By who?"

Paula put her face in her hands and started a nervous heel tap. "I don't want to talk about it."

Carrie sat back. "I know it's hard. But I think you'll feel better."

"I just need you to help me get rid of it," Paula said, her voice muffled. "I can't have this . . . thing."

Carrie leaned forward and put both hands on the desk. "I know the prospect of having a child conceived from rape is difficult, but I have to tell you, no one is going to perform an abortion at this late stage. How far along are you—seven, eight months? You can always give it up for adoption."

Paula laughed again, sharp and humorless. "True. The humane society's right next door, isn't it?"

Carrie didn't know what to say to that. She watched as a single tear spilled over Paula's cheek. She swiped it angrily away with the back of her hand.

"Can I go now? I'd like to take a shower and crash. I'm tired."

"Yeah. Yeah, you bet. I'll get you a towel and a hospitality kit. The bathroom is a shared one. Don't be scared if somebody walks in on you. There's no locks on any of the doors."

"It's fine," Paula said, accepting the little bag of donated hotel soaps and shampoo. "I'll just be glad to get clean again. Thank you."

You and me both, sister, Carrie thought. "No problem. Give a holler if you need anything else."

Carrie went back to the office and, after giving the room a shot of air freshener, sat down and searched the shelter database for Paula. No records found. She spent about twenty minutes creating a file and prepping Paula's intake paperwork. Then she settled into the novel. Cujo was just showing the first signs of rabies. She'd read it at least a half-dozen times.

A scream split the silence. Carrie jerked in her chair, knocking her water bottle off the desk. She ran into the hall and saw Tula Mae standing in the doorway of the bathroom, her youngest in the crook of one arm, her other hand clapped over her mouth.

"What's the matter?" Carrie asked. She pushed Tula out of the way and put her own hand to her mouth.

"Oh my God."

Paula Davis was hunched on the floor against the wall underneath the towel dispenser, her legs splayed. Blood pooled around her, almost black against the white linoleum, and continued to flow in a steady stream from her exposed vulva. One blood-stained hand clutched the crumpled hospital scrubs; in the other, she gripped a wire coat hanger, now twisted into a glittering hook. A brownish pink hunk of flesh clung to the end like some ghastly piece of bait.

Tula's other two children, a boy and girl, ran up, craning their necks to see. The little girl, maybe six, got an eyeful and emitted a prolonged shriek rivaling any fire whistle. The boy stood agog, Darth Vader clutched against his chest.

"*Get those kids out of here!*" Carrie yelled. She pushed Tula down the hall to get her going. Carrie knelt beside Paula. The woman was looking down at her spasming belly and panting.

"What the hell are you doing?" Carrie hissed.

"What's it look like?" Paula said between gritted teeth. "Getting rid of it."

Carrie stood. "I'm calling 911. I'll be right back."

She spent the next few minutes answering the dispatcher's questions as patiently as she could. When another scream cut the air, Carrie told the woman she had to go. She ran back to the bathroom to find things were progressing. The baby was crowning.

She knelt again by Paula, trying to keep out of the blood spreading around the woman, and put her hand on her arm. She had absolutely no idea what to say.

"Try and take even breaths," she said finally, knowing it was woefully inadequate.

"Fuck that," Paula said, rolling her eyes toward Carrie. "And fuck that ambulance, too."

"Paula," Carrie said. "You'll bleed to death."

"I don't care," Paula said, tears squeezing from her eyes. "Just make sure *it* doesn't live, either."

They heard two short siren blasts, announcing the ambulance. Carrie stood; just then Paula's body convulsed violently. She gave an agonized cry. The baby was coming, paramedics or not.

Carrie yelled for Tula. "Let the paramedics in!"

Carrie got some towels and piled them around Paula's legs. Pitiful, threadbare donations, they were immediately soaked. She folded one and put it directly between her legs. The air was thick with the smell of blood, and something else: a flesh smell, the smell of viscera. Carrie felt her gorge rise.

The baby's entire head appeared. The rest of the body came free with one final bloody contraction and a wail of relief from Paula, and then Carrie realized something was wrong, terribly wrong.

Her first thought, giddy and hysterical, was: *That's the ugliest baby I've ever seen.* Then, as her brain registered what she was seeing, she snatched her hands away with a mixture of horror and revulsion.

"Oh," she breathed. "Oh my. I don't—oh that can't be."

Paula moaned thickly. "Is it dead Carrie? Please tell me it's dead."

The little creature on the towel stirred and made a feeble squawk. Carrie's heart went out to it, despite its . . . its . . . well, everything. She picked it up and wiped the little face with the towel. The baby's hands and feet were badly deformed, the outer fingers and toes fused together, leaving a split down the middle. And the face—

The EMTs appeared, startling Carrie so she almost dropped the baby. A man and a woman, they filled the room with a sudden, comforting presence. Tula stayed in the doorway, one hand fluttering at her throat.

"Holy crow," the man said. "What a mess."

Carrie half-turned, presenting the infant. "It's born," she said. "There's something wrong with it—"

Paula's left foot shot out like a piston, striking the baby's head. There was a faint snap, like the breaking of a toothpick. Its little arms sagged.

"*No!*" Carrie cried. The female EMT swept in and took the infant from Carrie. Working quickly, she cut the umbilical cord and then ran from the bathroom. That was the last Carrie saw of the baby.

The other EMT began working on Paula. Blood continued to pour from her loins. Paula herself seemed not to notice. She slid sideways, her hair plastered to her head in a sweaty helmet, eyes vacant and glazed. He patted her cheeks.

"Come on honey. Stay with me." He looked at Carrie. "Hand me my bag, will you?"

Carrie numbly did as she was told. She saw the coat hanger again, and the hook with its ragged piece of flesh. She made it to the toilet just in time and vomited forcefully.

The lady EMT returned and began helping her partner. The front door buzzed; Tula Mae went to get it, and soon two cops appeared.

One of them touched Carrie gently on the shoulder. "Why don't you come with me."

Carrie allowed herself to be led back to the office, where fifteen minutes ago, things had been relatively sane. She sat down at the desk and put her head in her hands.

"Can you tell me what happened?" he asked.

Carrie recounted the events. "The baby's dead, isn't it? She kicked it. I was holding it and she kicked it."

The officer had an iPad and was busily typing in her statement. His phone sounded. He looked at it and sighed. "Yes, it's dead. And so is the mother, apparently."

3   CARRIE SAT ON THE SHELTER'S FRONT stoop, her arms wrapped around her knees. The night was warm, with a light breeze ruffling her hair now and then. Overhead, nighthawks swooped for insects, just beyond the halo of the streetlamps. Their sharp calls took her back to her college days when she and a gaggle of friends would be coming back from the bars. To her, the sound meant summer and cavalier youth. She hoped tonight wouldn't sully the memory.

Everyone was gone; the ambulance with its sad cargo, and the EMTs, bloodied and weary. The policemen, awkward in their comforting. Carrie had to wait for the shelter director. She'd called Anne and told her what happened. Anne said she'd be down as soon as she could. She would assume the rest of the night's duties herself, so Carrie could go home. Anne was a hell of a director and a counselor to the bone.

When she arrived, she gave Carrie a long hug. "Are you okay?"

"I guess," Carrie said. "I think I'm still in shock."

"Call me tomorrow, when you have time. We'll need to fill out a report, and you'll need to process this."

"Counseling for the counselor," Carrie said ruefully. "I'll try. I have to work."

She thought she saw Anne wince a little at this. She gave Carrie another quick hug and then went inside.

Carrie lingered on the stoop, studying the night sky. It was closing in on ten o'clock. She'd called Ben and told him she'd be early—there'd been an incident. He hadn't sounded too concerned, for incidents weren't uncommon. *Not like this one*, she thought. *Yowzah.*

A figure appeared out of the dark, his bicycle looping wide arcs in the parking lot, reminding her of the swooping nighthawks above her head. It was Reggie Spavine, the ever-present GT draping his shoulders like a king's mantle. Reggie was a frequent visitor to their lot, the mental health facility being just two blocks away. He never stayed long and didn't bother anyone—he just liked to ride circles in their parking lot. Anne had seen no harm in it.

"Hi Reggie," Carrie called. "You're out late tonight."

"Hello night lady," Reggie said, never pausing in his pedaling. He referred to any volunteer after five as a night lady. "It's late all right. What are you doing out on the stoop?"

"Thinking. Getting ready to go home."

"Mmm. Big doings afoot tonight. Lots of flashing lights. That cannot be good."

"Right," Carrie said. "Big doings. Not good at all."

Reggie looped and spun. GT yawned. "Lots of bad coming. You best go home, pretty lady. The night is not your time anymore. Not with your genes."

Carrie looked down at herself. "My jeans? What's wrong with my jeans?"

"Mmm. Nothing is wrong with your genes. You are a ripe apple. It would be best to get on home."

Carrie felt a chill. Reggie wasn't looking at her, but he was riding his bike in tighter circles. Now he was between her and her car.

"I think I'll do that," she said, standing. Reggie pedaled closer and then eased his bike to a stop about ten feet away. His face was ghostly pale, and God, he was thin. His clavicles jutted above the raggedy white t-shirt he wore, and shadows darkened the flesh beneath his cheekbones. High cheekbones and his smile revealed good teeth. *Good genes*, she thought.

She gave a start. "Oh."

GT turned his yellow eyes on her. His tail flicked at Reggie's chin like a serpent's tongue.

"Did you know the girl who was here tonight, Reggie? Do you know what happened to her?"

Reggie looked off into the night. "I did not know her. But I do know from where she came. She came from Round Top. I saw her come out of the woods. I followed her here."

"Round Top. You mean Radio Tower Hill?"

Reggie shrugged. "Call it what you like, night lady. It is Round Top."

"What's up there?"

A smile stole across Reggie's face, a slippery shadow. "The People are there. They live in The Warrens, underground."

"What people—the pig people?"

"Mmm." Reggie rolled back and forth on his bike. "I know you are skeptical, but they are real. Very real indeed."

Carrie felt the hairs on her neck stand up. She remembered the baby's face. Its fused fingers and toes. How they'd looked, well, cloven.

"My brother used to tell me about them. How they'd get me if I was bad. It scared me—clever tactic. How do you know about them?"

"I have shunned the Control System, and therefore my energy field is high. I can move freely between worlds. I have seen The People and know what they are up to."

"And what is that?"

Reggie gave her a sad look. "They are using human beings as their tools. Genetic playthings. They want to assimilate and walk above ground like men."

Carrie decided she'd heard enough. "I'd like to get in my car now, Reggie. Will you let me by?"

The young man hesitated so long Carrie feared he wouldn't. Normally she wasn't afraid of Reggie, but she was alone, it was dark, and the smell of Paula Davis' blood hung about her face like a pall.

At last, he eased his bike into motion, rolling another slow figure eight. Carrie walked quickly to her car and got in, popping the lock as soon as she shut the door. Reggie rolled up and tapped the window. She let out a startled yip.

He leaned in so close his breath fogged the glass. His voice was dim and muffled.

"You be careful, Miss Good Genes. You could be one of the chosen. There are no more women on Round Top, not anymore."

He offered a sad smile, his oddly perfect teeth glinting in the light of the streetlamp. Carrie started her car and sped away, leaving tire marks on the pavement.

✻

Ten minutes later, she pulled into their drive and parked next to Ben's aging Subaru. She could see light flickering from inside the house: the television. He was up.

Their house was a two-story stick-built, big for just the two of them, on the north end of town. They had no close neighbors. Beyond their road, Pennsylvania farmland unfurled, checkered with pockets of deep woods run through with winding streams. Good country, soft and rolling, with voluptuous growth in the summers and thick snows topping the hills like buttercream in winter.

Carrie walked through the kitchen, dropping her purse on the table, and headed for the living room where Ben waited on the couch, watching Law and Order through half-lidded eyes. He was handsome and boyish in his PJ bottoms and t-shirt, lean and athletic in build, competent to a fault in most everything he tried, except folding laundry and wiping off the counter. He stirred and sat up.

"Hey," she said, collapsing next to him. "You didn't have to wait up."

"It's not that late, and you sounded pretty shook up. What happened?"

He whistled and shook his head when she finished telling him. "That's some hardcore shit. You okay?"

"No, I'm not. I'm going to tell Anne I'm done volunteering. My motives aren't pure. I'm not a counselor. The job I liked is never coming back. Looks like I'll be stuck with this crappy notary job for a while."

Ben put his hand on her thigh. "Something better will come along. You've got a degree, experience."

"And good looks. Don't forget good looks."

He grinned and slid his hand further up her thigh. "Fuck that. Downright hot."

She kissed his cheek. "You're sweet. I don't think it's going to get me much. I know it sounds like a handy excuse, but even at thirty-eight, I'm turning into a bit of an old horse. The job market's tough. All those fresh-faced college grads out there have an edge.

Energetic, trainable. To an employer, I'm set in my ways and want too much money."

"That's pretty cynical, babe."

Carrie shrugged. "What can I say? I'm a realist."

He gave her thigh a final squeeze. "Okay realist—let's get to bed. It'll all look better in the morning."

"Yeah, and I have to work tomorrow."

He looked at her, startled. "You're going to work? After a night like tonight?"

She smiled grimly. "No time off at Bert's little house of horrors."

Ben shook his head. "What an old crank."

Carrie shrugged again. "She's a realist."

**ANDY LAY IN HIS TWIN-SIZE BED,** staring up at the same ceiling he'd stared at for the first eighteen years of his life, listening to his mother putter around the kitchen downstairs. The smell of coffee drifted to him but did not entice. It was decaf, and freeze-dried. His parents had started drinking it after his mother's coffee pot privileges were revoked last year when she filled the reservoir with bleach instead of water.

His parents lived in a two-bedroom modular on a quiet little street called Sunnyside Avenue, about a mile and a half from Rolling Meadows Retirement Home, where Andy hoped they'd agree to install themselves within the year. The end of the week would be preferable, but Andy was not so much a realist as an out and out pessimist. His folks doggedly refused to do the right thing, which was

die

acknowledge they couldn't live on their own anymore. Not that he didn't love them, but it was difficult. His dad was maddeningly hard of hearing and had grown more irascible as his arthritis advanced. Never one to mince words, he had gotten downright nasty. There had been no congenial conversations at the Korn dinner table for several years now. Mostly they were one-sided shouting matches, Andy's father—Bill—excoriating his wife for burning dinner again, or to pass the goddamned salt. Fortunately, in a way, Judy Korn had fallen so far down the dark well of dementia she seldom registered these outrages and would merely ask Andy—for the fifth time just since the meal began—if there were many black people living in upstate New York.

His bladder finally prodded him out of bed, and he padded down the short hall to the bathroom, clad only in his boxers. Above the sound of his own pissing, he could clearly follow the Today Show. Probably so could the neighbors. He knew his father was hunched in front of the TV, maybe five feet away from it in his recliner with a tray in front of him, clutching the remote and occasionally jabbing it at the screen.

"Judy!" he bawled. "Bring me the goddamned paper!"

A pause. Andy couldn't make out whether his mother had gone into the living room or not. He did know it was going to be a scorcher in the mid-west. Al Roker said so, at about eight hundred decibels.

"What?" Another pause. "*What?*"

Andy sighed and flushed. *Another day in my new life.*

He showered, thought about shaving, and dismissed the idea. He donned a pair of jeans and a t-shirt and then braced his way to the kitchen.

"Good morning, dear," his mom said, ruffling his hair as he sat down at the table. "Would you like some coffee?"

"Just some OJ. I'll get it."

She patted his hand. "Don't be silly."

She went to the refrigerator and set a carton of sour cream in front of him. "There you go."

"Thanks." He waited until she'd turned back to the stove and then exchanged the sour cream for the plastic jug of Tropicana. Behind him, his father bellowed for the paper again.

"Mom, is the paper here?"

She stared at him, wide-eyed and blinking as a fawn. "What paper?"

"The newspaper," he said wearily. "Dad wants his paper."

"Oh." She drifted to the kitchen door and looked out on the front porch. "I don't see it."

Andy rose and pushed past her, not unkindly. The paper was there, rolled and tucked in its blue cellophane wrapper. Evidently, his mom's eyesight was just as bad as his dad's hearing. They made a fine pair.

He tossed the wrapper in the trash and read the headline as he walked into the living room, and then stopped just short of his dad's chair.

TRAGEDY AT LOCAL SHELTER

He skimmed the story, which seemed plenty horrific, but what held his attention was the picture. There were two, actually: one of an ambulance with several police officers crowded around it, clearly taken at the hospital. The other was of some woman he didn't know—the director of the shelter, the paper said—at an unrelated speaking engagement. It was an older photo—apparently the only one the paper could get a hold of on short notice. Off to the side, almost out of focus, was a face he did know. It was the woman from the notary, the pretty one who'd waited on him.

He read the story more closely. The woman wasn't mentioned by name, but he remembered it from the business card she'd given him: Carrie. Evidently, she moonlighted at the shelter. He studied the picture a long time, remembering the instructions she'd given him about his truck. He'd not done a thing she'd told him. Apathy had long fingers, and they dug deep.

"Is that my paper?"

Andy looked up, blinking much like his mother. "Huh?"

"I said, *is that my paper!*"

"Oh. Sorry. Here." He handed it over, feeling thick-headed. His father snatched it, pawing past the front page.

"I don't care about any of that claptrap," he said. "I just want the obits. Maybe I'm in there. Here—take this. It's the help wanted section. Give yourself something to do today."

Bill Korn's upper lip curled back over his dentures in what passed for a smile. Andy felt hot blood crawl up his cheeks.

"Fuck you, dad," he said.

"What?"

"I said thanks, dad."

He went back into the kitchen. His mother was stirring something into her coffee and frowning. "This is the worst creamer."

He looked. It was flour. "I'm going out for a while, mom. I'm not sure when I'll be back. Maybe after lunch. I have some stuff to do at the notary and then I might work on the boat for a few hours. Dad says the oil needs to be changed."

His father had never said any such thing. He might not even remember he owned a boat. It had been given to him by Chuck Pettit, the owner of the marina, in lieu of paying the brokering fees when Bill had sold Chuck's house two years ago. It had been dry-docked at the marina ever since, a big old Bayliner that may or may not float. It had never seen the water as far as Andy knew.

"All right, that's nice of you dear," said his mom. "Will Melinda go with you, or does she have to work?"

His shoulders stiffened. *It's not a dig,* he thought. *It's mom talking, not him.*

"No, mom. Melinda and I got divorced, remember?"

"You did? My goodness, when did that happen?"

"In January. Eight months ago."

He grabbed his wallet and keys before she could ask about Billy.

❋

Andy had every intention of going to the notary first, but when he reached the T in the road he turned left instead of right, toward the lake. His parents' address said Conneaut Lake, but they lived nowhere near it. Houses on the lake were expensive, and Bill Korn would rather go bird watching or nap in his car than push houses for Baker Realty back in his day. Hence the shoebox five miles from the beach.

Even though the boat wasn't in the water, Andy still liked to sit in it. It was *close* to the water, and all the accompanying sounds and smells. He could pretend he was floating, a childish thing, yes, but in his present state of moroseness, he considered it a minor detail.

He pulled into the marina and parked. The day was bright, warming nicely, and the place was busy for a weekday, bustling with transplants from Pittsburgh, mostly. The water was a deep blue, a light breeze ruffling the surface. Andy waved to a few people he recognized but did not know.

The boat, named the *Wishy Washy*, set off by itself at the back of the parking lot on the trailer that had come with it. A canvas cover kept it out of the weather, secured by heavy snaps which Andy now undid, folding the heavy muslin neatly back. He kept a little stepladder nearby and used this to climb aboard. A few pine needles had found their way in; he brushed these away before taking a seat on the vinyl-covered stern lounger.

The view was lovely. He could unobtrusively watch his fellow boaters as they came and went, usually laughing and chatting happily, though on more than one occasion he'd witnessed some pretty vigorous arguments. These usually occurred at the end of the day, after the beer had been flowing for most of the afternoon. Andy himself typically had a six pack to keep him company. It was a little early for that today, though he was dimly aware cocktail hour was creeping up earlier and earlier, and if things continued to go the way they were, noon might seem like a perfectly reasonable five o'clock somewhere.

He'd been there for about a half-hour when a familiar voice hailed him. "Ahoy! Anybody home?"

Andy stood. "Hey, Jason."

Jason Carter was a psychiatrist with his own private practice and had been Andy's closest friend growing up. They'd gone to college together, but Jason had come home and Andy had left. They'd kept in touch, their friendship the easy sort that allowed them to pick up right where they'd left off, no matter how much time had passed. They hung out quite a bit now since Jason set his own schedule and Andy had all the time in the world, courtesy of unemployment.

Jason climbed carefully into the boat. "When are you going to get this suds bucket out on the water, anyway? Does it have a hole in the bottom, or what?"

"I don't know. I don't know anything about boating. I'd probably sink it."

Jason gave him an exasperated look. "And you're not capable of learning?"

"Did you come out here because you needed someone's ass to ride?"

Jason sighed. "No. Sorry. It'd just be pretty sweet to be out on the water instead of sitting in the ass end of a parking lot in what is probably a perfectly operable boat. God forbid you enjoy yourself."

Andy leaned back and gestured at the view. "I am enjoying myself."

Jason raised an eyebrow. "Yeah? How's dear old dad?"

"Boy, you didn't waste any time today, did you? Started right in. What's eating you?"

"Nothing." He held up his hands. "Again, sorry. I just hate to see you like this."

"Is this like an intervention or something?"

Jason laughed. "No. Forget it. What's new—anything?"

"Nothing much. I'm going to the notary today to get my PA plate. It'll be official."

"Well, that's progress."

"Yep." Andy hesitated. "The woman who waited on me last time was pretty nice."

Jason's brow went up again. "Oh yeah? Hot?"

"Yeah. Doesn't matter, though. Married."

"Oh. Well, maybe he's an asshole."

Andy laughed. "Right."

They lapsed into silence. Andy knew he should ask after Jason's wife, Cassandra, but he didn't want to. He knew things were irritatingly perfect. Cassandra was an herbalist with her own shop, stunning and excruciatingly nice. He'd never met anyone so without apparent flaw. Unless perfection itself was a flaw, which he knew to be true only to the jealous and underachieved.

Jason and Cassandra also had two children, a boy and a girl, ages ten and eight. He definitely didn't want to ask about the boy, for he was the same age Billy would have been. He suspected Jason knew this and refrained from bringing up Matthew unless Andy was in an extremely good mood. Which was infrequent.

Andy stood. "I guess I better get moving. This isn't as much fun as I thought it was going to be."

Jason also stood to go. "I ruined your good time, didn't I?"

"No," Andy lied. "Just a good dose of reality. I need to find an inspection mechanic and then go home and work on my resume. What do you say we get some beers and reconnoiter back here around four?"

Jason grinned. "Deal. You're welcome to come over to my place after, for dinner. I think we're just having burgers. Nothing special, but, you know."

"Yeah. Maybe." He wouldn't, and knew Jason knew he wouldn't.

They climbed down the ladder and walked back to their respective cars. Jason paused at the door of his Lexus. Andy cringed a little, bracing for some last bit of unsolicited advice from his well-meaning friend. Which he got, though not what Andy expected. Instead, Jason brought up the notary again.

"You should find out about her a little. She might be one of those women who just wears a ring to keep the losers away."

"Oh, well, then she's wearing it for me."

Jason shook his head. "Get off it, will you? Christ. Things will look up. You'll get a job. Once you move out of that psychiatric ward and get your own place, you'll feel better. Your old man is a daily dose of poison. You don't deserve this, Andy. You're a good guy."

"Yeah. Tell that to my wife. Tell that to my dead son."

He got into his truck before Jason could protest.

 **CARRIE STOOD AT HER WORKSTATION,** watching an old man make his way across the parking lot toward the office. She liked to make a game of guessing what customers might want. In her limited experience, an old man wearing a hat and carrying a big folder spelled car title transfer. The wife was probably dead since he was alone. Had, maybe a car, a truck, and about three trailers. Some in his name only, some in both names. Possibly smelling of pee.

Carrie threw a glance at Lola/Jennifer, who was counting weight class stickers like her life depended on it. "What do you think, Jen?"

Lola/Jennifer looked up briefly. "Oh, that's a title. Wife's dead. All yours."

Fuck you, Carrie thought, and then put on a smile as the man walked in the door. "Hi! Help you?"

"Oh, I'm beyond help," the old man said, grinning proudly at this trite witticism.

Carrie winced inwardly, and her smile tightened. Every day was the same. The people wore different skins, but inside they were all basically the same: baby birds, mouths gaping with their incessant needs. And she was the worm.

The man's paperwork took a half-hour; people came and went. Bert came back from lunch, reeking of cigarette smoke and fried chicken. Throw half a six pack every afternoon on top of this daily physical assault and call Bert's very existence a miracle. Carrie envisioned an hourglass suspended over Bert's head, the sand running out of it in a steady stream. Carrie imagined all the people she saw every day, going about their business, each with their own hourglass, the sands at varying levels. Old, young—even children.

She suspected Bert's glass was pretty bottom heavy by now unless she'd stoppered up the hole with sheer orneriness.

Bert cast a critical eye about the office. "Lola, do you have to bring out every goddamned sticker just to count them? Christ, the place looks like a going out of business sale."

Lola/Jennifer made no reply, her lips moving silently as she counted. Every now and then, just for fun, Carrie would bark out a random number to throw her off, which was too easy. She supposed it was no cleverer than the old man's stale wisecrack, but she didn't care. It was her way of accepting the new low she'd sunk to.

The doorbell jangled and the cute man with the truck title and the funny name came in. He smiled when he saw her.

"Hi. I was in the other day to register my truck. I brought the form you gave me."

He set it before her, along with his title, driver's license and insurance card. Carrie had liked him before, but now she liked him even more. He'd listened and was prepared.

She glanced at his license. Andy Korn. Right. Unfortunate name. He'd seemed sad that day, and indeed, as she met his gaze again, there was still something haunted working in his eyes. She would tread lightly.

"Well, you're the big winner. Looks like you've got all your ducks in a row." She scribbled some numbers on a piece of paper. "These are the fees you'll be paying. I'll just copy your license and insurance and I'll have you out of here in about ten minutes."

He stood before her silently as she processed the paperwork. She could feel his eyes on her and felt a blush creep up her cheeks.

"Have you worked here long?" he asked.

"Just about three months. I'm still wet behind the ears. Thank you for not having something complicated."

She looked at him. "Where do you work?"

It was his turn to blush. "Nowhere yet. I'm looking."

"What's your field?"

He took a deep breath. "Well, in my other life, I was a financial advisor."

She cocked an eyebrow. "Ah. A numbers guy. One of those people."

He smiled. "What have you got against numbers guys?"

She shrugged demurely. "I was a Communications major. I can't even count."

Behind her, Bert grunted in agreement. Carrie threw a look over her shoulder. "Hey. I heard that."

She turned her attention back to him. His troubled eyes had become lively with their banter. "So anyway, I bet you'll find something in no time. That's a marketable skill. I have none myself, which is why I'm here."

"I heard that," Bert said.

They both laughed. "You must have family here, then," Carrie said. "The only reasons people move here is either for work or family and if it ain't work it must be door number two."

His smile faded a bit. "My parents live here. I grew up here."

She looked at him more closely. He seemed to be about her age. "What year did you graduate from high school?"

"Nineteen-ninety. I went to Conneaut."

"Mmm. I went to Meadville. Eighty-six."

She found the fact that he was younger than her depressing. The sand in her own hourglass seemed to trickle a little faster. She finished his work and hit the print button.

"Okay. You're all set. Here's your credit card and your registration, plate and receipt. You have ten days to get the truck inspected. Anything else?"

He hesitated. He looked down at her left hand and bit his lip. She followed his gaze to her wedding ring.

"Do you wear that for show?" he blurted suddenly.

She blinked. Even Lola/Jennifer paused in mid-count, and behind her, Bert snorted.

"I—well, to show I'm married, yes."

He turned such a sudden deep shade of red Carrie feared his head might explode. He gathered up his things.

"Have a good day," he stammered and bolted for the door.

After the door swung shut, Carrie glanced at her co-workers. Bert shook her head.

"What the hell was that?"

"I don't know," Carrie said. "He's an odd one."

"He likes you," Lola/Jennifer offered.

"No shit," Bert said. "Stay in your lane, Lola—keep counting them stickers."

"I like him. Not that way," she added hastily when the two older women eyed her shrewdly. "But there's something sweet about him."

She stood musing for a bit and then started putting together his paperwork.

Later, at home, Carrie nuked some leftover chicken for dinner and watched TV until nine. Ben was at his weekly bowling league and wouldn't be home until late.

And yet, as she lay in bed, sleep wouldn't come. Andy Korn and his funny remark stuck in her head. Customers seldom touched her, literally or figuratively, yet he had done both. There was definitely a mystery there.

Hopefully nothing like the one at the shelter, she hoped. Nothing could top that. She'd not followed up with Anne and gotten any counseling, which she knew was probably a mistake. She kept putting it off, and so the nightmare clung to her like some nasty oil she couldn't wash off. And Reggie Spavine's talk of her good genes. The People he alluded to. How they were coming into town now. And Paula Davis' baby. Let's not forget that. The baby who had resembled, well, Porky Pig, drawn by a madman.

"That's not possible," she said to the dark room.

No, of course not. Vampires were more believable than what she was conceptualizing. One thing nagged at her—other than the glaring fact of the baby—was that Reggie had been, at one time, quite smart. He might be crazy, but crazy wasn't usually stupid. It was possible he was making stuff up, but why? To get attention? Probably.

She rolled over on her side and wondered briefly, before sleep finally took her, if any more women had gone missing from town.

※

The next morning, she and Ben had coffee on the porch. She had slept like a dead thing, not even waking up when he came home. She felt better, but not enough to feel enthusiastic about facing down the daily horde at Bert's. Ben went in before her, and when she had drained the last drop, she went in and found him in the bedroom, packing.

"Something I said?" she asked, smiling.

He gave her a patient look. "I'm going to Hershey for a couple days, remember? For training?"

She rubbed her forehead. "Shit. I forgot all about that."

He kissed her cheek. "No worries. You've been pretty busy these last few days. I've got to be out of here by eight—the training starts at one. We don't get out until five tomorrow, so by the time I grab some dinner, it'll be close to eleven by the time I get home."

She pouted. "Maybe I'll go see a movie. I hate being here by myself. It's spooky lately."

"Don't let Reggie Spavine's bullshit get in your head. He's a schizophrenic crackhead, nothing more. He probably sees spiders in his Cheerios and knows where Hoffa's buried."

An hour later, she bade him goodbye and headed off to work. As she pulled into her usual spot in front of Bert's, she noticed something on the doormat of the office entrance. She got out and bent to inspect it. It was an ugly reddish-brown mass with fur sticking out in several places. Two long ropes—entrails, she assumed—extended out from the pile in straight, gray lines.

"God," she murmured. "What the hell is that?"

Lola/Jennifer had pulled up in the meantime and joined her. She looked for a moment and then smiled. "It's a hat."

Carrie stared at her. "A *hat*? That is not a hat."

"Sure it is. It's one of those Sherpa hats. See? Those gray things are the ties. Somebody must have thrown it away."

Carrie looked from Lola/Jennifer to the thing at their feet. "Back when I was a younger lass, I used to hunt, okay? That's a gut pile. Or a carcass of some sort. It looks like it's been turned inside out, whatever it was."

Carrie opened the trunk of her car and retrieved an ice scraper. She poked at the thing and managed to turn it over, exposing the remnants of a tail and a single paw. A chill went up her spine; something tweaked her memory, something old and familiar, and frightening. Then it was gone.

"It's a cat," she said. "Definitely not a hat, Sam I am."

Bert pulled up and got out amid a cloud of smoke. "What are you two looking at?"

"Somebody left us a present," Carrie said. "Lola thinks it's a hat."

"I don't think it looks like a hat now," Lola/Jennifer protested. "At first I did."

Bert gave Lola/Jennifer a dull, bulldog look. "That's the ugliest hat I ever saw. There's a shovel out back. Scrape it up and throw it in the dumpster."

She waddled on into the building. "Christ, I hate people."

The rest of Carrie's day passed with the routine onslaught of humanity. Bro's Notary was seldom slow, there being few full-service notaries in town, other than AAA, which, Carrie had heard, had been taken over by some huge conglomerate and was losing its hometown touch. Carrie wouldn't know—she'd never set foot in the place. If this were true, it would explain the steady increase in Bert's business, despite Bert being a colossal grump. She knew what she was doing and charged a fair price. Plus, people seemed to be amused by her gruffness. The more she barked at them, the more charmed they seemed. Perhaps they viewed it as some refreshing form of honesty.

Carrie, on the other hand, lied routinely to her customers. She hated waiting on them—anyone, no matter how nice they were—and could easily be nominated for an Oscar for every performance she delivered. She couldn't bring herself to be blunt like Bert—she knew if she tried that, someone would key her car, or worse. And Bert would yell at her, despite probably having just delivered a scathing lecture to someone who had forgotten their insurance card. Every word out of Carrie's mouth was countered by an inner dialogue:

"Hi, can I help you?"

Go away.

"Yes, I have a big problem."

Yes, your mother carried you to term.

"I'm sure it's nothing we can't handle!"

"I lost my registration and I'm getting my car inspected tomorrow."

I guess you're fucked. And I don't give a shit.

"Oh, that's no problem. I can fix you right up."

"Really? That's great! I love coming here!"

Sure you do, you lousy fuck, because you're stupid and you lost the dumb thing in the first place. Who can't keep track of their car registration, for God's sake? Now just stop talking and let me fill out the stupid form. I don't care about your stupid wallet and how you should've gotten a new one but you love this one and now look, you're showing me a picture of your granddaughter, no I don't think she's cute, no I don't care, all I want to do is finish this, take your money and tell you to have a wonderful fucking day so I don't have to look at you anymore, you loser.

"There. You're all set. Is there anything else I can help you with?"

"No, miss, you've been so helpful. Thank you!"

"Have a great day!"

Drop dead.

And those were the nice people. The ones that stuck with her the most were the bad ones, the assholes, the people Carrie wished the most insidious diseases upon. The ones who looked at her like she was less than, the ones who knew she was weak and would take it, because, these days, Carrie *did* feel less than, and they could smell it, like the end coming off a deathbed. Her *knowing* she was somehow less than, because she was here, talking to them, trapped behind the counter like an animal backed into a corner in this narrow chapter of her life that seemed without end. Carrie often wondered, as she stared at some jerk fumbling for his money, who was authoring this story, and what kind of a mean bitch was she?

Despite all this, what made it worse in a way, was she knew she was lucky. She could be homeless, she could be alone. She could be like dead-as-shit Paula Davis. She had a nice house, a nice car, and a husband who loved her. Her proverbial health. All this, and still she managed to have a scorching case of first world woe is me.

The day finally drew to a close, and Carrie was released into the remainder of the afternoon. She got in her car and noticed the ice scraper she'd tossed on the floor of the passenger side. She picked it up and winced. A single white whisker stuck to the blade. Muttering in disgust, she got back out and threw the scraper into the dumpster, where the cat itself had found its final resting place, or close to it.

She got back in her car but sat a moment. Bert had not been overly perturbed at the discovery, but it made Carrie uneasy. Who would do such a thing, and why? Bert had dismissed it as an unhappy customer, which was likely—people hated the state and the state's messengers. But to Carrie, it seemed more than that. She remembered Tula Mae and her story of the stolen cats and shuddered.

She wondered if it was merely the first of three.

**THE DAY AFTER HIS VISIT TO** the notary, Andy spent most of the afternoon on the *Wishy Washy* with Jason until Jason had to go home. Not ready to face another dinner with his parents, Andy headed for a bar/restaurant called The Timberland, which was right next to the multiplex. He figured he'd kill the rest of the night with a few more beers and the most mind-numbing movie he could find.

The bar was cool and dark, nicely done in hand-hewn beams harvested from old barns. Just after five, the place was mostly empty, a condition which would probably change in another hour. He had his pick of seats; a lone wine glass stood at half-mast, the occupant either in the bathroom or recently departed. He took a seat a respectful distance from it.

He ordered a draft and sipped judiciously, buzzing already. He cast an eye about the place, looking for anyone he might know.

The ladies' room was at the far end of the bar; the door opened and the woman from the notary came out. She walked past him, rummaging through her purse, and then took the seat stewarded by the wine glass. He shifted on his stool, suddenly agitated, looking everywhere but at her. He caught his hollow-eyed reflection in the mirror across the bar. *God, is that me?*

He turned away and found her watching him. She smiled.

"Hi. Andy, right?"

He smiled, pleased she remembered. "Right. Carrie?"

"Yep. Get your truck inspected yet?"

"Um, no. Not yet. I forgot about that."

She tapped an imaginary watch. "Nine days left. Clock's ticking."

"Yeah." He found himself squirming a bit and stopped. "Hey, I guess I should apologize for that dumb thing I said yesterday. About your ring. I don't know why I said it."

She glanced at it. "A lot of women do that, actually. I probably would, too. It might keep a lot of the riff-raff at bay."

"It didn't stop me."

She laughed. "No, it didn't, did it?" She gestured to the seat next to her. "Join me?"

"Sure, I guess. You're not waiting for someone else?"

"My imaginary husband, you mean? He's in Hershey until late tonight. I've had a rough week and can't bear the thought of staring at the TV another night. So, I thought a few drinks and maybe a movie would do the trick. Take my mind off things."

"Sounds like a plan." He took a big swallow of beer and then moved down to the stool next to her. "I was thinking of something along those lines myself."

She sipped. "Oh yes? Rough week too?"

He considered. "Rough year."

"Sorry to hear that. I have to admit, you seemed like you had a lot on your mind when you first came in the office."

She was right, of course, but he didn't want to talk about it. He imagined telling her about his mother's dementia and his father's relentless disappointment. About how his wife, Melinda, had cheated on him and married her lover. How he'd left New York, unemployed, racked with guilt and shame, and returned home as an act of self-punishment. She would drain her glass in one hasty gulp, scatter bills across the bar and run for the door. He would only respect her more for it.

"I saw your picture in the paper the other day," he said. "That story about the women's shelter. Do you work there, too?"

She sighed. "I used to. I was the Volunteer Coordinator. Then we lost a bunch of state funding and they had to lay me off. I was volunteering to sort of keep in the loop, but it got to be too much. The notary job really sucks the life out of me. And that night—"

She shook her head and shuddered. "It was awful. If you read the paper, you know what happened. I saw the whole thing."

She paused, remembering. "I've never seen so much blood."

"I shouldn't have brought it up. Let's talk about something else."

She hesitated, looking as if she did indeed have more to say. He waited, unsure of how to proceed. Up close she was even prettier, a few thin lines around her eyes marking her passage out of girlhood and giving her a look of awareness and humor women in their twenties did not possess. He felt the ache of longing start somewhere beneath his sternum and knew sitting here in a bar with a pretty woman he couldn't have, who probably wouldn't want him anyway, was just one more item on the list of things he deserved.

"There was something wrong with her baby," she said finally. "It was, I don't know, like a circus freak or something."

He hadn't expected that. "Really? How?"

She gave him a sheepish look. "You'll think I'm a conspiracy theorist, or plain wacky. I've probably had too much wine. It looked like a little pig. Like a cross. Like a cross between—oh hell, I don't know. Forget it."

She rubbed her hand across her face and then dared to look at him. He laughed. After a moment, she joined him.

"I'm sorry, you think it was like a pig person?" he asked.

"I don't know. And, just to add to the weirdness, this homeless kid came along afterward and started talking about the pig people on Round Top. Do you know that story?"

"Sure. It was part of the science curriculum at Conneaut." She laughed again, and he went on. "Not really. But yeah, we all had our versions of the story. Some people say there was a leper colony up there, but I don't know how that fits with the pig people."

Carrie shrugged. "I don't either. Anyway, this kid, Reggie Spavine is his name, told me he knew the girl had come from there. I mean, I know the pig people story is just that—a story—but it is a weird coincidence."

"Synchronicity," he offered.

She looked at him, and he felt an instant connection, a moment of complete understanding. A thrill of excitement shot up his spine. He sensed she felt it too.

"An inexplicable, strange circumstance," she said. "Yes. That's it. Like this, too, perhaps."

"Yeah." He raised his glass. "Let's hope this is the good kind. Serendipity."

She toasted it. "It feels good. Something about you touched me the minute I saw you. I think you're a good egg, Andy Korn."

He frowned; the moment dampened a bit. She studied him, a bemused look on her face.

"What?" she asked.

"Nothing. I just really hate my last name."

"It is a little unusual. Did you get teased a lot as a kid?"

He picked up his glass. "Oh yeah."

"It could always be worse. It could be Cox or Butts."

He almost choked on his last swallow of beer. "Right. I could be Harry Hoar."

The bartender came by, and Carrie scooted her empty glass toward her. "Please," she said. "And a refill for my new friend here."

Andy flushed with pleasure. He liked the idea of being her friend. He cast a glance at the swell of her breasts pushing against the white t-shirt she wore and the ache he'd been feeling deepened.

An alert sounded on her phone. She opened it and studied the screen briefly. He hoped it wasn't her husband. "My brother," she said as if she'd read his mind. "He wants to know where I am."

"Does he live around here?"

"No," she said absently, tapping a reply. "Baltimore. What difference does it make where I am, I wonder?"

She shook her head and looked at him. "What movie were you going to see?"

"I didn't have any one in mind, particularly. You?"

She shrugged. "Nope. If you want, we could pick the dumbest one playing and throw popcorn at the screen. I bet we'll have the theater to ourselves, it being midweek and all. What do you think?"

"That's a great idea," he said. His heart was racing. Did she really like him? What was this: a date? Or was she just bored and he was the only option in the room? He was feeling too much like a fourteen-year-old girl. He stood, his barstool scraping loudly against the ceramic tile. She watched him with interest.

"I have to go to the bathroom," he said. "I'll be right back."

He did have to pee, but what he most needed was to pull himself together. After relieving himself, he stood at the sink, letting cold water run over his hands and wrists. He splashed his face several times and then studied his dripping reflection.

"Her husband is an asshole," he said softly. "He takes her for granted. He doesn't get her. They're growing apart. That's why she's here. I get her. *I* get her."

He stepped back from the mirror and slapped himself, first one side, then the other to even things out. He dried his face on a paper towel and exited the men's room, two high spots of color on his cheeks.

She was still there; he studied the arched curve of her back and the wave of brown hair cascading down its middle. He imagined it in his fist.

She smiled as he sat down. Her phone was out again. "The dollar theater is playing Dumb and Dumber To. Have you seen it?"

"No, but I heard it was pretty, well, dumb."

She laughed. "Right. I think it's exactly what we need right now. I bet there won't be a soul in there—we can throw all the popcorn we want."

He drained his beer and set the glass down with a bang. "Let's do it."

She giggled. "Wait. I can't chug Chardonnay like that. It'll kill me."

"Oh, come on, you can do it." He leaned in close and whispered: "Do it for the pig people."

She snorted into her glass and downed it in three big gulps. "Oh God. I'll pay for that."

They paid their tabs and walked outside. The afternoon light was just starting to tilt, and the parking lot was mostly deserted. Andy had parked midway between the bar and the theater—he pointed out his truck. She laughed—her Honda was right next to it.

His thoughts turned back to synchronicities. Fate. Luck. He was feeling very lucky at that moment. She chattered on about something, but he couldn't hear over the din of his own thoughts as they pinged around inside his skull in short bursts of energy. Something else was building inside him, within that cloud of longing: hope, sizzling like a kernel of popcorn, quivering in hot oil, crackling and swelling.

The theater was cool and equally deserted. Andy thought he saw her do a quick scan, perhaps looking out for someone she might know. It dampened his spirits a little. Then she smiled and pointed.

"There's the dollar counter over there."

They bought their tickets separately and then split a big tub of popcorn. They were just in time—the show started in ten minutes.

Much to Andy's delight, they did have the place to themselves. Carrie led them to seats smack dab in the middle and plopped down with an exaggerated sigh.

"Let the dumbness begin."

They didn't have long to wait. The dollar theater skipped the previews and got right to it. The movie was dumb, but not without its laughs, particularly since he was seriously buzzing, buzzing enough to let his inhibitions slip from him like a coat in too hot weather. He leaned into her, shoulder to shoulder, whispering jibes and sarcastic remarks she seemed to find uproariously funny. It was like a miracle. He'd found some part of himself, long lain dormant.

She leaned back, wiping tears from her eyes. "Quit it, seriously, I'm going to pee my pants."

She had her legs drawn up on the seat, tucked against her. Her skin was bronzed and looked as smooth as blown glass. He looked up and saw she was watching him.

She extended one leg and rested it on his knees. "I just shaved them this morning. Check it out."

The movie, blaring, suddenly faded to dim background noise. He ran his hand over her shin, and then beyond the knob of her knee. He ran it back down, marveling at the impossible smoothness of it. Their eyes met. His hand traced the same path back up and then continued, stopping at the hem of her shorts, which were quite short. He squeezed, feeling the supple muscles of her thigh. He waited for her to push him away. She didn't.

He leaned forward in a rush and kissed her. She met him open-mouthed; her tongue touched his, and he felt a searing jolt of pleasure. His hand left her thigh to cup her breast, its swell a perfect fit in his palm. He kissed her over and over, moving down along her neck and throat. God, he was so *hungry*.

She cupped his face in both hands. Something cold pressed against his cheek: smooth, precious metal. He felt another slap then, not of his own doing, but of reality, shocking him out of his beer-infused fog. He reared back and looked at her. She sat before him, legs open, nipples poking through the thin fabric of her tee, lips parted. Her eyes were wide and just as confused.

"Oh God," he said. "What am I doing? I'm sorry. I have—I have to get out of here."

He stood. The tub of popcorn, forgotten, tumbled from his lap, spilling in a drift across the floor. He lurched away, gripping the backs of seats to keep from falling.

"Andy. Andy, wait."

She caught up with him in the lobby and walked silently beside him until they were outside. The light had faded to rose; the security lamps had come on in the parking lot, casting brightening circles as darkness came on. He made for his truck, hands stuffed in his pockets, head down.

"Andy, stop." She grabbed his arm and turned him so he faced her. He couldn't look at her.

"I'm sorry," he said. "I don't know what's the matter with me. I'm fucking drunk, for one thing. You're married, goddamn it."

"I know. I'm sorry, and I'm a little drunk, too. This is my fault. I started it, and I don't know why."

He lifted his eyes. She looked to be on the verge of tears, her mouth turned down and trembling. Even now, in his welling shame, he wanted her.

"Are you, like, unhappy or something? With your marriage, I mean?"

She uttered a humorless laugh. "No. I'm not. I love the hell out of Ben. I'd die before I'd hurt him."

He swallowed hard. "Then why—this?"

She looked off into the coming night. "I don't know. I like you. A lot. But that's not it. I'm not unhappy in my marriage, but my life is definitely not going in the direction I'd hoped. None of that matters, though. This was wrong."

He leaned back against his truck and looked at the sky. Stars were coming out, twinkling in the cornflower blue. "My ex-wife cheated on me. I'll never forget that awful feeling when she told me she was in love with the guy. Like someone's turned your life upside down and emptied it out on the ground. How everything you thought was true, isn't. And the worst part, knowing it was me that drove her away. And I still didn't see it coming."

He looked at her. "I don't ever want to be the cause of someone else's pain. I don't want to be that guy. I like you, too. I feel a real connection with you. You're beautiful. And I haven't touched another person in over a year. Not even a hug from my grandmother. Who's dead, by the way, so I guess that's a good thing."

He offered her a sad smile, which she returned. "I'm gonna go home now and try not to beat myself up over this. I've got plenty of material already. I want to make this a good memory, okay? I don't have many."

She stood for a second, and then wrapped her arms around his neck and hugged him, molding her body to his. He held her for a long moment, willing himself to remember all of it: the push of her breasts against his chest, the smell of her hair, the feel of her thighs against his. He held her for a kernel of a lifetime.

She backed away, her eyes locked with his, and then got in her car and drove away without a backward glance. The sound of the engine blended with the other cars on the highway leading back to town and became meaningless.

He lingered a moment and then hit the key fob to unlock the door. He glanced up and froze, his hand on the handle, his blood suddenly gone cold in his veins and the hairs on the back of his neck raised and stiff.

He'd parked his truck on the outer edge of the lot; beyond it was a stretch of grass about fifty yards deep, at the end of which the woods began. The grassy area was lit at one-hundred-foot intervals by security lights. In the halo of one of these, about twenty yards away, was a man. Even at a distance, Andy could tell he was large, though the light was such his face was cast in shadow. Despite this, he sensed the man was watching him.

The feeling of being caught doing something illicit shot through him in a bolt of adrenaline. He clawed the door open and flung himself into the truck, stabbing at the lock. *It's her husband. He came home early, knew she was at the movies, thought he'd surprise her. Oh Jesus, please.*

He started the engine and backed out, careful not to hit another car—that would be just about par—and stole another glance at the man. He was still there, shoulders hunched, head lowered like some predatory animal, arms loose at his sides. A low whine escaped Andy's throat as he threw the gearshift into drive and punched the gas. He looked back once.

The halo of light was empty.

**TWO DAYS LATER, ANDY HAD WORKED** himself into such a state of paranoia he could barely eat. He was afraid to even go to the boat, his only sanctuary, for fear an angry husband might be waiting for him, though how an angry husband would know about the boat, Andy didn't know; nor did he want to find out. He stayed mostly in his room, sequestered and crawling with guilt.

Finally, he couldn't take it anymore. Goaded by unbearable curiosity or the need to get away from his parents' maddening isms, or a bit of both, he decided to go to the notary and ask Carrie if the man had indeed been her husband. Logic and rational thinking told him it was unlikely, if not impossible, but logic and rational thinking were not in the driver's seat.

When he opened the door to Bro's Notary, he could tell something was wrong. The two older women were there, working silently at their stations. Four customers sat in chairs along the far wall, waiting for their paperwork to be done. There was a solemn air about the place, and when he closed the door, both women looked up at him, their faces drawn and pinched. Of Carrie, there was no sign.

He approached the counter and stood before the older of the two women, the one he presumed to be the owner. "Excuse me," he said. "Is Carrie here?"

The women exchanged a glance. The older woman looked back at him with sad, rheumy eyes.

"No," she said. "She won't be back for a while. Is there something I can help you with?"

A deep feeling of unease settled in Andy's gut. The image of the man rose in his mind. "No. I really need to talk to her. Is she—is she ill?"

The woman looked at her co-worker, who gave a small shrug. "No. Are you friends now, or what?"

"I'm—sort of. Can you just tell me?"

The woman glanced at the row of customers, who were eavesdropping shamelessly. She leaned toward him. Andy caught a whiff of stale cigarettes.

"Her husband was killed two nights ago. Car accident. Evidently, he was on his way home from Hershey when he lost control of his car. Carrie had gone to see a movie. The state troopers were waiting for her when she got home."

All the strength went out of Andy's legs. He gripped the counter to keep from sliding to the floor. "Oh," he said. "Oh my God."

The woman looked at him sympathetically. "The obituary's in today's paper. There'll be two viewings tomorrow. Marshall's Funeral Home. Though I guess—" She cleared her throat. "I guess it'll be a closed casket."

Andy barely heard her. He managed a thank you and stumbled out the door. He got in his truck and sat, numb with shock. Images flickered through his mind, both real and imagined: his hand sliding up her thigh, cupping her breast, his tongue in her mouth, probing lustily at the exact moment her husband swerved off the road and hit a tree at some ungodly speed, his body catapulting through the windshield and landing in a ditch where he lay, gasping for breath through torn lungs, while Andy held his wife in a parking lot, making memories of her body with his hands.

He started the truck and drove aimlessly around the parking lot before making a decision. He drove to the nearest Sheetz and bought a paper. He laid it on the seat without looking at it and drove to the boat. Only when he was situated on the vinyl lounge, late summer sun on his back, did he open it directly to the obits.

Ben Owens, 38, passed away unexpectedly because of a car accident on August 13th. A graduate of Penn State University, Ben was an avid golfer and bowler. He is survived by his wife, Carrie Owens, and his parents, Ed and Alice Owens, of Lancaster, Pennsylvania, a brother, Eric Owens of Richmond, Virginia, and a sister, Trudy Kent of Columbus, Ohio. He is preceded in death by his grandparents, George and Edna Owens. Viewings will be held at Marshall's Funeral Home on August 16th from 2 to 4 P.M. and 7 to 9 P.M. Memorials may be made . . .

Andy skipped the remainder and read the rest over again. He let the paper fall from his hands and sat, thinking, looking out at the lake. Then he got out his phone and texted Jason.

Twenty minutes later, Jason walked across the parking lot, a six-pack of Coors Lite in one hand and a McDonald's bag in the other. He climbed into the boat and without a word handed Andy a beer. Andy popped the top and drank nearly half of it.

"Must be pretty bad, whatever it is," Jason remarked. He hoisted his own beer briefly. "Cheers."

"I need your opinion on something," Andy said. "Remember the woman I told you about? The one at the notary?"

"The hot one. Sure."

"I ran into her a few days ago. At The Timberland. We really hit it off. I—well, to make a long story short, we ended up making out."

"No way!" Jason said his brow arching. "I told you the ring was fake."

Andy shook his head. "No, it wasn't. She is—was—married. That same night her husband was killed in a car accident. I found out today because there was this guy standing in the parking lot, watching us, and I thought *he* was her husband, so I freaked out and went to the notary today to ask her and she wasn't there, and—"

"Wait a minute," Jason said, holding up his hands. "You better give me the long version. You're not making any sense."

Andy started from the beginning. He was halfway through the six-pack by the time he finished. Jason doled out Egg McMuffins and sat, considering, while they ate.

"What are you going to do now?" he asked.

Andy gestured helplessly. "I don't know. I really feel like I should talk to her. I want her to know how sorry I am."

"Sorry for what? Sorry for making out with her? Or sorry for the coincidence?"

"For all of it, I guess. For Christ's sake, her husband is dead."

Jason studied him closely. "You're acting like that's your fault. He didn't die because you made out with his wife. Not cool, but probably not karma, either. If karma was at work, *you'd* be dead."

"Then what? It's too much of a coincidence. And who was that guy by the light?"

Jason shrugged and dusted crumbs from his hands. "Just some guy. Some pervert, waiting for the Disney movie to let out. Let's go back to the husband. Straight up, no bullshit: how sorry are you he's dead?"

Andy stared at his friend, a vigorous protest on his lips. Then he slumped and put his face in his hands.

"I really, really like her," he said, his voice muffled by his palms. "That makes me an even bigger asshole than I already am, right? A damn vulture. But I can't help it. I can't fucking help it."

Jason nudged his shoulder. "You're human. Be patient. Wait it out. Give her some time, a few months, and then drop by the notary. Stick your toe in the water. See how she is."

Andy straightened up. "A few months? I feel like I should talk to her now. She needs to know that I know what happened. How fucked up I think it is. I just don't want her to take it the wrong way."

"What way? That you're the vulture you just indicated you don't want to be? Hell, go to the viewing. Give her your number over the casket."

Andy made no reply. Instead, he gave Jason a sheepish look. Jason stared back at him with dawning alarm.

"Oh no. You can't be serious. Do not go to the viewing, man. That would be extremely bad taste."

"What other options do I have? I don't know where she lives, I don't know her phone number. She's not in the book—I looked. All I know is where she works, and she isn't there."

"That's better than the damn funeral home, Andy. Christ, have you lost your mind? Think about it. Better yet, forget about it—her, everything. It was a mistake. There'll be other women."

"There haven't been," Andy murmured.

"That's because you're not trying. Have you asked anybody out on a date since Melinda?"

"No."

"I didn't think so. And believe me, there won't be any Carrie What's-Her-Face either if you show up at the funeral home. How are you going to introduce yourself in the receiving line? 'How do you know the widow, sir? I was trying to screw her in a movie theater the night her husband died tragically. Isn't it a small world!'"

"All right, all right, I get it. It was just a thought." He tried to smile and ended up wincing instead. "At least I know it wasn't him in the parking lot."

Jason eyed him critically. "Yes. That's the takeaway."

By one o'clock the next day, Andy's resolve to avoid the funeral home had withered down to a nub. He sat in his room, watching the time click by on his clock by the bed. At one-thirty he rose and put on a pair of khakis and a blue sport coat and a red tie. He was sweating.

His father was in the kitchen, eating a tuna fish sandwich. He looked up at his son suspiciously.

"Who died?"

Andy paused, surprised. "How did you know?"

His father shrugged and turned back to his late lunch. "Somebody must have. I doubt you're going to a job interview."

"Very funny," Andy said and walked out.

He drove to Marshall's, crackling with nervousness. He had to park down the street; the funeral home's lot was packed. He sat for a moment.

"I'm making a mistake," he said aloud. "This is going to go wrong because everything I do is wrong. I can't remember the last good decision I made."

He got out of the truck and walked to the funeral home like he was going to his own. People were streaming up the walk from all directions. Ben Owens must have been popular.

He got in line. The day was another hot one; the sun beat down on him, and he could feel the sweat beading at his hairline and dampening his already damp armpits. People filled in rapidly behind him. The man ahead of Andy turned and smiled sadly at him.

"Lot of people," he commented. "I figured there would be. I thought I was going to be early."

"Yes," Andy said politely.

"How did you know Ben?"

"I um, I know his wife. She did some notary work for me."

"Oh. I used to be their neighbor. I moved after my divorce a year ago. Such a shame. Ben was a fantastic guy. I feel so bad for Carrie. All alone now. Though not for long, I suspect."

Andy flinched. He searched the man's face for judgment and got an admonished smile.

"I shouldn't say that I know. But she is quite a catch, don't you think?"

What kind of a line am I in? Andy looked at the other men around him and saw birds on a wire, hunched and beady-eyed, the smell of death wafting to them on the breeze. Waiting for the meat to ripen just a little bit more . . .

"I don't know much about her," Andy said, and turned away.

The line began to move. Shortly he saw people emerging from a side exit, some of them crying, others chatting briskly. He shuffled into the building's cool interior and fought the urge to loosen his tie. Marshall's was one of the oldest funeral homes in town, done up in Early American Death. Wallpaper with vines and pink flowers crawled up the walls, lit by low-slung chandeliers and sconces. The carpet was another floral horror, and the smell of funeral arrangements was cloying. Andy felt like he'd fallen into a pitcher plant.

The foyer was filled with the low hum of murmured voices, spiked by the occasional burst of subdued laughter. What was normally divided into two viewing rooms had been opened to accommodate the crowd, and as Andy approached, he was confronted by the guest book. The Good Neighbor ahead of him signed and then handed the pen to Andy. He hesitated and then scrawled his name in a burst of resolve.

The receiving line loomed ahead. Carrie was not in it. He craned his neck to see and then ducked away before he was propelled in front of Ben Owens' family. He wound his way through the crowd, looking for her, and found himself suddenly and quite by accident in front of the casket.

It was open, contrary to the notary's prediction. Andy stood before the dead man, staring at his gummed eyelids with morbid fascination. Ben Owens had been good-looking. Whatever trauma took his life must have occurred elsewhere on his body, for his face was unmarked. It was still the face of a dead man, though, caked with make-up and unanimated. Andy looked at the photographs next to the coffin. Here was Ben Owens at graduation. Here he was as a little boy on some beach with dad, grinning like he had the world by the tail. And here he was at his wedding with the love of his life: Carrie, smiling at the camera, her long hair done up in fetching curls, her body ensconced in white satin and lace.

His arm was suddenly caught in a forceful grip. Andy turned to face a man about his own age, maybe a few years older, dressed in a black suit. Andy saw a resemblance to Carrie right away.

"Excuse me—hi. I'm Chris Barrett, Carrie's brother. She's asked me to tell you to leave."

Andy's heart sank. He looked past the man and saw Carrie. She was sitting down, surrounded by women. She was glaring at him, her face contorted in grief, and now, shock. Her brother followed his gaze and then turned back to him.

"As you can see, she's very upset. Would you please go?"

"I'm sorry. Yes. Of course, I'll go. I made a mistake."

He fought his way through the crowd and out the exit. Chris Barrett was right behind him.

"Hold on a minute," he said and caught Andy's arm again. "Who are you?"

Andy turned and held up his hands. "I'm nobody. Really. I barely know her and I didn't know her husband at all. I made a mistake. I don't belong here."

Chris was not to be dissuaded so easily. "You're damn right about that. Where did you meet her?"

Maybe it's none of your business, Andy thought. "Look, I just know her from where she works. That's all, I swear."

"I think you're full of shit. But I guess that's where we'll leave it, for now."

He turned to go. It was Andy's turn to grab his arm. "Could you tell her something for me?"

Chris studied him. "What?"

"Just tell her—tell her I'm sorry."

"That's it?"

"Yeah."

Chris bit his lip, still eyeing him curiously. "Okay. I don't like this. Stay away from her."

"I will," Andy said.

Chris went back inside. Andy went to his truck. He looked at himself in the rearview mirror. His eyes snapped through with red and hung with purplish bags.

"That went well," he said.

**CARRIE'S NEW LIFE STARTED LIKE THIS:** she came home from the movies toting a mixed bag of feelings. There was guilt, of course, the old handmaid, not to mention her good friend fear—fear she might have been seen in the arms of a man, not her husband. And with that, exhilaration, and the pleasure of being desirable to someone who was not obligated.

But when she pulled into the driveway and saw the police car there, alarm had sent that bag flying out the window. Panic set in when the state troopers took off their hats and waited for her to get out of the car, their looks somber. She would never forget their words as long as she lived:

"Ms. Carrie Owens? Your husband is Benjamin Owens? We have some terrible news. Your husband was killed this evening in a car accident."

The details rushed by her in gusts of air. She heard none of them, not even the troopers' names, though she imagined they told her. The only thing she heard was her own voice, repeating through it all, no, no, it's not possible, not Ben, not my Ben, he's on his way home from Hershey, he'll pull in the drive any minute, you'll see, it's all a mistake.

They nodded sympathetically, even as they loaded her into the back of their patrol car, and she kept trying to convince them, even as they pulled into the coroner's office, even as they led her down the hall, even as they pulled out the slab. When she saw Ben's face, a single drop of blood on his cheek, the words dried up. She turned and vomited up movie popcorn and wine into a silver bucket, strategically placed perhaps for just such occasions.

"Is this your husband?" the coroner had asked. A ridiculous question, now that she had puked up the remnants of her sordid little tryst. No, she wanted to say. This is what I always do on my weekly visit to the morgue.

Then she'd lost it, just completely lost it. They tried to console her, but even through her hysteria, she sensed the routineness of it for them. They didn't know her. They didn't know Ben. They never would. All they could do was take her home and ask if there was anyone they could call so she wouldn't be alone. She thought of Andy. *I'm sure he'd come right over*, she thought, and hated him, and hated herself, too.

No, she'd said, there's no one. No one she wanted to wake up in the middle of the night. Of course, she would have other calls to make: Ben's parents, and his brother and sister. She would call her own brother, Chris, in Maryland. She winced. He would come and take over in his usual big brother fashion. He could wait until morning. Their parents were dead, gone for decades now. Ben could tell them himself. Ha!

The troopers stayed long enough for her to make the call to Ben's parents, waiting respectfully in another room, but she still felt self-conscious. It went as one might expect such a call to go. Afterward she told the troopers they could leave, she would be fine, and they did so with obvious relief.

She called Chris first thing in the morning and he was at her door by noon. The senior manager of a pharmaceutical company, he was used to being in charge and giving orders, a trait which had irritated her in the past. Now, she was grateful for it and watched him go to work, making arrangements, helping her write the obituary even. He drove her to the funeral home and helped her pick out a casket, a nice oak one with a silver satin lining. Ben had died from blunt force trauma to the chest. The police said he'd lost control of his car for unknown reasons, though it was likely he'd swerved to miss a deer. He hit a tree full on, and the car had simply crumpled like a beer can—an older model Subaru before the advent of airbags, the steering wheel had crushed Ben's chest. How he'd loved his vintage cars.

His face had been relatively unmarked, however—what a blessing! The funeral director said they could have an open casket viewing if they wished. Chris had looked at her, his shoulders hunched, as if this was somehow a critical question. She couldn't decide. Chris said yes.

Then came the onslaught of people and their food and their flowers and their sympathy and disbelief. How could this happen? She didn't know. Not Ben. Yes, Ben. What was she going to do? She didn't know.

When she saw Andy at the viewing, she'd felt a momentary thrill: He came! How sweet. Then she saw him standing over her dead husband, looking at the pictures of their life, scrutinizing them like some perverse archeologist, and rage had filled her. How dare he look at Ben! He had no right. She was sitting because she had nearly fainted at one point, overcome by the people and their pressing in, and she had gripped the arms of her chair to keep from leaping to her feet and screaming at him to get out, get away from poor Ben who couldn't see and couldn't defend himself against the prying eyes of a morbidly curious suitor. She'd sent Chris after him and Chris had done what big brothers are good at.

And now she was home, in a house which had always been too big for them and now seemed positively cavernous. Everything creaked at night in ways she was sure they'd never creaked before and she heard it because she couldn't sleep even though she was exhausted. Chris took a week off work and stayed with her, sleeping in the spare bedroom. He'd asked who Andy was only once, and she produced a lie so smoothly it shocked and shamed her. He used to be in Ben's bowling league and Ben had never liked him. He cheated.

Chris helped her go through her finances and make calls to their insurance companies. Unbeknownst to her, Ben had two life insurance policies, one through work and one he'd taken out himself, each for five hundred thousand. Carrie found herself a bittersweet millionaire.

"If you invest this carefully, you should be all right, financially," he said, leaning back in Ben's chair at Ben's computer. "This is good news. He really took care of you. You might not even have to keep working at that shit job at Bro's Notes, or whatever it's called."

"So, this is the best thing that ever happened to me," she said.

"No, no, that's not what I mean, of course." He looked at her reproachfully. "Give me more credit than that, Carrie. I just mean you're not screwed. You can sell the house if you want, but you don't have to. You can stay here until things settle down. Or forever. I probably wouldn't quit your job yet, especially if you get your health insurance through them."

She shook her head. "I got it through Ben's work. Bert doesn't offer benefits."

He shrugged. "Well, there's always government healthcare, or whatever they're calling it now. It's better than nothing, you can afford it and you have to have it. Let's get it set up as soon as possible."

"No more today," she said. "I'm feeling overwhelmed. I need a drink."

He frowned at this. He didn't drink and didn't approve of her drinking. *Tough shit on that one, brother,* she thought. *I'm a rich widow.*

She went to the kitchen and poured herself a glass of Chardonnay from an open bottle in the fridge. Outside, the day was ending, a late summer chill seeping into the air. Carrie felt it through the breeze coming from her open kitchen window. Pumpkins were cropping up everywhere, and Walmart was already advertising Christmas stuff. She felt a pang. Christmas. Christ.

"Do you feel safe staying here alone?" Chris asked.

She sipped. Her mouth filled with creamy oak and vanilla. "I guess so. It's not a bad neighborhood. The house is set off a little from everyone else on the street, but it's not like I'm on a deserted island. I guess I could get robbed here just as well as any place else."

"That's not what I meant." He hesitated. "I'm talking about the missing women."

Carrie shrugged. "I'm not worried. I don't fit the profile."

"What profile? Granted, some of them have been low income or homeless, but a few have been similar to you. Take the last one—she was at a bar when anybody last saw her."

"I don't hang out at bars," Carrie said, and then winced.

Chris looked at her narrowly. "You were at a bar the night Ben was killed. You texted me from The Timberland."

"That was one time. I'll be fine. Don't worry."

"Do you have a gun in the house?"

"Ben keeps—kept—a shotgun by the bed. I've fired it a few times. I'll put it on my side."

"I think you should consider moving to Baltimore. You can stay with me."

Carrie shook her head. "No. I don't want to. Besides, Rachel doesn't like me, according to you."

He gave her a direct look. "That won't be a problem."

She sighed. "I can't think about it right now. It's too much."

"You need to be more proactive. You never think ahead. This could be just what you need right now. I can help you find a good job. We can go to the Chesapeake and eat blue crabs—it'll be fun."

Carrie looked at him like he was crazy. "Fun? My husband just died. I'm not interested in having fun."

Chris said nothing to this, but to Carrie, he looked like he had plenty to say. "What's the look for?"

He shook his head. "Nothing. Tell me you'll think about it."

"Fine," she said. "I will. Please don't start planning the rest of my life for me."

Two days later, Chris left. She watched him load his bags into the trunk of his Toyota with a mixture of trepidation and relief. The coming night loomed large even though it was nine in the morning on a fine August Sunday.

"You'll call me when you get home?" she asked, trying not to sound as anxious as she felt. Sending loved ones off in cars had become a scary proposition.

"Yep." He shut the trunk and gave her a long hug. She started to cry, unable to help it. "You're going to be fine, Carrie. Call me whenever you want. Anytime—day or night. I'll try and come up again soon so we can put those checks to work for you."

He pulled away and looked at her. "Then we can start talking about the holidays. Okay?"

She sniffled. "Okay. I love you. Call me."

"Love you, too." He got in the car then and pulled out of the drive, giving her a wave. She returned it, alone in the driveway—her driveway, now—and then went inside.

The silence loomed immediately, unbearable. She stumbled into the bedroom—*her* bedroom—and flung herself onto the bed, sobbing uncontrollably. She stayed that way for an hour until the pillow was soaked and the pile of tissues by the bed had become a sizeable mound.

She rolled onto her back and stared at the ceiling for a long time, her mind empty, her cheeks and eyes raw. Slowly, her gaze drifted to the gun propped in the corner in its new place on her side of the bed. It stood, a mute guardian, useless without her wherewithal. She imagined grabbing it as an intruder—some hulking man-pig, perhaps—crawled through her window in the pitch-black dark, probably armed with whatever weapon man-pigs were favoring these days. Imagined her terrified screams as she brought the barrel around, fumbling for the safety. Missing entirely. And then, God knows what.

Inevitably, as one often does in dark moments, she considered what it might be like to put both barrels in her mouth. She rejected the idea at once as cowardly. There again—what if she missed somehow, perhaps merely clipping her brain stem, rendering herself a vegetable? Unable to feed herself but still able to register the pitying looks of her caregivers?

She turned back to the ceiling. "Dammit, Ben. What am I going to do?"

The next morning, having survived her first night alone without incident, she drove to Bro's Notary to check in with Bert. Lola/ Jennifer greeted her with a warm hug that went on too long, and then Bert herself emerged from the back, a stack of passenger plates in her hands. Carrie expected the usual brusque greeting, but instead was enfolded in Bert's large arms, swathing her in the smell of Pall Malls.

"How are you, girl?" Bert asked, her usual growl softened into a rumbling purr.

"I'm all right," Carrie lied. "Keeping it together, anyway. Can I talk to you for a minute?"

They went into Bert's tiny office in the back of the building, a closet-sized horror of bulging files and license plates that would give an auditor a coronary. A sun-faded poster of Dale Earnhardt decorated one wall—the only attempt at decorating, unless you counted the withered fern in the corner—and lastly, Bert's pet goldfish Arnie, suspended in a bowl perched precariously atop a stack of Car and Driver magazines.

Bert moved a mass of papers from a sagging chair and motioned for Carrie to sit. She settled her own bulk behind her ancient desk and folded her hands in her lap. "Are you quitting?"

"Not now," Carrie said. "Maybe never. I don't know. I do need to sort things out. I need to find a financial planner or an accountant. Someone to help me figure out where I'm at. Do you know anyone?"

Bert rummaged through a drawer and planted a business card in front of her. "My cousin. Eddie Norris. Works out of his house, cheap. He's been doing my taxes for years. He can line you up. It's none of my business, and you don't have to tell me, but was there insurance?"

"Some. Look, Bert, this is nothing personal, but you know I don't enjoy this work. I'd like to keep on for a while, but if I figure out I can be okay and maybe do something else, I probably will quit. I just don't want you to think I'm in this for the long haul if I don't have to be."

"I know," Bert said gruffly. "I'm not blind. I know you're smarter than this job. College-educated, management experience. I didn't figure I'd have you for long. But we both needed each other, right?"

"Right."

Bert nodded. "You do what you have to do. Me and Lola can get along. Stay as long as you need to. You're a good worker. Are you seeing a counselor? For your grief?"

"I—no, I'm not. Do you think I should?"

"Hell, no. Waste of money. Just cry it out. Best thing to do and a hell of a lot cheaper."

Carrie couldn't help but smile. She wondered what it would be like to have Bert for a mother. A lot of tough love, no doubt.

"Thank you, Bert. I'll be in tomorrow, I guess."

Bert walked out with her. Quite a line had formed, mostly men, and Lola/Jennifer had her hands full. Bert was unmoved. She put her hand on Carrie's shoulder.

"Take your time with things. Word gets out you're a widow, these nut sacks will be on your doorstep with their dicks pressed up against the glass. Don't pick the first asshole that comes along just to warm the bed. That's my advice."

"Thank you, Bert. I'll remember that."

Carrie had to push her way through the men to get to the door. She could feel their eyes on her, and suddenly she felt very small.

 **AFTER THE DEBACLE AT THE FUNERAL** home, Andy spent most of his time on the boat. He brooded much of it, playing the scene over in his mind, and cocktail hour had crept steadily closer to noon. He considered taking up smoking, just to nail things shut.

One day, having drunk just enough to become emboldened, he got in his truck and drove to the notary. He walked in the door and had been in line for ten minutes before he realized he had not contrived a reason to be there. He stood, shifting his weight from one foot to the other, his slowed mind churning. Carrie was there, looking very pretty in a pumpkin-colored sweater and jeans, her hair swept up in a ponytail. The man she was waiting on was leaning across the counter, chatting her up in a way that was irritating. He hoped she would look up and see him, but she didn't, concentrating on her work.

It was his turn in line, but the fat old lady who owned the place called for him to come over. He hesitated, wanting to wait for Carrie, but whatever she was doing was involved. He stepped up to the counter, feet away from her, having no idea what he was going to say.

The woman looked dubiously at his empty hands. "How can I help you?"

Flustered, he looked around. There was an assortment of local souvenirs lining the back counter, a nod to the area's thin tourist trade. "Postcards," he said. "I'd like a postcard."

He continued to stare at Carrie, hoping she would look up at the sound of his voice. He knew the old lady was watching him, and he sensed she didn't like him.

"A postcard." She turned to the display behind her and gestured like a skeptical Vanna White. "All right. Which one?"

Andy barely glanced at them. *Come on, Carrie. Look at me.* "Any one. I don't care."

The woman blew air forcefully out through her nose and snatched a postcard off the rack and slapped it down in front of him. "That'll be a buck six."

Andy gave her a five. She got his change and then looked at the guy Carrie was waiting on. "Get your dirty elbows off my counter. It's gettin' crowded in here."

The guy gave the old woman a look, but he did step back. Carrie handed him his paperwork for his signature and then afforded Andy one small glance. She seemed to register nothing.

"Will there be anything else?" the woman asked testily.

"No," Andy said. "I guess not."

He took his postcard and walked out. He got in his truck and then sat, staring at the rectangle depicting some church in town he didn't recognize. He slowly tore it into pieces and let them fall to the floorboards.

A rap on his window made him jump. Carrie stood outside. He fumbled for the ignition, turning it briefly so he could roll the window down. A breeze brought a faint tickle of her perfume.

"What are you doing?" she asked.

"I'm sorry. I don't mean to bother you at work."

"I guess it's better than the funeral home."

He blanched. "I know. I'm sorry about that, too. I don't know what I was thinking. I just wanted to tell you how sorry I am."

"That's a lot of sorrys. About what?"

He groped for an answer. "I—for your loss?"

He hadn't intended for it to come out like a question. Jesus, he was burying himself.

"My loss. Okay. Anything else?"

He gripped the steering wheel with one hand; the other was restlessly rubbing his thigh as if trying to get rid of something.

"Yes," he said, his voice low and tight. He tried to look at her and found he couldn't. "I'm sorry for that night. You know I was, even then. But now I'm doubly sorry. For the timing. I feel terrible.

I don't want you to think I don't care. I don't want you to hate me. I don't think I could live with myself."

She folded her arms across her breasts. "You want to kill yourself because you think I'm mad at you because we made out the night my husband died?"

"Well," he admitted, "it does sound excessive when you put it like that."

She sighed and looked off across the parking lot. "I don't hate you. There have been moments when I've hated you, but I'm mostly hating myself. You already apologized. I'm the one who should be ashamed."

He looked at her at last. "I don't want you hating yourself. I'd rather you hate me if those are the only choices."

She studied the ground. "Sometimes I wonder, you know, what it's like to be dead. I wonder if you can look down on the people you love and know what they're doing. What they have done. And I think of Ben, looking down on me, and knowing what we were doing while he was dying. How hurt he must be. I can't stand that."

"Maybe if he can see that much, he can see into your heart and know how sorry you are."

She swiped at her eyes. "Sorry doesn't count for much when someone is dead, Andy."

"I know that," he said. "Believe me, I know."

She looked at him curiously, but he said nothing. He bent and picked up a piece of postcard and wrote his cell number on it.

"Here," he said, handing it to her. "I know you have a brother who takes care of you, but if he's not around, you can call me. I'm pretty handy—I can fix some things, or even if you just can't reach something on the top shelf, I'd like to help. Or maybe you need someone to talk to. Okay? Would that be okay?"

She hesitated and then opened her mouth to say something. He held up his hand. "I'm not looking for anything else. I want to help if you need it. That's all. I'm not leaning across your counter, you know?"

This made her laugh a little, and he was glad. She nodded and tucked the paper into her jeans pocket.

"Okay, Andy. I am struggling with this. Ben and I know a lot of people, but we don't have a lot of friends, you know what I mean? I didn't even realize it until this happened. And now, even those friends don't know how to act around me. Everything is so awkward. It's like death might be catching."

She looked at him. "You know something about it, don't you? Death."

His mouth tightened into a grim line. "I do."

"Was it your wife? I thought you said you were divorced."

"Not my wife," he said, starting the truck. "My son. Another time."

She nodded and backed away. "All right. I better get back inside. I'm sorry for being hard on you."

"You weren't."

He watched her go, swarmed with mixed feelings. He'd lied to her.

He was practically draped across her counter.

※

Three weeks went by before she called him. He was on the boat, as usual, but this time the boat was in the water. His conversation with her had sparked enough hope in him to do something constructive, and, perhaps garner another reason to see her. He'd had the marina's mechanic look ol' *Wishy Washy* over, and it turned out all she needed was an oil change, gas, and a new battery. He paid a month's rent for a berth, hoping the rest of September and at least some of October would be nice enough to take her out. Then he'd persuaded his father to sell it to him—God forbid the colossal prick give it away. Now all he needed was a notary. If she didn't call him of her own accord, at least he had a legitimate excuse to see her.

But she did. He was tightening some loose fittings on the handrail when his cell began to ring. The number was local. His hopes soared.

Her voice was hesitant and embarrassed. "Hi. It's me. Carrie. Am I interrupting anything?"

"No—no, not at all. Just working on my boat. Is everything okay?"

"I—well, mostly. I'm trying to mow the lawn and the mower won't start. You said if I needed something I could call you. But if you're busy—"

He was already climbing onto the dock. "Where do you live?"

She gave him her address and he told her he'd be there in ten. He trotted to his truck, the fastest he'd moved in two years, his heart skipping. He pulled up to the house and liked it immediately. It was cedar-sided with a big porch and an attached two car garage. Well-tended flower beds ran the length of the front and flanked both sides. Ben must've had a good job; Andy wondered if she would be able to stay.

She stepped out of the shadows of the garage just as he killed the truck's engine. The day was warm, and she had on a pair of olive green shorts and a white tee. She smiled tentatively as he got out.

"I'm really sorry," she said, wringing her hands. "I didn't know who else to call. My brother's in Baltimore, and I don't think he knows any more about lawnmowers than I do. I don't know our neighbors very well, so."

"It's okay. I'm glad you called. Let's take a look at it."

The mower in question was out back, sitting in front of the small shed from which she'd pushed it. It was a new John Deere rider, like the one his dad owned. *Please God, let me be able to fix this thing.*

He swung onto the seat. "Does it even turn over?"

"Sort of. It starts to and then nothing happens. I'm embarrassed to admit I've never used it. Ben always mowed the lawn. I might not even be doing it right, for all I know. I did get the manual out, and it *seems* like I'm doing it right, but, no go. It's probably me, I'm so stupid not to know how to do it. It's a fucking lawnmower for God's sake, not rocket science."

She stopped then and took a deep breath, her cheeks coloring, and at that moment, he fell in love with her, his heart dropping like a single, perfectly round stone into a still pool. *Plunk!* The day brightened; everything became acute. He saw her very clearly:

nervous, and behind that, looming like a caul, raw, black terror at her own perceived helplessness. He fought the urge to kiss her.

He pushed in the throttle with his foot and turned the key. The engine cranked and stalled. He glanced at her and saw her relief.

"That's what I did. Good. At least I'm not a total idiot."

"You're not an idiot." He got off and lifted the mower's hood. "Do you know when he changed the sparkplugs last?"

She arched her brow and put her hands on her hips. They both laughed. "Right," he said. "Is there a workbench around, in the garage maybe? Where he keeps stuff?"

She led him back to the garage, and indeed, there was just such a bench along the back wall with a red metal storage cabinet underneath, the kind with deep shallow drawers. He began opening them one by one, feeling a bit like he had at the funeral home, an intruder poking into a dead man's space. He closed them and then scanned the top of the bench, drumming his fingers on one thigh. There was a plastic Home Depot bag tucked amid a random pile of work gloves, duct tape, and hand tools. He opened it. Relief filled him. Inside was an unopened package of plugs. Evidently, Ben Owens had been planning on changing them but had died before he could get to it.

He held them up for her to see. Her eyes widened. "No way! Oh, I hope that's all it is."

"Only one way to find out." He walked back out and swapped out the old plugs with the new ones. He climbed back on and turned the key. The Deere sputtered once and then roared to life.

He let it idle for a minute and then shut it off. When he looked up he found her wiping her eyes.

"Sorry," she said. "I'm such a baby. Thank you."

"I wish you'd stop apologizing and calling yourself names," he chided. "I'm just glad I could fix it."

"I would've spent fifty bucks on a repair guy to pick it up and take it to a shop. Ridiculous."

"Do you want me to mow the lawn while I'm here?"

"Oh, gosh, no, I've already messed up your day." She gestured around her. "It's a big yard. Front and back takes, like, over an hour."

There was a set of ear protectors hanging on the steering wheel. He put them on and grinned, firing up the engine again. "Sorry, can't hear you!"

She shook her head and rolled her eyes, but stepped back as he put the mower in gear. He gave her a wave and watched as she walked back to the house, unable to help but notice the shapely curve of her legs.

An hour and a half later he backed the mower into its shed and walked to the house just as she emerged with a couple of beers. She handed him one.

"I seem to remember you're a drinking man."

He accepted it, wondering how the reference was intended. Her tone belied little. She took a long pull and then gestured to the deck. "Sit for a bit?"

He followed her, taking a seat at an octagonal glass-topped table. The deck looked new—smelled new, too, the not unpleasant odor of treated lumber filling his nostrils. He drank and studied her. She sat one chair away from him, squinting across the yard.

"Nice job. I guess I'll be mulching leaves pretty soon."

"It's coming," he agreed. "And the snow after that. Who plows your driveway?"

"I don't know," she said vaguely. "Some guy. There's a lot I don't know, I'm discovering. I don't do much around here except clean the toilets, I guess. Ben took care of all the finances. I didn't even know who our mortgage was with. My brother had to help me figure it out."

"I'm sure you do more than you think," he said.

She shrugged and smiled grimly. "I do now. I just never paid any attention to that stuff. And Ben didn't push it. Funny how we feel so invincible. And then *bam*, you get the rug jerked out from under you."

"That's true." He took a sip. "Will you stay here?"

"For now. I do like it here. I have—there was life insurance. I just have to figure out how to manage it. Chris—my brother—says I should get a financial advisor. He's right. I don't know how to invest money."

She looked at him. "You're an accountant, right, or something like that? Do you know anything about investing?"

"I am—or was—such an advisor, and I do," he said. "I'll help you if you want."

She was silent for a time. He could tell she was working it out, the pros and cons, whether she could trust him or not. He waited, giving her space, his outward appearance hopefully one of indifference. Inside he was roiling with eagerness.

"Let me think about it," she said. "No offense, but how do I know you know what you're doing?"

He let his breath out slowly. "Oh. I can give you some names and numbers of past clients if you like. That's pretty standard procedure, actually."

He hoped she wouldn't want any. He could get them, but it would require some footwork and he would have to contact his old firm, something he didn't want to do. He hadn't left on the greatest of terms.

He could also tell she was waiting for something else, and he knew it was time to tell her about Billy. God knows he didn't want to—it might end everything right here. He could tell she wanted to trust him, and he wanted her to be able to. He took a big swallow of beer.

"So, I told you I had a son. Billy. He was five when he died. We lived in New York, near Syracuse. I was working at a big investment firm in the city, and Melinda was a nurse at Syracuse Main. We had a nice house in the country, around twenty acres. I had a tractor—a good-sized Kubota for hauling firewood and brush-hogging. Billy loved the thing."

He took another swallow and heard a dry click in his throat. "I always knew it was a bad idea to let him ride with me while I was working, but sometimes it's damn hard to say no to your kid. Melinda hated it—it was the subject of a lot of arguments, for sure. But I did it anyway, you know, figuring I've got him, nothing's going to happen. And one day, I hit a chuck hole and I lost him. I just—lost him."

He closed his eyes. "I remember it like it was yesterday. He pointed up at the sky at an airplane. I leaned back to look—I had my arm around his waist—and the tractor lurched hard. And he was gone. He made one little sound: 'Da.' Then the rear tire rolled over him. I killed him. I killed my boy."

He opened his eyes and found her looking at him. Her expression was intense and sorrowful but without recrimination. He stood.

"Can I get another one of these?" he said, holding up his empty bottle.

"Sit," she said. "I'll get it."

He sat back down and rubbed his face. She soon returned and set two fresh bottles on the table and then put a warm hand on the back of his neck. He looked up at her and tried to speak, found he couldn't, and cleared his throat.

"I was afraid that's where the story was going," she said. "Tell me the rest."

He took a sip of the fresh beer, and she took her seat again. His skin tingled where she had touched him.

"After the accident, Melinda and I drifted away from each other. I couldn't forgive myself, and neither could she. She tried, I think, for a while, but there are some things you just can't get past. I considered killing myself but couldn't muster the balls even to do that. I got depressed, and that's hard to live with. One day I came home from work early—the numbers weren't making any sense—and I found her in bed with some guy. Our bed. She actually looked relieved when I walked in. So, we split the house and the cars and the savings account. I quit my job just ahead of the firing squad and got the fuck out of there."

"Why back here?"

He shrugged. "It was home. I think I told you I grew up here. I moved back in with my parents to save money until I could find a job—at least that's what's on paper. The real reason is to punish myself."

She smiled. "That bad, huh?"

"Real bad, actually. My parents are . . . difficult. My dad was always an asshole, but now he's raised it to a fine art. Can't hear for shit. And my mother has dementia. She can't remember anything from one day to the next. She asks if I'm going to pick Billy up from school every single day."

"Oh God," Carrie said. "How awful."

"Yeah. Exactly the kind of punishment I'm looking for. As good as any jail sentence."

He fell silent, wondering how he must sound. Self-pitying, he supposed. Not a good catch. Damaged goods. Baggage. Not a good replacement for the no doubt perfect Ben Owens.

"You look like you're waiting for something," she said finally.

"I am," he said, a little too sharply. "I'm waiting for the boom to fall. For the judgment."

She shook her head. "You'll get no judgment from me, Andy. What happened was an accident. A terrible, tragic accident, one that happens all the time, unfortunately. I can't comprehend the pain you must feel, every day. I've never had a child. I've lost my parents and now a husband, and those are each their own kind of grief. Losing your child is another kind. But you can't torture yourself for the rest of your life. You've got to live."

"Blah blah, yeah, you're right." He felt anger rising in him. "It sounds good, doesn't it? I don't deserve to move on, don't you get it? My son is dead. I killed him. That thing you said the other day, about the dead being able to look down on you and see what you're doing. Christ, what if my son is watching me right now? How would he feel if he saw me yucking it up and having a good time, knowing he'll never have a chance at anything? I can't bear that, no more than you can."

He stood. "I better go. I'm sorry I told you. Call me, I guess, if you want me to look at your books."

He walked around the side of the house to his truck, his vision blurring. He was behind the wheel before he realized she'd followed him.

"What?" he said.

She looked off across the yard, chewing her lower lip. "Grief is like a mean jack-in-the-box, you know? You think you're managing, getting it together, and then surprise! It jumps out at you. I was brushing my teeth the other night and saw Ben's toothbrush still in the holder next to mine. And I lost it. Crazy, huh? Undone, by a toothbrush."

She turned to him. "I want you to help me. I like you, Andy. Okay? I like you even more than I did before. Thank you for telling me. I know it was hard."

He sat, watching her, and saw himself. "What did you do with it?" he asked. "The toothbrush."

Her hand went to her mouth, where it fluttered like a bird. "I slept with it under my pillow for two nights and then made myself throw it away."

She went into her house. He drove home. There, he opened the drawer of his bedside table and pulled out a coloring book, the faded crayon wandering outside the lines here and there. He leafed through it, his throat working, and then held it over the trashcan, where it hovered uncertainly. He put it back in the drawer and slammed it shut. Then he lay down on his narrow bed and stared at the ceiling, tears leaking unheeded down his cheeks.

 **CARRIE LET TWO WEEKS PASS BEFORE** she called him to set up a time for him to come over and look at her finances, not so much because of their conversation but more out fear of what he might think of her shabby organizational skills. Ben had kept everything in such neat order; now, in a matter of a few weeks, his office looked like it had been ransacked, and it pretty much had. Her attempts at sorting through files in search of passwords and things had resulted in chaos. Particularly since these attempts were made after a long day at work, with a glass of wine to keep her company.

Andy had sounded dull when he said Saturday afternoon would be fine. The calendar had made the turn into October, but it remained warm. She thought she might have him stay for dinner if things went well, a simple gesture of gratitude for his help. Nothing more, she told herself. She put a roast in the slow cooker that morning and bought some good bread. She even went so far as to make an apple pie, a little embarrassed at her extensive efforts. But, she hadn't cooked much since Ben's death, and it had been pleasurable to fix a meal for someone.

He rang the bell promptly at three. He looked tired, and her heart went out to him. *You're not sleeping much, are you?*

"Wow," he said, pausing in the kitchen. "It smells amazing in here."

"Thanks," she said, well-pleased. "I got the urge to cook today. I was wondering if you'd like to stay for dinner if you have no other plans."

"I'd like to," he said and then dropped his gaze. "I'm sorry I left the way I did, last time. It still gets me pretty upset."

"It's all right. You didn't say how long ago it was."

"Two years in June."

"Do you ever hear from Melinda?"

"No. I heard she married the guy she was, you know, fucking. That's all I know."

"And there's where we'll leave it," she said. "Come on and take a look at the mess I've made. You'll wish you never set eyes on me."

She led him to the office with considerable trepidation. "I tried to clean it up a bit for you, but I think I keep making it worse. Believe it or not, this was actually quite tidy until I got my hands on it."

He surveyed the damage. "Okay. Geez. Where do you want to start?"

She pointed to two very big checks sitting side by side on the desk. "With those. What's the best thing for me to do with those?"

She watched him absorb the amounts. "That's a million dollars."

"Yes," said simply. "Ben took care of me. My brother says if I invest properly I should be okay, maybe even better than okay."

He sat down at the computer and did a Google search on investment companies. A bunch came up, Charles Schwab, Fidelity to name a few. He explained how they worked.

"Basically, you can manage your wealth on your own, if you know what you're doing. I know, you don't. But I'll help you, and these companies have people you can talk to. What are your goals, short and long term? No holds barred. We'll work back from there."

She thought a minute. "Seriously? The American Dream, I guess. I want to quit my job, pay off my house and go to the French Riviera every summer. Is that possible?"

He grinned. "Maybe not the Riviera part. Not right away, and not *every* summer. But maybe the house and at least get you down to part-time. How much do you owe?"

She surrendered everything to him. He went over her debt, which wasn't much: a mortgage three-quarters' of the way paid off, a car payment—Ben liked vintage, she did not—and about three grand in credit card debt. He seemed pleased, and she enjoyed watching him work. He navigated the sites deftly, explaining types of investments and where he thought she should put the money to garner the highest yield. She felt excitement building in her, and relief.

He touched the checks lightly. "Take these to your bank on Monday and put them in your checking account. Then I'll help you distribute the funds. It sounds like you want to simplify things, so I'd take one check and pay off the house and your car. That will still leave over half of it. The rest of it you can put in a place where it's handy but will still grow. The other check we'll put away for your nest egg and see how it takes off."

He paused. "Are you sure you want me to do this? I mean, you can get a broker, or your bank will have options. You'd have to pay for their help—I don't want any money—but I won't be offended."

"I don't trust anybody else."

"You don't even know me, Carrie."

She looked at him steadily. "Yes, I do."

She insisted he look at all her bills to make sure nothing was lurking in some file that would bring her to financial ruin, but he declared her solvent, compared to most people. She credited Ben, praise which Andy acknowledged solemnly. They retired to the deck, he with a beer, she with a glass of wine. It was going on five o'clock—he'd also helped organize her files, a task which had taken the better part of an hour on top of the financial discussion.

"So, I have a favor to ask you," he said, settling into a chair.

"Ah, here it comes," Carrie said, smiling.

He grinned a bit sheepishly. "Not really. Maybe. I hope not. A small favor. I think I mentioned I have a boat. It's my dad's boat actually, but he's agreed to sell it to me. The trailer, too. I was hoping you'd help me with the notary work."

"Oh. Well, sure—that's not much of a favor at all. It's my job."

"There's a bit of a wrinkle. My dad won't go to your office to do the work. He has no excuse—he just likes to make things difficult for me. I was hoping you could come to the house. I have both titles."

She thought a minute. "Notarizing the titles is simple enough. I can do that at the house, and I can pilfer the forms from the office. The boat commission is easy—you can just mail the application in. PennDOT is different—I'll have to slide your work in with some other outgoing stuff so you won't have to pay Bert's fees."

"I don't mind paying. I don't want you to get in trouble."

She shrugged. "I won't. The fees get expensive. I'd like to cut you a break where I can."

"Thank you."

She took a deep breath. "You have no idea how grateful I am for your help. My brother tried to help a little when he was here, but he gets so impatient when I can't find something fast enough. I feel like he's judging me."

"Don't get too excited. What if I bankrupt you?"

She laughed and then ventured out on a limb. "You said you haven't worked in almost two years and you seem to be doing all right. Granted, living with your parents, but that's about something else. It's also financial prudence. And your truck isn't exactly a beater."

He nodded around a mouthful of beer. "Very observant. I'm not running on fumes, it's true. I actually am pretty good at what I do, all modesty aside. I need to get back in the game soon, though. I'm blowing through my retirement. I'd sort of given up on the idea."

He looked at her. "Things have changed in the last few weeks."

A thrill of excitement ran up her spine. She hoped it was because of her but didn't dare pose the question. She felt suddenly shy, afraid a different answer would douse the ray of hope she had. He did seem to be waiting for something, perhaps nurturing hopes of his own.

"I'm glad," she said.

He relaxed visibly and took another swallow. They sat that way for a comfortable time, settling into one another. The air was cooling rapidly; soon it would be time to eat. She was finding it difficult lately to relish moments—there were precious few worth it—instead looking ahead to when something might end. When the time came for him to go, for instance, and leave her to face another restless night.

She looked down and saw her glass was empty. How many was this? The first? It must have been a big pour because she was feeling it. She pointed questioningly at his bottle and he nodded.

"Thirsty work, all this wheeling, and dealing," he remarked.

She laughed and gathered his empty. On her way by, she gave his shoulder a brief squeeze. She fortified their refreshments and checked on dinner. It was bubbling nicely, so she shut off the cooker. The petite loaf of Italian she'd bought had been warming in the toaster oven, wrapped in foil. She turned the heat off but left it in until they were ready.

"Dinner'll be ready in about ten minutes," she said, back outside. "Do you want to eat out here?"

"If you don't mind. It's pretty here." He paused. "I was thinking, if you're not busy tomorrow, would it be a good day to do the title work? We're supposed to have another warm day and I'd like to take the boat out. I may not get many more chances this year. You could come with me if you like."

She hesitated, not from doubt, but from the logistics. Getting into the office would be no problem—Bert, in lieu of flowers perhaps, had given her a key—but she still felt like she would be trespassing.

"Not like a date or anything," he added hastily. "I mean, you don't have to if it makes you uncomfortable. Or we could do it another time. The title work, I mean."

"No, no. I want to. I'd like that very much. I haven't been on a boat in a million years. What time tomorrow?"

"Eleven, maybe? I could pick you up and bring you over to the house. I could pack us a lunch and then we could tool around for the afternoon until we get bored, or it sinks, or you throw me to the fishes."

"I doubt any of those things will happen. That sounds perfect. I'll swing by the office first thing and get what I need." She stood. "Let's eat."

They brought dinner out to the deck and ate in relative quiet after Andy pronounced her an excellent cook. She believed him—he went at the roast like it was his last meal. Afterward, they brought coffee and pie out. She lit a couple of candles and studied his face in the flickering light while he ate.

He pushed his plate away and heaved a contented sigh. "That was amazing, Carrie. I'll put on ten pounds if I keep hanging around you."

She blushed, pleased. "You can handle it. You're a pretty lean machine."

They lapsed into silence. She was thinking about the coming day and what to wear when there came a rustling from the edge of the yard. She sat up and looked uneasily into the darkness.

Andy followed her gaze. "What is it?"

"I don't know. Did you hear that?"

"I guess," he said, and turned back to her, his brow knitted. "I was sort of distracted. Do you want me to have a look?"

"No," she said, her hands gripping the chair. "God, no. It could be a bear. Or something else."

"Like what?"

She stood abruptly, banging her thighs against the table hard enough to send coffee sloshing. "Let's go inside, shall we?"

He followed her obediently, hands full of cups and plates. She locked the door firmly and stood looking out. He came up beside her, having deposited the dishes in the kitchen.

"What's out there?" he asked softly. "The boogeyman?"

She glanced at him and saw he was teasing her. She uttered a shaky laugh and shook herself off.

"Wouldn't you be embarrassed if it was. I'm turning into a paranoid. I just, I don't know. I've had this weird feeling of being watched. It's almost every night now. I thought I heard something the other night, and finally got up the nerve to look out the window, and—"

She stopped and shook her head. He was looking at her with mild concern, his humor gone.

"And what?" he asked.

"I did see something. Maybe it was just a deer. But when I woke up the next morning, I found this—this smear on the windowsill. It wasn't really a handprint but I don't know what else would have made it."

"Is it still there?"

"No. I washed it off. I couldn't bear to look at it." She swallowed hard. "I know I'm lonely and things always seem worse at night, right? It's just that with all the things that've been happening, the disappearances, I can't help but feel a little freaked out. Am I being a baby?"

He touched her face. "Not at all."

He was looking at her with those fine gray eyes, and for the first time in a long time, she felt like she was really being seen. She tilted her head back, extending an invitation she knew was too soon in the making and not caring.

He took her face in both hands and kissed her, enveloping her in his strong embrace. It was an embrace she remembered well, had tried to forget, one that had gouged her with guilt. Now it was food for her. She could feel it in him as well, his need to be touched and held.

She broke the kiss, flustered. He continued to hold her, stroking her hair and pressing his lips against the top of her head, her forehead, her cheeks, before he sought her mouth again. Her heart hammered against her ribs so hard she feared she might be having a heart attack. She found one last shred of control and pushed him back, her hands on his chest. She was near tears and cursed herself for it.

He gave a slight but firm nod. "I know. I should go."

"I don't want you to," she said, her voice tremulous. God, she sounded on the verge of hysteria. "But I'm kind of drunk and I don't want to make a mistake. Not that this is a mistake—I don't mean that, Andy, I don't. It's just—it's too soon, isn't it? Is it?"

He took her hands away from his chest and held them. "I can't make that decision for you. It's nobody's decision but yours. I don't want to be a mistake. God, we're right back where we started."

He swallowed hard and looked out into the night. "I care about you a lot, Carrie. *A lot*. As for tomorrow, sleep on it. When you wake up in the morning, clear-headed, and you still want to spend the day with me, call me."

He looked at her, his eyes searching hers. "All right?"

"Okay," she said weakly, swiping at her eyes. "I care a lot about you, too. I *know* I do."

He kissed the tears from her hands and then walked to the front door. "Good night, Carrie. Sleep tight."

She closed the door and leaned against it for a long time. She made sure all the doors were locked and then got ready for bed. She went to the window and stood looking out at her darkened yard. Eyes stared back at her, and she gave a start. Then she laughed—they were her own eyes, reflected in the glass.

She drew the blinds and crawled into bed. There, she lay staring at the ceiling, remembering Andy's touch. She ran her hands over her body, imagining his weight on top of her, his mouth on her.

She felt those eyes upon her again, boring into her despite the blinds. She moaned and rolled onto her side, drawing the covers over her head.

"I'm sorry, Ben," she said. "I'm sorry."

11

WHEN ANDY GOT HOME, HE WENT straight to his room, not even bothering to announce his return. His parents were cloistered in front of the TV, absorbed in some show, unidentifiable to Andy despite the volume. He locked the door behind him and shed his jeans. He stretched out on his bed; relief came in a jarring spasm within about thirty seconds. He lay breathing in harsh gasps, one arm thrown quivering over his face.

He pulled on a pair of sweats, feeling drained but unsatisfied. He went to the bathroom and brushed his teeth, looking at himself in the mirror, thoughts rumbling through his mind in a black, awful train: *What if she doesn't call. What if I never see her again? What if? What if?*

He crawled into bed and curled onto his side like a boy, his hands tucked under his pillow. Moonlight shone through his window, striping the worn carpet. He wondered at her, just a few miles away, in her own bed, thinking God knows what, making a decision he could neither argue for or against. It was, as he'd said himself, hers alone to make. If the answer was no thank you, he decided he would drive a hole through the bottom of the boat and watch it sink, like all his hopes of anything good.

Dawn came with a cottony mist that was supposed to burn off by late morning. He showered and shaved, his phone close by. Nine o'clock came, and his hopes began to flag. Nine-thirty it rang. It was her. He snatched it up too quickly, and it danced from hand to hand, mocking him.

"Hi," she said, her voice far off like she was driving. "I'm on my way to the office to get my stuff. Is that still okay?"

He sank onto his bed. "You bet it is. And—and the boat?"

He could almost hear her smile through the phone. "I think it's a great day for a boat ride. I'll see you at my house at eleven."

She ended the call. He sat cradling his phone, and then raised both hands and allowed himself a small whoop of delight.

When he pulled up to her house, she emerged with a yellow folder in one hand and her purse slung over one shoulder. She was wearing a light short-sleeved sweater and shorts. She climbed into his truck and laid her things on the floor.

"Hi," she said. "Ready?"

"I am." He paused, wanting to kiss her, but not badly enough to endure the disappointment if she pulled away. Maybe once they got on the boat they could talk about things. Where she stood. She snapped on her seatbelt, and he put the truck in reverse. "Let's do this thing."

The drive to his parents' house was mostly silent, punctuated by bits of trivialities that felt strained to him. He wondered if she was having second thoughts. Weariness settled over him, a feeling which intensified as he pulled into their white gravel driveway. He watched as she surveyed the house.

"Not much, is it?" he said.

She shrugged. "It's not nothing. It's fine, really. I should be living in such a house."

He doubted as much. She started to get out but he put a hand on her arm. She looked at him questioningly.

"Listen," he said. "Before we go in there, I just want to remind you my dad can be kind of a dick. If he says anything to you, don't take it personally. It'll be a dig at me if anything."

"Why don't you two get along?"

He sighed, resting one arm on the steering wheel. "Who knows. I'm their only child. Honestly, I think it started when I got my growth spurt. He's always been self-conscious about his height. I think he liked me better when I was shorter than him. And he resents my hair."

"Your *hair*?"

He ran his hand through it reflexively. "He was bald by his late twenties. I'm thirty-five and still have all my lustrous locks. He makes little jabs about it all the time. Calls it my girly wig. Shit like that."

"Wow," Carrie said. "That's messed up. Anything else?"

"Oh, sure. He never went to college. He's 'a self-made man.' He didn't need college to get his education. My BS in accounting stands for bullshit, and so on. He thinks accountants are all shysters, even though he hires some guy in town to do his taxes every year. He won't let me touch his money."

"Wow," Carrie said again. "He is a dick."

"Yeah," Andy said, smiling ruefully. "On that note, let's go meet him!"

They got out of the truck. The sound of the television could be heard from the yard. Carrie cocked her head to one side. "Seinfeld," she said, and quipped, "No soup for you."

Inside the noise was deafening. He directed her to the kitchen table and pulled out a chair. "Wait here."

He went into the living room and hit the mute button on the remote. His father reared back in his Lazy Boy, his eyes narrowed behind his bifocals. "What the hell are you doing?"

"The notary is here, dad. For the boat and the trailer."

"*What?*"

Andy's shoulders slumped. Louder this time. "I said, the notary is here! About the boat title! You said you'd sign off on the titles if I brought a notary to the house!"

"I don't remember that," Bill Korn muttered, but he got slowly to his feet. He shuffled to the kitchen. Andy pulled a chair out for him and he eased into it with many affected groans. Andy watched Carrie assess his old man. She lifted her chin and her brown eyes grew dark. Then she smiled politely.

"Hello Mr. Korn," she said, very loudly.

Andy's dad stirred and looked at her. He offered a brittle smile. "So you're in cahoots with this runt here. Stealing my property. Think I'll just sign off on it, do you?"

"Yes," Carrie said, planting her words like bricks in cement. Andy watched with growing fascination. Gone was the trembling woman from the night before. In her place, a lioness.

"Yes, you've agreed to do that—the boat and trailer for the combined agreed upon price of five hundred dollars." She looked at Andy. "I need the titles and both your driver's licenses."

"I don't have a driver's license," Bill muttered, looking askance.

Andy sighed. "Yes, you do. Where's your wallet?"

Without waiting for an answer, he began rummaging through kitchen drawers and soon found it. He pulled out the license and handed it to Carrie, along with his own. Carrie studied them and then wrote their names in her notary register. All business, she gave them back to him.

"I'll need copies of those, front and back. Do you have a printer with copying capabilities?"

"Yes," he said. "In my room."

"Good. We'll do that later." She marked x's where they needed to sign on the titles. "Mr. Korn, you need to sign right here on this one and here on this one."

She put her finger next to the mark and didn't move it, despite Bill's efforts to dislodge it. "No, here," she said firmly. "Right here."

He signed both titles, along with the boat commission form; only then did Andy begin to relax. Carrie signed, dated and stamped them, and then tucked them in her folder. She looked up at Andy.

"We can get your signature later. Let's get your licenses copied, and then we're done here."

She turned to Andy's dad. "Thank you, Mr. Korn. You're all done. You can go back to your program."

Bill Korn made no move to rise. Instead, he studied her with his flinty gaze, probably expecting her to wither beneath it.

"What's a looker like you doing with this runt here?" he asked.

Andy watched blood creep up Carrie's neck to her face. It was not the blush of embarrassment. He realized she was furious.

She put her hands on the table. "Helping him deal with your bullshit."

Andy's mouth fell open, but Bill Korn merely grunted. He continued to stare at the woman before him, tracing his gnarled fingers across the faded oilcloth.

"When I was in the workforce, we knew what to do with little gals like you. Grab you right where it counts and give a little squeeze. Worked every time."

"Okay dad, that's enough," Andy said. It was all he could do to keep from throwing his father across the room. Carrie, on the other hand, seemed very cool, though she was throwing off enough sparks to ignite a bonfire. She stood, bracing her hands on the tabletop.

"I see little bald cranky fucks like you at work every day," she said. "You come shuffling in, trying to convince the world it's your dick swinging below your knees instead of your ball sack, but everybody knows. Everybody knows from the kiddies to the biddies you're scared shitless. Eternity's a dark place, Mr. Korn. You're scared of the dark, aren't you?"

She looked at Andy. "Where's your room?"

Andy led her upstairs and showed her in. She sat on his bed while he made the copies, gripping the mattress, her elbows locked. He stole glances at her from time to time, still shocked by her outburst. He sat down in his desk chair and looked at her full on.

"Where did that come from?"

She let her breath out in a giant rush as if she'd been holding it. "I'm sorry. I usually have more self-control. If I didn't, I'd have been fired a long time ago. I just hate it when people think they can say shit like that and get away with it."

"I'm sorry for what he said. I knew he might be ugly, but not that bad. It's embarrassing. I should've made him come to the office, though he might have been just as nasty."

Carrie clasped her hands between her knees. "It wasn't so much what he said to me. I didn't like him calling you names."

Andy smiled. "Runt? Yeah. He's always called me that."

Carrie shook her head. "I could see it if you were short. But you're like, what, six two?"

"Three. It's not my height he's referring to."

She arched her brow. "You're of no consequence? Emotionally puling? Weak of spirit? What a shame he doesn't see what a fine son he has."

Andy felt himself blushing. He looked away and touched the paperwork. "Do you want to finish this up here?"

They swapped seats. She filled out the forms and then motioned him over for his signatures. She made no move to relinquish the chair; when he leaned over to sign, he could smell her perfume again. His throat tightened.

She only moved away when he needed to write the checks, and when she resumed her place on his bed again, he was keenly aware of it.

When he was finished, she got up and put everything back in her folder. "Okay," she said. "I'll mail this stuff in for you on Monday. Here's the green slip so we can take the boat out today. We are still doing that, aren't we?"

"I'm game if you are. I packed us a lunch—I hope you like ham and cheese."

Her gaze softened. "How sweet of you. Ham's great. I'll pretty much eat anything."

They walked back out to the kitchen. Bill Korn had retreated to the living room, where Seinfeld was ending. Andy's mother was at the kitchen sink, picking glasses out of the dish drainer and looking at them as if she'd never seen them before. Andy sighed. *Here we go,* he thought. *Round two.*

"Hi mom," he said. "What are you looking at?"

"Hello dear. These glasses—are they new?"

She turned. Her face lit up when she saw Carrie. "Why, Melinda! When did you get here?"

"This isn't Melinda, mom," Andy said. "This is my friend Carrie. She's a notary. She came out to take care of the boat and trailer titles."

"What boat?"

"Never mind. It's not important. Carrie, this is my mom."

Carrie smiled and offered her hand. "It's nice to meet you, Mrs. Korn. You have a lovely home."

"Thank you, dear." Judy Korn looked curiously at her son. "Where is Melinda, honey?"

Andy felt the beginnings of a headache forming at his temples. "In New York, with her new husband. We got divorced, remember?"

"For heaven's sake! You didn't tell me that. Well, is Billy with her?"

"Yes," he said. "He's with her. We're going out for a while. I don't know when I'll be back."

Andy grabbed the cooler with the lunch he'd packed and ushered Carrie out the door. Her expression was sad and sympathetic, and at that moment, he knew he was done living with his parents. He had a flash of something, not quite a premonition, but a feeling something was going to happen. It was as frightening as it was exhilarating, and for the moment, he was glad.

12 THEY DROVE TO THE MARINA IN silence. Carrie didn't know what to say to him. No words of comfort seemed adequate. She couldn't imagine living such a horror, someone asking her, every day, *Where's Ben?*

He pulled into the parking lot and shut off the engine, his hands resting on the steering wheel. He looked at her, silent, waiting.

"You have to get out of there," she said.

"I know. Funny, seeing things through other people's eyes. I mean, I knew it was bad when I moved in. That's *why* I moved in. Now that I don't want to be there anymore, I'm a little afraid to leave them alone."

"Would they go to a home?"

"I don't know. I haven't talked to them about it yet." He shook his head as if trying to clear it. "Come on. Let's hit the water."

They walked out to the pier side by side. He led her to a big white motorboat, much bigger than she'd imagined, over twenty feet. He helped her aboard, stowing the cooler near the front. For the first time in a long time, she began to feel excited—almost giddy, in fact.

"Wow," she said, taking it all in. "This is nice."

"Thanks," he said, looking pleased. "It's all mine, thanks to you. It even has a cabin so you can sleep on board and a head. That's the bathroom, in boat talk."

She laughed. "Right—the important stuff. As long as I can get to the head and the galley, I'm good."

"Ahoy, Captain Korn," said a voice. She turned to see a man of about fifty approaching, wearing a t-shirt sporting the name of the marina on it.

"Hi Chuck," Andy said. He held up the temporary registration. "She's all mine."

"About time," Chuck said, but he was clearly more interested in Carrie's presence than the piece of paper. "I see you have a first mate."

Andy nodded, a bit shyly, Carrie thought. "Carrie Owens, this is Chuck Pettit, owner of this lovely marina. Chuck, Carrie."

Carrie shook his hand. "Nice to meet you."

"For sure, for sure." He appraised her bemusedly. "So, you're not scared to go out with this bloke on his maiden voyage?"

"Maiden voyage?" Carrie asked. "You've never had her out?"

"Nope," Andy said, grinning. "You're my first victim."

"Oh boy," she said. "Lucky me."

Chuck laughed. "Don't worry. He can get you out of the harbor, at least. I have seen him do that."

He helped them cast off, and Andy started the engine. The boat came to life with a satisfying rumble. Chuck waved to them as he backed the *Wishy Washy* carefully out to open water. Once out, Andy throttled up and they moved briskly toward the middle of the lake. Normally crowded, it was all but deserted, this being the off-season. Other than a fishing boat or two, they had the water pretty much to themselves.

Carrie smiled, enjoying the feel of the sun and wind on her face. She watched Andy navigate, admiring the comfortable way he sat in the captain's chair, the wind blowing his hair back. He had fine, chiseled features and full lips. She'd been disappointed he hadn't tried to kiss her, or even touch her at all. Perhaps he'd been having second thoughts, or maybe he was nervous at her meeting his parents, and with good reason. She hoped for the latter.

Andy nosed the boat into a little cove and dropped the anchor. It was just after noon by her watch. He got out the cooler and handed her a sandwich and a bottle of water. He'd also packed an array of chips. She picked a snack-sized bag of Baked Lays and settled back, alternating between bites of sandwich and chips, enjoying the view. Expensive houses lined the shore, outlined prettily by trees lit with autumn's fire. The sky was clear and brilliant, the air hovering right around seventy degrees.

"I still can't believe this is October," she said. "Maybe it'll forget to snow. Global warming's not so bad, after all."

"That's a hoax, you know," he said. "Right up there with that moon landing thing."

For a moment he looked completely sincere. Then he tipped her a wink, and she burst out laughing. He joined her, and she couldn't seem to stop. After a minute she wiped her eyes and shook her head.

"God, I love you," she said.

Andy had taken another bite of sandwich; he froze in mid-chew around a mouthful of ham and swiss. He stared at her.

Her smile faded, and she knew it, knew just as surely as she was sitting there, it was true. Her skin prickled all over and her heart went into overdrive.

"I do," she said. "I really do. I love you, Andy."

He didn't say anything, and for a moment she was afraid. Then he swallowed the bite in one hard gulp—she tracked its progress down his throat with some alarm. He took a swig of water, rinsing his mouth, and then scooted across the bench and kissed her.

"I love you, too," he said. "The minute I walked into your office I knew we had something. It sounds like a cliché, but I don't care. I'm yours, Carrie—however you want me, you've got me."

He kissed her again and ran his hand over the side-swell of her breast and then down to the warm place between her legs. When he tried to move it, she kept it firmly there.

"I want you to make love to me right here on this boat," she said.

He hesitated, and she was instantly mortified at her own forwardness. He bowed his head and she was about to back-pedal when he spoke.

"I want to. But I wasn't expecting—I mean, I didn't bring anything. You know."

Relief swept her. "Oh. That's okay—you don't need to worry. I can't get pregnant. And I don't have cooties, either. Do you?"

He relaxed visibly and then offered her an impish smile. "No— just the clap."

He took her down into the stuffy little cabin. She stretched out on the narrow berth and watched him undress, smiling a little because he looked like a giant in a gnome's house. He came to her and she helped him take her clothes off, arching her back to undo her bra for him. Then he moved over her and into her. The weight of his body on hers was a deeply satisfying comfort. He nibbled and kissed his way over her face and neck; she heard her name over and over, and the word love. The urgent rocking of his hips harmonized that of the boat.

Afterward, they lay in the puddled single sweaty sheet, she on her back, he on his side, his head propped in one hand. The other roamed its way across her body, caressing and exploring. She let him, reveling in the simple pleasure of being touched.

"My God, you're beautiful," he said.

She smiled. "You're not so bad yourself, fella."

"Thanks." He paused, his brow knitting. "I don't mean to keep hammering the subject, but what kind of birth control do you use? Are you on the pill?"

"No. Ben and I tried to get pregnant for about a year and a half with no luck. We went to a fertility clinic, and we're both viable, but apparently, my uterus is what the specialist called 'inhospitable'. We had just started exploring our options when the accident happened."

"Is it something you're still wanting?"

She could see he was anxious; the question carried a lot of weight. She stared at the low ceiling, considering how best to frame her answer.

"I don't think so, Andy. I'll be thirty-nine in a few months. Ben and I got a late start on the baby train, to begin with. At first, when I found out I probably couldn't get pregnant, it was hard. You make that big, scary life-changing decision and start all the planning, picking out names—you know. And then it doesn't happen."

He was silent for a moment. "You just said probably. There's still a chance you can get pregnant?"

"Not much of one. Like ninety-eight percent unlikely, which is almost the same percentage as getting pregnant while on the pill. Don't worry, Andy. If I was going to get pregnant, I would've by now."

He was again silent, and she could see he wasn't totally convinced. She rolled onto her side to look at him directly. "You're really worried about this, aren't you?"

He gave her that sad, haunted look she'd seen when she first met him. "I don't want to have any more kids. I don't think I could handle it. If something bad happened again, Carrie, I'd kill myself."

He took her hand. "I don't want there to even be a chance. I'll schedule a vasectomy as soon as possible. I've always planned on getting one, but up until now, I haven't had a reason. Until I do, I'll use a condom."

She kissed him. "Do whatever you need to do. I don't want anything to come between us."

He smiled, but she could tell by the way his throat worked he was upset. She wasn't doing much better. The talk of Ben and babies that weren't to be had stirred her emotions. She pulled him to her and kissed him again.

"I want you," she said, her voice thick. "So much. You don't need a condom or an operation. Trust me on this, Andy—we're not going to make a baby."

She watched him wrestle with it for a minute, and then she put her hands on him. Desire beat out fear as it usually did; he rolled on top of her again. When it was over, he held her for a long time, even dozing a bit. She lay with her head on his chest, the rise and fall of his breathing, his heartbeat, everything she needed.

A while later they emerged, tacky with sweat and grateful for the breeze. He started the engine and they spent the remainder of the afternoon motoring around the lake, exploring its many coves and islands. At around four-thirty, Andy pointed the boat for the marina. Chuck was there when they arrived to help them tie off.

"You're all in one piece I see," he said with a smile. "Must've done all right."

"He's a fine captain," Carrie said as he helped her ashore. "Best afternoon ever."

He and Carrie walked to his truck. He set the cooler in the back and then stood before her awkwardly, his hands limp at his sides.

"Do you have plans this evening?" he asked.

She looked at him for a minute and then laughed. "Yes. I was hoping someone would come over for dinner. I have a lot of leftover roast beef."

"Yeah, okay," he said, smiling, but still clearly troubled. "And then?"

"I'd like you to spend the night. I know what's bothering you. Which bed, right? Let's worry about that when the time comes. If sleeping in the master bedroom is uncomfortable for either one of us, there are two spare rooms we can choose from. How does that sound?"

"Sounds fine," he said. "I just don't want to overstep my, I don't know. Bounds. Welcome. Whatever."

She wrapped her arms around his waist and pressed her face into his chest. "I don't want to spend another night in my house alone. And I can't stand the thought of you tossing and turning in that little boy's bed at your parents' funhouse. Stay with me. We'll figure it out."

But when they got to her house, Andy stopped the truck at the head of the drive. There was another car parked in front of the garage. A Toyota with Maryland plates.

"Goddammit," Carrie said, blind-sided. "What's my brother doing here?"

"You didn't know he was coming?" Andy asked unhappily.

"I had no idea," she said and picked up her purse. "Of course, I haven't looked at my phone all day. I didn't even think of it."

There was a single text, posted an hour ago: I'm here at the house. Thought I'd surprise you. Where are you?

"Fuck," Carrie muttered. She looked at Andy, who was visibly uncomfortable. "You better take me in there."

She knew what he was thinking and didn't blame him. She was suddenly nervous herself, for Chris could be a hothead. An overprotective hothead, which came in handy sometimes. Now, not so much.

"I guess this squashes our plans for tonight," Andy said.

"No. No, it doesn't. He can stay in a hotel."

"Carrie—"

"No," she said firmly. "It will be all right."

Chris was sitting on the porch but got up as Andy parked the truck. He walked toward them casually enough, though the look on his face was one of suspicion.

"Hi," he said, giving Carrie a hug. "What's going on here?"

Andy came around the front of the truck and stood by her, hands stuffed in his pockets, his gaze shifting from her brother to the ground. Chris was at least a good two inches shorter than him, but Andy seemed to shrink beneath her brother's cobalt stare. She found herself irritated at both of them.

"This is Andy," she said. "You might remember him."

"I sure do," Chris said. He didn't offer to shake hands. "Andy what?"

Andy sighed. "Korn."

Chris barked a cruel laugh. "With a c or a k?"

"Cut it out, Chris," Carrie said. "There's no reason to be nasty."

"Oh really? I'm sorry. It's just that I remember walking him out of Ben's viewing at your request. Your *frantic* request, in fact. And yet here he is. I don't get it."

"Andy's been helping me. He replaced the sparkplugs in the mower last week."

She knew that sounded lame. She groped for something more official, more sensible. And then she made a mistake.

"Andy's a financial advisor. He's been helping me with the insurance money."

Andy made a small noise in his throat and looked away. Chris stared at her, incredulous.

"Your *money*? Holy shit. Okay." He looked at Andy. "What firm are you with? Someone around here?"

Andy shifted. "I'm actually kind of on my own right now."

"You're unemployed. I see. That's great. It's actually pretty clever of you. Stalking fresh widows at funeral homes and then going to work on their finances. Genius!"

Carrie turned abruptly to Andy. "I think you better go. I'll call you later, okay?"

It was clear he couldn't get out of there fast enough. "Okay. Um, see you, Chris."

"Yeah," Chris said. "You bet."

Carrie watched Andy pull out of the drive and then turned to her brother. "Why are you here? Surprise, my ass. Surprise inspection is more like it."

He tapped his chest. "I was going to help you with those checks. Not some total stranger."

She rolled her eyes. "Oh, like if I went to some firm in town and handed over those checks to one of those total strangers, it would be okay?"

Chris shook his head. "Not the same thing, Carrie, not the same thing. Those guys are insured by their companies. They have accountability. What does this guy have? *Nothing.* I still don't get it. How do you know him? Why the one-eighty?"

"I did his title work for him when he moved back here from New York. We kind of hit it off. He offered to help me if I needed it."

"I bet. That still doesn't explain why you wanted him gone at the funeral home. You said he was in Ben's bowling league. That's bullshit, obviously."

She took a deep breath. "It's none of your business."

Chris looked at her long and hard, his blue eyes turning violet in the deepening shadows. He continued to stare, his brain clicking away, reading her like a book until she felt hot blood crawling up her cheeks and she had to look away.

"Oh Carrie," he moaned, and put a hand to his forehead. "For Christ's sake."

"I don't want to talk about this," she said, her voice shaking. "You should go."

She turned but he caught her arm. "What, you had an affair with him? When?"

"*No.* We just—I ran into him at a bar. I'd had a bad week. I—I needed to blow off some steam. Ben wasn't home. We went to a movie. And we—we—"

She stopped, afraid to go on. How could this day go so horribly wrong? One minute, things seemed to be making sense, and now it was all a shambles, lying at her feet like so many fallen leaves. Chris had systematically dismantled her, like he always could.

He was looking at her now with growing revulsion because he was so *fucking* smart. *Well, why not,* she thought. *Why not?*

"When was this?" he asked. "Ben wasn't home? It was the night he died, wasn't it? The night I texted you at The Timberland. That was him? My God. I'm gonna kill that motherfucker."

"This is none of your business!" she cried, spraying spittle. "It wasn't his fault. It was all mine, okay? You're not my keeper anymore. You have no right!"

She stopped, her chest heaving, eyes wild. He was looking at her like she was crazy, and maybe she was. She felt like she was coming unglued, all her parts loose and flapping in the wind like some unhinged scarecrow. The strain of the last few months, simmering so long unheeded, now boiled over. She wanted to claw her own eyes out and brought her hands up to do just that. Chris caught her, yelling for her to stop. He slapped her, and she slapped him right back. They stood panting, regarding each other balefully.

"I can't believe Ben's only been dead a couple of months and you're already fucking him. Do you know how that looks?"

"I'm so sorry I embarrass you," Carrie said. "Go fuck Emily Post and leave me alone. You can let Rachel watch."

Chris leveled a finger at her. "Watch your mouth, kiddo. You've needed someone to take care of you your whole life. First, it was me. Then it was Ben, and now him."

His face twisted into a mockery of a pouting child. "Because you can't fuck *me*."

"That's it, Chris. Go home. Get off my property. You son of a bitch. I don't want to see you again, maybe ever. We're done."

She turned and walked into the house and slammed the door, locking it. She leaned against it and put her face in her hands, waiting for his knock. When it didn't come, she walked to the kitchen on rubbery legs and poured herself some wine, the bottle clattering briefly on the lip of the glass. She drank it all down, one steady gulp after another, not tasting it. She poured herself another, gripping the counter. Then she picked up her phone and called Andy.

He picked up on the first ring. "Are you okay?"

"No," she said through wine-numbed lips. "No, I am not."

"What happened?"

"We had a pretty bad fight. About you. And me. Ben makes three."

She uttered a high-pitched laugh. "I think I've gone insane in the last ten minutes."

There was a pause on his end. "Is he gone? Your brother, I mean?"

This brought on another titter. Of course, he meant Chris. Ben was dead. Gone, but not forgotten!

"Carrie."

"Yes, he's gone. He hit me. And then I hit him, so I guess we're even."

"He *hit* you?"

"It's all right. Just big brother, little sister stuff. You know. Or I guess you don't. You were an only child. Lucky you."

There was another long pause. "Do you still want me to come over?"

"No. I mean yes. Just—just give me a little while. I need to take a shower. Calm down. Sober up. I've had one glass and I'm half-drunk already."

"Christ, Carrie."

"That's what all you boys like to say." She shook her head. "I'm sorry. Give me a couple hours. Say eight o'clock?"

"All right. Will you call me if he comes back?"

"Yep."

"All right. Carrie? I love you."

"Love you too, Candy Andy."

She hung up and knew that was a terrible thing to say. She almost called him back because she didn't want it to end that way.

What do you mean? asked a voice inside her head. *The call? Or the two of you?*

She bowed her head. Her brother's disapproval loomed like an all too familiar shadow.

"I don't know," she said aloud. "Now I don't really know."

She drained the second glass and stumbled for the shower, the seed of doubt her brother had planted growing in her belly like some poisonous plant. It was his way of controlling her.

It always had been.

13

UNTIL CARRIE CALLED HIM, Andy had been driving aimlessly around town, unsure what to do or where to go. Leaving had been chicken shit, he knew, but he also knew staying would not have helped. Things had apparently escalated badly enough.

When she did finally call, it took everything he had not to go to her immediately; later, he would give anything to have done so. But now, he respected her wish, half-scared she would change her mind and call to tell him to forget it. Forget everything. If the conversation with her brother had gone anything as he feared, it was a distinct possibility.

Eight o' clock finally came, and he drove to her house armed with a pizza. He didn't want her to feel she had to cook for him, even if it was just leftovers. He fairly trotted up the walk, glad to see there was no car sporting Maryland plates in the drive, but when he got to the porch, he came to an abrupt halt. He stood looking at the door for a long time, his mind slowly absorbing what his eyes were feeding it. Then he looked around, unsure for a moment if he was at the right house. He approached slowly, the pizza box drooping in his hands.

Carrie's front door was the heavy metal variety with a brass knocker. It was fronted by a storm door made of a single pane of clear glass. This door stood open on one broken hinge and hung askew like a leaning drunk. The glass was splintered up the middle, amid a kaleidoscope of spidery cracks. The main door was ajar, more than halfway. There was utter stillness about the house, a vacuum of silence as if whatever had come to pass had done so mere minutes before.

"Carrie?"

Her name came out in a cracked whisper, and he tried again, louder. No answer. He set the pizza down on the porch and stood facing the open door, unease building around him in a static charge. He studied the storm door and imagined what force it must have taken to rip it half off. It was not a cheap product. He started to push the main door open, and then Jason's voice—always his voice of reason when circumstances demanded it—spoke up:

Don't touch anything.

Andy curled his fingers into a fist and knuckled the door open. The foyer was empty, but a little bench Carrie kept there was overturned, stiff-legged and mute.

Something broke loose in him; he ran through the house, calling her name. He checked every room, rooms he'd never visited, and then stood in the kitchen, looking wildly about. Her car was in the garage. Her purse sat on the kitchen table, along with her car keys and phone. Unmindful now of fingerprints, he picked it up and tapped it open. She didn't use a lock screen, thank God. He did a quick search. The only recent call was to him. He wet his lips and then found her brother's number in her list of contacts and dialed it.

He answered on the first ring, his voice wary. "Hello?"

"Chris, it's Andy. Is Carrie with you?"

There was a pause. "What the fuck are you doing with her phone?"

"I'm at her house. She isn't here. Is she with you?"

Another pause. "No. What do you mean, she isn't there?"

"Her car's here, and her purse and her phone. But she isn't. Something's happened. The front door's busted in. You're telling the truth: she isn't with you?"

"No! I left a few minutes after you did. What's—"

"I'm calling the police."

Andy ended the call, panic galloping through him. He put down her phone and pulled out his own. Then he dialed 911.

Andy was waiting by his truck when the police pulled up and got out, two township officers, one young, one old. They approached him cautiously; he held out his hands for them to see.

"Good evening sir," said the younger one. "I'm Officer Mead and this is Sergeant Taylor. Are you Andy Korn?"

"Yes. Thanks for getting here so fast. My—my girlfriend is missing. Something bad has happened, I think."

The officers followed him around to the porch. Sergeant Taylor grunted when he saw the door. They both stood looking for what Andy thought was an eternity, hands on their hips. Then Taylor started through the open door, and both officers disappeared inside. Andy could hear them murmuring to one another. Mead stuck his head out.

"You've gone through the house?"

"Yes. I searched every room."

"The surrounding area? The yard?"

"No."

Both officers came out. Mead walked to the cruiser, his phone to his ear. Sergeant Taylor took out a small notepad and came over to where Andy stood.

"Your girlfriend is a Miss Carrie Owens? She's the owner of this house?"

"Yes."

"When did you see her last?"

"At about five-thirty. We spent the afternoon on my boat and then came back here. But her brother was here. Chris Barrett. They started arguing, so I left."

Taylor's bushy gray eyebrows shot up. "Arguing? About what?"

"About me. Chris doesn't like me much."

"And why is that?"

"He just doesn't." Andy stopped. Chris's Toyota was flying up the drive. "Here he is. I called him to make sure Carrie wasn't with him before I called you guys."

Chris got out of his car and walked rapidly toward them. He slowed as he passed the porch, taking in the scene, and then resumed walking, fists clenched, his face a ball of rage.

"You son of a bitch, what did you do to her?" he snarled. He hit Andy in the chest. Andy stumbled back; anger flooded him. He hit Chris back and sent him staggering. Sergeant Taylor stepped between them.

"All right—just calm down everybody. We need to find out what happened here tonight, and this isn't helping. You're Carrie's brother? When was the last time you saw her?"

Chris ran a hand through his neatly clipped hair. "I don't know. I left here around six, I think."

"And how was she when you left?"

"She was—" Chris glanced at Andy, and his face reddened. "She was upset. We were having a discussion. About money. Her husband was killed a couple of months ago. She got a big insurance settlement. And this guy has been trying to get his hands on it."

Andy's mouth fell open. "That is not true."

"It is! You were sizing her up at the funeral home, for Christ's sake. She *demanded* I escort you from the premises. But you've still managed to worm your way in, haven't you? Did you get her to sign those checks over to you? And now she's missing. What have you done with her?"

Andy looked at Sergeant Taylor, who was watching him. "Officer, none of that is true. I swear. Those checks are in her office, probably in a drawer. Check and see. I haven't done anything with them. Carrie and I were going to go to the bank tomorrow and deposit them in *her* checking account. I was going to help her invest them. Nothing more."

By then, Officer Mead had joined them again. At a slight nod from Taylor, he turned and went inside the house. Two state police cars eased up behind the township car. Two troopers got out and approached, Forbes and Malloy by their name tags. Both were the size of Russian tanks. They sized up Andy and Chris before turning to Sergeant Taylor, who filled them in. Officer Mead came out of the house and whispered something into Taylor's ear. The Sergeant nodded.

"Did you find the checks?" Andy asked.

Taylor cleared his throat. "Not yet."

"They have to be there," Andy said, trying to keep his voice steady. "Where else would they be?"

It was a foolish question, one Chris leaped at. "You've got them. Search him. I bet he's got them in his damn pockets."

Andy raised his arms. "Go ahead. I don't have the checks. What's wrong with you, Chris? Carrie's *missing*. All you care about is the damn money. Look at the door. The bench. *I* called the cops, not you. And she told me you hit her."

Fresh rage bloomed on Chris's face. "I did not hit my sister."

"She called me after you left. She said you hit her and then she hit you. Why would she say that? And what's that mark on your face?"

Chris's hand went to his cheek. "Okay. I slapped her. Because she was hysterical. She knew you were stealing from her."

"I think it's time to take this little party downtown," said Forbes. He looked at Malloy. "Would you bring Mr. Barrett down to the barracks, and I'll bring Andy, here?"

Andy allowed himself to be led to a cruiser. Forbes didn't cuff him, so at least he wasn't a suspect, officially. A person of interest, perhaps. At the barracks, he was taken to a small conference *interrogation* room, where Forbes invited him to have a seat and offered him coffee, water, tea? Andy accepted a small cup of water and drank half of it. Chris had presumably been taken to some other room. Andy hoped whoever was talking to him was a Nazi.

Forbes, on the other hand, seemed pleasant enough, taking down Andy's basic information: address, phone number, etc. Andy had the sense he was waiting for someone else, and sure enough, about fifteen minutes later, a plainclothesman came in after a brief knock. He was also a big man, though not as big as Forbes, clean-cut and sharp-eyed. He nodded at the trooper and then extended his hand to Andy.

"I'm Detective Mike Ross. Please, keep your seat." He sat down across from Andy and set a small tape recorder on the table. "I understand you've had a rough evening so far. I'm sorry to hear it."

"Thank you. I'm pretty shaken up."

"I bet. It's a pretty unnerving scene, from what I've been told. I haven't been out to the site yet, but I will after we're finished here. I understand your vehicle is at the house. I'll drive you there so you can pick it up."

"Thanks."

Detective Ross nodded genially. "So what we're doing here is just a little information gathering. You're not under arrest or even suspicion. I just want to know everything you can tell me about tonight and anything relevant leading up to tonight. Will it be all right with you if I record our conversation?"

"Yes. Is someone talking to Carrie's brother?"

"My partner, Evan Clark. Tell me how you know Carrie Owens. Don't leave anything out. Even the smallest detail could be important."

Andy took a deep breath and told him everything. How he'd met her at the notary office, and how things had happened fast between them—faster than he'd realized until he tried to explain it, and he wondered how it must sound. He told them about the checks, and Carrie's willingness to trust him. The only thing he omitted was the night at the theater. He couldn't bring himself to talk about it, and anyway, it didn't seem relevant. Then he told them about today, his face reddening when the detective asked if they were involved sexually. And finally, the altercation with Chris.

"I don't know why he's so wound up about the checks," Andy said. "I mean, it's a lot of money, but they can be reissued if they were stolen. His sister is missing, for God's sake."

Ross shrugged. "The money is relevant as a possible motive. Whoever took Carrie—assuming someone did take her—might have taken the checks, too. They might try and force her to transfer them into a different account. Maybe they just happened on the checks while they were abducting her. I'm sorry, Andy, I know that's upsetting. Who else knows about this money?"

"No one, as far as I know. Carrie told me she doesn't have many close friends. I suppose she could've told somebody."

Ross pursed his lips. "So, it's likely the only people who know about this million dollars are you and her brother. Correct?"

Andy felt the room turn to quicksand. "I don't have the money. And I don't have Carrie. If I did, why would I have called you?"

Ross ignored this. "The Conneaut Lake address—how long have you lived there?"

"A few months—it's my parents' house. I'm staying there temporarily."

Ross scanned some notes. "And, it says here you told Trooper Forbes you took Miss Owens out for a boat ride today. Does this boat have living quarters?"

Andy saw where this was going, and he felt anger rising in him. "Yes. Feel free to search both places. You don't even need a warrant. Just take it easy at my folks' place—they're elderly. I don't want you scaring my mother."

Ross smiled. "That's generous of you, Andy, and we wouldn't dream of scaring your mother. I'm not sure we need to talk about search warrants yet—technically, we can't even list Miss Owens as missing for twenty-four hours. We are treating the house as a crime scene because of the forced entry. What else can you tell me?"

Andy thought for a moment, his hands clasped before him on the table. "Carrie mentioned she had the feeling she was being watched. One night she got up to look outside and she thought she saw something—or someone—at the edge of the yard. The next day she said there was a print of some kind on her windowsill. I asked to see it, but she said she washed it off."

Detective Ross exchanged glances with Trooper Forbes, who still stood in the doorway. "When was this?"

"I—I don't remember. A couple of weeks ago, maybe? She also told me she'd been a volunteer at the women's shelter. She used to work there, but she got laid off. Anyway, she was working the night that woman and her baby died. Do you know what I'm talking about?"

Ross shifted in his seat and sat up a little straighter. "Yes."

"She said afterwards, she was getting ready to leave and this kid—Reggie somebody—the street kid who rides around on a bike with a big cat on his shoulders—showed up and started telling her about how she needed to be careful. How 'they' would like her because she has good genes."

Ross looked at the trooper. "Do you know anything about this Reggie kid?"

Forbes nodded. "Reggie Spavine. Homeless guy. The city cops know him well. I know about him because my youngest went to high school with him. Got into drugs, I guess. Damn shame. He's quite the character. The paper interviewed him once about the disappearances, and he had quite a colorful theory."

"The pig people," Andy said, nodding. "Up on Round Top."

Forbes chuckled and then coughed politely. "Uh, yes. Radio Tower Hill is what it's called on the map. It's a bit of an urban legend, sir. A good campfire tale. You're not familiar with it?"

"No. I'm from Ohio," Ross said. He looked at Andy. "You think, what?"

"I don't know what to think. I do know Carrie said that baby looked, well, like a hybrid."

Ross raised an eyebrow. "Like what? A pig person? The Davis baby suffered from some significant deformities, it's true, but nothing out of a sci-fi novel."

While the detective had been talking, Andy had gotten the feeling he recognized the man from somewhere. Suddenly it came to him.

"I saw you on TV," he said. "You were on the news. You're investigating the missing women, aren't you?"

"My partner and I are, yes," Ross said. "There have been nine over the course of the last fifteen years."

"And Carrie makes ten," Andy said weakly. "Oh my God."

"There are similarities, I'm afraid," Ross admitted. "Which is why we wanted to clear you and her brother as soon as possible. This business of the checks doesn't fit the profile, however."

"Has anyone really looked for them?" Andy asked. "She probably put them away somewhere. She wouldn't just leave them sitting out."

"That aspect is still being investigated," Forbes said. "The only reason why it's being given so much attention is because Mr. Barrett is very concerned about it. He insists on pointing the finger at you."

Andy gestured helplessly. "He doesn't like it that I'm sleeping with his sister. I can't help him there."

Detective Ross shut off the tape recorder and stood. "Well. I think we're finished here. Let me check in with my partner and then Andy, you and I can head back to the house."

He left for a few minutes and then returned. "Evan is finishing up with Chris. We can get a head start on them if we leave now."

Ross pulled his Chevy into Carrie's driveway ten minutes later. They got out, surveying the scene grimly. Other vehicles had arrived; one had Crime Lab printed on the side. The porch had been roped off with yellow crime scene tape, and people went in and out of the house like ants, all busy and efficient. Andy felt sick to his stomach.

"She's dead, isn't she," he asked dully.

"We know nothing of the kind, Andy," Ross said. "You have to remain hopeful."

He put his hand on Andy's shoulder. "I have your contact information. I'll be in touch."

The detective left Andy to stand in the yard. He stared at the woods, the trees looming like sentinels, and wished they could speak, for whatever had happened, they'd born witness to it. Their dying leaves rustled together, making whispers out of the breeze.

He turned back to the people moving silently in and out of the house and hoped the process would work, that they would find answers. And even as he wondered and hoped, he still couldn't believe it was happening. That it had happened.

Carrie was simply gone.

PART II

**CARRIE'S NEW, NEW LIFE BEGAN** like this:

Consciousness came in a slow unfolding, each of her senses awakening to send bits of information to her stunned brain: Prickling across her back, making her shoulders twitch, and the awareness she was lying on something hard. Smells came next: damp earth, overlaid by mustiness. Stale air.

She didn't want to open her eyes. Her ears registered silence, interrupted by an occasional rustling. A dry cough. Then a groan.

She lifted her hand and put it to her face, searching her forehead until she found the sizeable lump there, the source of the dull ache nestled like a rotten egg. *You fell*, she thought. *No. You were pushed.* She opened her eyes.

Her first thought was she was in a barn. Growing up, she'd been friends with a rather poor girl who'd lived on a ramshackle farm with a menagerie of animals. Cows and horses were kept in box stalls made of cast-off lumber of varying widths and origins, held together with rusty nails of similar repute. Where she lay reminded her of that, except the ceiling was far too low, and the rear wall was not made of wood, but of dirt; she could just make out a tree root jutting from the black hardpack. The fourth wall was no wall at all. It was made of thick woven wire fencing, the kind people used to keep goats or sheep. A crude door had been cut in the center, framed with stout pieces of treated lumber. The only light came from two battery-operated camping lanterns hung from hooks in the ceiling.

Carrie sat up. She'd been lying on a thick bed of straw, the source of the prickling and the mustiness. In one corner of her room

pen

was a water bottle and a paper sack. Next to these was an old wool army blanket. Otherwise, the place was unfurnished. Beyond the wire, she could see nothing but darkness; and yet, she sensed the place was larger. Faint echoes came to her, and an occasional low whistling, like the wind in a stovepipe. With these, she caught whiffs of fresh air.

Her memory of what happened was hazy and brief. She remembered talking to Andy and being a little drunk. She'd taken a long shower and changed into the French terry pants she was still wearing, and a fresh t-shirt. And then—

She closed her eyes. Fear swept her, and her hands began to shake. The doorbell had rung. The clock said seven-thirty, which made her smile. Andy was early, unless it was Chris, coming back either to apologize or give her more grief. She'd opened the door with no hesitation, prepared for either one, but not for what was standing on her front porch.

At first, she thought it was a prank, an early Halloween trick from someone, a neighbor perhaps, but she didn't know her neighbors well, and who would do such a thing? Her memory of the creature looking in on her through her storm door was vague, but the visceral feeling of terror as it reached for the door handle was stark and clear as the moon on a cloudless night. The eyes were what got her: eyes that stared out at her from a malignant and tortured face, hellish eyes the color of embers, but flat and cold, with a different kind of heat.

She didn't remember screaming, though there was a scream as the storm door was ripped from its hinges with enough force to send the man-thing rebounding into the glass, which splintered. It lunged at her, and then she did scream and turned to run. She'd felt a hand close on the back of her neck, and then there was a terrible weight and then nothing.

She crawled to the water bottle and unscrewed the lid. She sipped cautiously—it was cold and good. Suddenly mad with thirst, she took it in both hands and drank, much of it running down her chin and soaking her shirt. She opened the bag and pulled out a sandwich. Ham and cheese. Startled, she dropped it and looked around.

"Andy?"

There was a faint rustling sound. "Hello?" she said tremulously.

The reply was low and hoarse, but distinctly feminine. "Shut up, newbie."

Carrie tried again. "Where are we?"

The answer was simple and discouraging: "Hell."

Carrie heard a door open and close, and on the heels of that, a rush of fresh air. The sound of footsteps on hardpacked dirt. She instinctively moved to the far wall and crouched against it.

She did not recognize the thing that materialized out of the dark to stand in front of her cage. He was huge, with broad sloping shoulders and long arms. His features were different from the other one, as far as she could see: more human, though he still bore tusks and a profound underbite. His body was covered with a light coating of stiff reddish-brown hairs that thickened on his crown. He wore a pair of camouflage pants and a flannel shirt open at the neck, revealing a powerful chest. His hands were relatively normal, each finger ending in a thick yellowed nail. His eyes were a deep midnight blue that seemed to change and pulse as they caught the faint light of the lamps.

It's true, she thought, horror ascending through her like an arc of electricity. *It's all true. Crazy Reggie Spavine was right.*

He stood, watching her intently, and, a little sadly, she thought. He stood there for so long Carrie began to relax a little; there was nothing threatening in his gaze, but there *was* something. She sensed he was trying to send her a message of some sort, the weight of his stare pregnant with meaning. Whatever it was, it was lost on her.

He lifted his head and turned, watching something beyond her sight. His ears flattened and he backed away, throwing her one more sad and almost desperate look. Then he was gone.

There was another sound then, a shambling step which elicited a flight of frightened moans from the unseen woman. Carrie braced herself against the dirt, fear skipping along her spine like a flat rock across still waters.

The thing that had rung her doorbell like some madhouse trick-or-treater was pale, luminous in the dim light glinting off the stiff white hairs coating its body in a panoply of iridescence. She could see the skin beneath, pink and smooth. The face was a dreadful convulsion of features: a wide nose with flared nostrils that worked the air; a pronounced underbite flanked by yellowed tusks; rounded, very human ears; and finally the eyes, glittering red rubies set deep within an overhanging forehead. Carrie remembered back to the unfortunate farm girl. She'd had a rabbit with snow-white fur and pink eyes. An albino.

The man-beast's body was muscular and compact. He wore a pair of cargo jeans, work boots, and a shirt with a logo that read, *Don't blame me, I voted for Mickey* across the chest. His hands had a thumb and four digits, but the fingers were fused into two, like the Vulcan greeting. They each culminated into a single thick nail, forming what resembled a deeply cloven hoof. He stepped forward and curled these through the wires of her cage, pressing his face against the metal hard enough to dimple the flesh.

Seconds ticked by. Carrie cringed against the dirt, panic snapping through her as if she'd sat on a hand buzzer. Every nerve screamed for her to run. *Run.* The thing's tongue slid out and ran wetly over its snout. Carrie began to whimper.

He reached into a pocket and withdrew a key to unlock her door. He had something in one hand, but Carrie was so frightened she couldn't focus on what it might be. He approached her and dropped it on the straw before her.

It was a dead cat. Carrie stared at it for a long time. *That's two,* she thought. It was a gray tabby, its lips pulled back in a death snarl. The man-beast—she couldn't bring herself to say 'pig man,' she just couldn't—seemed to be waiting for her to do something. Finally, he gestured at the cat and then to her.

"Remember?" he said.

She jumped. She hadn't expected him to speak, though his voice was so low and guttural she could hardly understand him. He gestured at the carcass and said it again.

She shook her head slowly. "I—I don't remember. Remember what?"

This seemed to vex him severely. He picked up the cat and affixed it to the door with some baling twine. It hung limply, regarding her through slitted yellow eyes.

He grunted and pointed a finger at her. "You are mine. No one else's."

"No. I don't belong to you."

Those red eyes watched her malevolently. "Yes, you do. There will be no need for the others, now."

He took hold of her ankles and dragged her to the middle of the pen. Carrie began to shriek and flail. He hooked a hand into the front of her pants, unaffected by her blows. He leaned close to her, his hot foul breath in her face. She pummeled him as he tried to unbutton his pants with one hand.

"Stop," she sobbed. "Please. Don't rape me. Please stop. You're hurting me."

And though his breath was coming in short, urgent gasps, he did stop and looked at her quizzically. "Hurting you?"

"Yes. This hurts me. Why do you want to hurt me?"

"I don't want to hurt you. I'm loving you. I've waited a long time."

"This isn't loving," she said, knowing she had hold of a thin edge. He still had his hand down the front of her pants, his knuckles resting on her pubic mound. One wrong move and he would be on her.

She dared to look into his eyes and saw her reflection, a tiny image in a volcanic stew. There was torment there, and in it, she found a bit of hope.

"I can tell you don't want to do this," she said. "I can see it in your eyes. You know it's wrong."

He shook his head violently. "I don't want to hear this talk, Carrie. You are mine now. No one else's. I have seen to it."

How do you know my name? she wondered, but then he was pulling at her pants again, exposing her. Her foot shot out and connected with his groin. He let out a terrible roar of pain and rage. She crawled away from him, emitting a high terrified whine. He grabbed her and threw her up against the wall amid a shower of dirt, his face inches from her own.

"You bitch," he hissed.

A dark memory fluttered through her, like a bat against a starlit sky. His hand was on her throat, and she squeezed her eyes shut against his penetrating stare.

"No," she whispered. "Please, no."

"I will have you, Carrie," he said and jerked his thumb over his shoulder. "That could be Andy instead of a cat."

He left then, locking the door behind him. Carrie relaxed, and with it came the shakes. She put her face in her hands and tried to slow her breathing, for she was threatening to hyperventilate.

"Hey," called a voice, the woman from before. "Hey, new girl. Are you okay?"

"No," Carrie said. "I don't know. I'm alive."

"Your name is Carrie?"

"Yes. What is this place? Caves, tunnels, what?"

"I've heard Shaw call them The Warrens. I think they're mostly man-made. Old aqueducts, maybe? But I really don't know."

"Shaw?" Carrie said. "Is that his name?"

"The dark one, yeah."

"How long have you been here?"

There was a pause. "I don't know. There's no way to separate the days. No windows, no light. It feels like years. The last thing I remember was leaving The Firehouse. Then I woke up here, and it's been hell ever since."

"Oh," Carrie said and groped for the woman's name. "You're— you're Emma?"

"Emily," she corrected. "Emily Dawson."

"I remember. I read about you in the paper. That was, like, three months ago."

At first, Emily said nothing; then, Carrie thought she heard a muffled sob. "I'm sorry," Carrie said. "It's been unspeakable, hasn't it?"

"He rapes me almost every day," Emily said, her voice thick. "He's trying to impregnate me. For *them*. For the good of The People. To improve the line."

"Where are they? The People. And where are the other women? In some other part of this place?"

"I don't know. I've never seen them, but I hear them. The People, I mean. I've never heard any other women. Maybe they're dead. Maybe once they have their babies, Zane kills them."

"Zane," Carrie said. "The white one?"

"Yes. He scares me, worse than Shaw. Shaw calls him his killer side." Emily paused. "I heard Zane say to you now that you're here, there's no need for the others. What did he mean by that?"

"I don't know," Carrie said.

"I hope I'm not one of the others. If I am, then that means he doesn't need me anymore. I haven't gotten pregnant. What will they do with me if I don't?"

"I don't know," Carrie said again. Hopelessness overtook her, and she sank to the floor. She was becoming a statistic. "I'm sorry. I don't know."

Emily began to cry. "I don't want to die in here. I'm sorry I was nasty to you earlier. I'm just so scared."

"It's all right," Carrie said. "I don't blame you. We'll get out of here. I have a boyfriend. I'm sure he's looking for me."

"They never found the others. And they never found me."

"Yet," Carrie said. "They haven't found you yet."

Emily was silent for a long time. "All right. Yet. Don't take this the wrong way, but I'm glad you're here. At least I have someone to talk to. And you stopped Zane. He didn't rape you."

She thought of Andy, and how Zane had just threatened him. Of all the times she'd felt like she was being watched, particularly the night when she and Andy sat on the deck.

Carrie let her head fall back against the dirt wall. "Not yet."

**MONDAY MORNING, AFTER A WRETCHED,** sleepless night, Andy called Jason and met him at his office.

Jason closed the door and offered Andy a chair. "What's up, my friend? You look bad."

"Carrie's gone missing, Jay."

Jason sat down behind his desk and looked at Andy quizzically. "Carrie who?"

"The woman I started seeing. The widow. Remember? From the notary? I wanted to go to the funeral home and you told me not to."

Jason nodded. "Right. You're seeing her now? When did that happen?"

"Yesterday, officially. It sort of started a few weeks ago. I offered to help her if she needed anything, and she took me up on it. We fell for each other. I'm in love with her, and she told me yesterday she loves me. And now she's gone. They took her."

"Who took her?"

Andy's gaze roamed the room. "I'd rather not say. You'll think I'm crazy. You're already psychoanalyzing me, I can tell by the look on your face."

Jason sat for a moment, drumming his fingers on his desk. "Maybe you better get me up to speed. I've got twenty minutes before my first patient. Go."

Andy told him everything in short, breathless bursts. When he was done he took the bottled water Jason offered him and drank gratefully. Jason himself sat pondering, his head tilted to one side, regarding Andy with the same look that the police had given him.

"So you think your girlfriend was kidnapped by a mutant species of pig people, whose existence is based on the secondhand ravings of a poor drug-wrecked mind of a homeless man. Have I got that about right?"

"I know how it sounds. I'm not saying I believe it. I'm just saying it's a possibility I'd like to explore."

"A possibility?" Jason leaned forward. "Forgive me for throwing out the clinical speak here, but it's lunacy, is what it is. Next, you'll be saying it's aliens."

Andy dropped his eyes. "I don't care. I want you to come with me and find that Reggie guy. I want to ask him about Radio Tower Hill. And then I want to go up there."

Jason studied him for a long time, and then checked his watch. "All right. What harm can it do? I'm finished at two. Pick me up here?"

Andy flushed with relief. "Okay—okay, great. I don't know if we'll even be able to find Reggie, but I'd like to try. And I want to go up on the hill no matter what. I just want to look around."

"I've been up there. Not since my high school parking days, but I doubt much has changed. There's nothing up there except some poor folk who probably don't have running water. A lot of woods. And the towers, of course."

He led Andy to the door and then paused. "In love, are you? None of my business, but it seems pretty sudden. Speaking strictly as a friend and not a psychiatrist, are you sure the both of you aren't just horny and lonely?"

Andy smiled grimly. "Both, yes, but not just. I love her, Jay. And I'm scared shitless something bad has happened to her."

At around two-thirty, Andy drove them down an access road to a rutted underpass beneath the Spring Street bridge on the west side of town. Andy had stopped at the men's homeless shelter after picking Jason up, and the sad-looking man at the front desk had suggested they look here.

"The young fellas like it," he'd said. "I think they pretend they're camping."

The day was cool, but not yet cold. Winter had settled its grip over the month but hadn't quite started to squeeze. Andy and Jason got out and looked cautiously around. The bridge spanned French Creek, a broad, shallow run that eventually emptied into the Allegheny River. There was indeed a cold fire ring with several battered lawn chairs around it, silent witnesses to God only knew what sort of postulations, exhortations, and summations such men of the underworld might put forth for one another. A red Igloo cooler sat tucked almost out of sight behind one of the bridge's concrete buttresses. Andy walked over to it and nudged it with his toe, imagining a portable meth lab.

"I hope you would not trouble another man's things, I hope you would not," said a voice.

Andy turned. Jason stood with his hands clasped behind his back, watching a young man on a bicycle approach: Reggie Spavine no doubt, for the big cat was draped over his shoulders. He pedaled slowly by them, getting perilously close to the edge of the road where it fell off to the creek's bank, taking them in with a sidelong stare. He turned and came back. GT impaled them with an impudent glare of his own.

"You're Reggie, right?" Andy asked.

"Who I am and who I may not be is up to you and your intentions, large man," Reggie said, spinning a slow tight circle. "You do not look friendly to me."

"I'm friendly," Andy said and licked his lips. "I'm a little nervous, is all. I'd like to talk to you if you don't mind."

Reggie slowed the bike and stopped a goodly distance from Andy and Jason. He studied them carefully from beneath the flat black brim of his baseball cap. GT jumped from his shoulders and stalked over to the cooler, observing the scene from this new perch.

Reggie watched his cat for a minute and then turned back to Andy and Jason. Andy noted he was not really a boy at all, more like twenty or twenty-five. The cap and the bike made him appear younger.

"You are out of your element, this is true," Reggie said. He nodded at Andy. "You smell of fear and a terrible unhappiness. And you," he added, nodding at Jason, "you smell like money."

Jason shrugged and offered a sardonic smile. "Thank you?"

"It was not meant as a compliment," Reggie said primly. "If you are not here to do me harm or take me someplace I do not wish to go, what can I do for you gentlemen today?"

"A woman went missing yesterday," Andy said. "She's very special to me. My girlfriend. Carrie Owens."

Reggie brightened. "Ah yes, I saw that on the TV this morning through the window at the magnificent Tim Horton's. I was eating a raspberry jelly donut someone had foolishly but fortuitously thrown away with only one bite taken. It was a misbegotten work of art, I can tell you."

Andy and Jason exchanged glances. "Yes," Jason said. "I bet it was."

Reggie eyed Jason shrewdly. "I do not believe I care for you." He looked at Andy. "I know the pretty lady of which you speak. She was one of the night ladies at the women's place. I have not seen her there in some time. She is your lady?"

"Yes," Andy said.

Reggie leaned back on his bike and took in a long deep breath and let it out slowly in a sigh of wistful satisfaction. "You are a lucky man, and now also a sad man. I understand now. I am sorry for your loss."

Andy felt a sickening drop in his gut. "Where is she, Reggie? Did the—" He glanced furtively at Jason. "Did the pig people take her?"

Reggie's eyes widened. "You know about The People?"

"I only know you told Carrie about them. And I know what I grew up hearing."

"Yes, I do remember having a conversation with the pretty night lady the night the sad pregnant lady died. The pretty night lady was afraid of me, but it was not me she needed to fear. I told her to beware the night, and she did not heed my advice."

"They took her from her home. She wasn't out."

Reggie sighed. "That is bad. They must have wanted her very much."

"For what?" Jason asked.

"To breed, sir," Reggie said. "To create the new People. For the second coming of Earth."

Jason leaned close to Andy's ear. "Can we go now?"

"Hold on," Andy said. "I want to go up there. To Round Top. I want you to come with me."

Reggie held his hands up in alarm. "Oh, I do not go up on Round Top. GT accompanies me wherever I go; therefore, I do not go there, as I am confident The People would enjoy feasting upon him."

"Your *cat?*"

"It is a terrible habit," Reggie agreed. "I believe it is a misinterpretation of cunnilingus."

Jason and Andy stared at him and uttered a collective, "What?"

"Eating pussy," Reggie said matter-of-factly. "They are imperfect in their assimilation attempts."

"Oh man," Jason said, stifling a laugh.

"What would it take to get you to come with us?" Andy asked. He pulled out his wallet. "I've got twenty-five bucks."

"I do not bow to the green overlord," Reggie said. Then he smiled slyly. "I might, however, consider accompanying you on your expedition for the procurement of two wondrous Wendy's Baconator sandwiches and a large Coke."

"Would you like fries with that?" Jason quipped.

"I do not eat of the lowly potato," Reggie said, sniffing.

Andy took a deep breath. "You've got a hell of a vocabulary, man," he said. "And one hell of an appetite. You and GT can have the whole crew cab to yourselves. We can put your bike in the bed. Let's go."

They hit the Wendy's drive-thru and got Reggie his payday. Then they doubled back and crossed the Spring Street bridge. Spring Street came to a T intersection at Cussewago Road, which ran concurrently with Route 102. This ran north and south and formed the very outskirts of that side of town. It was also the base of Radio Tower Hill. Andy turned left and drove for about a quarter of a mile and then made a sharp right onto Williams Road, which ascended immediately up the round little mountain.

Andy and Jason were serenaded along the way by the moans of profound satisfaction from the rear as Reggie made his way through his meal. Jason shook his head and winced.

"I think he's having an orgasm," he muttered.

Andy grinned. "They do smell good."

"Better than he does." Jason cracked the window a bit. "I bet he hasn't had a bath in a year."

"I take my ablutions monthly, thank you very much," Reggie said around a huge mouthful. "My spirit is clean and my soul is pure. I do not need to perfume my skin with unnatural scents that confuse my senses and have been tested on the flesh of my fellow creatures, caged in labs for the fickle whimsy of elitists such as you."

"I don't wear cologne," Jason shot back, irritated. "I'm talking about plain old soap. Hell, even Amish people use soap."

"The Amish are an arrogant, bloated people even more married to money than you are," Reggie said.

"You're just full of opinion, aren't you?" Jason said.

"Never mind," Andy said. "We're getting close to the top."

Lower down, there had been thick clusters of shabby houses; as they neared the top of the hill, they began to thin out until the road turned from buckled blacktop to dirt and the road was flanked on either side by deep woods. Many of the trees had all but lost their leaves by now, and the naked gray trunks stood thickly right up to the shoulder of the road. At the apex of the hill, the road banked left; on the right, the trees ended abruptly onto a vast open field, in the center of which stood three towers spaced about three hundred yards from one another.

"Are those cell towers?" Andy asked.

"Cellular, microwave—I don't know. All I know is I pay too much for my plan and I can't get WIFI when I need it."

"Reggie," Andy said over his shoulder. "Do you know where they are?"

"I do not know where The People reside. I believe they are underground and they do not come out during the day. They are not ready to approach the light."

"Why is that?"

"They fear you, and your so-called society, and its rules and tenets. They know in their present form they will be hunted down and driven into cells and institutions. They will be picked apart, dissected, and made sport of."

Jason half-turned in his seat. "They're kidnapping women to breed with to improve their race? To become more like us?"

"To become like *you*, yes. They are smart in many ways, but they are also foolish. They see you from a distance and see your fancy box houses and your rolling vehicles like this one that carry you over the earth at unnatural speeds. Which I do not like, by the way, it is making me uncomfortable and wishing I had not come. They see these things and want them for themselves. They crave the light, but they do not know light can create many dark and dangerous shadows. And yet, can one exist without the other?"

Having no answer for this, Andy parked the truck and killed the engine. He walked out into the field and stood looking, trying to get a sense of the place. It was unearthly quiet; no birds interrupted the fall air, and no wind moved the trees, even at this altitude, though as topography went it wasn't much. Andy guessed the hill rose no more than a thousand feet if that. A bit of an oddity in their part of the country, but not much of one. The hill itself was a long tabletop once you got up on it; in a western state, skinned of trees, it might resemble a rounded mesa of sorts. Here, in the Pennsylvania summers, it looked more like a big green Twinkie.

Reggie and Jason came to stand beside him, Reggie with the ever-present GT on his shoulders. Jason looked uncomfortable and out of place. He turned his head constantly as if expecting something to come rushing out of the woods and set upon them.

Andy turned to Reggie. "If The People took Carrie to—to breed with her, that means she's alive. Right?"

"That is right," Reggie said, looking at him sadly. "But, as you can imagine, it would be a terrible fate for a woman. Worse than death, perhaps. But I am not a woman and cannot know these things, though I have suffered many horrible torments. Many indeed."

"Jesus." Andy walked a few feet away and cupped his hands around his mouth. "Carrie! Carrie, I'm here! *Carrie!*"

"Andy," Jason said. "Come on."

"Best to let the man have his way," Reggie said quietly. "Though it will do no good. Round Top is too large a place for his voice to carry far enough. But he needs to feel he is doing something."

Andy began to walk the road, calling her name at intervals. He walked until the field ended and the woods began again; desperate, he button-hooked into them, stumbling over deadfalls and ugly snarls of grapevine. He called her name until his voice clogged in his throat and he sank to his knees on the cold dead leaves. He released her name one last time in a broken sob.

A hand fell on his shoulder: Jason's, warm and firm. "Come on, Andy. Let's go."

Andy got shakily to his feet and wiped his face on his sleeve. He searched his friend's troubled eyes. "Why is this happening?"

"I don't know," Jason said. "But I don't think the truth is up here."

They walked back to the truck. Reggie Spavine stood to the side, silent and respectful. Andy put both hands on the warm hood of his truck and braced himself, head bowed.

"She's here," he said, his voice barely audible. "I don't know whether that crazy story is true, but one way or another, she's here. Somewhere. I felt her back there. Just for a minute, but I did."

He looked at Jason. "You didn't?"

"No, I didn't. I'm sorry."

"Your ability is strong," Reggie said with quiet admiration. "You have a powerful connection with her. You are correct. She is here. Where, I do not know."

"Have the police been up here?" Jason asked.

"I doubt it. They looked at me like I was crazy when I suggested it. I don't blame them."

Andy turned and leaned against the truck. "I'm coming back up here tonight."

"Oh my, that is most unadvisable," Reggie nearly moaned. "A very dangerous idea, indeed."

Jason started to protest but Andy cut him off. "You don't have to come. I'll be all right."

Jason chewed his lip and said nothing. They got into the truck and started the descent back into town. The road was a big loop; on the way down, they passed several rundown shacks.

"People live up here?" Andy asked, hitting the brakes.

"They are hill people," Reggie said. "They will not talk to you."

"Please," Jason said. "Let's just get out of here."

Andy relented, looking over his shoulder at the sagging, paint-peeling houses. He let it go for now. But he would be back. He wondered at those silent walls with their opaque windows and sway-backed roofs. At their attics. And basements.

Carrie was here. He knew it.

THE SMELL WAS GETTING TO HER.

She had lost all sense of time, for, as Emily had pointed out, there was no change of light, or clock of any kind to mark its passage. She felt she might have been here a week—weeks, even. Or perhaps it had only been a day or two. However long it had been, it had been enough time for the dead cat to sour. She was afraid to ask Shaw to get rid of it—afraid to talk to him at all—and so it continued to hang, and swell, and stink.

Shaw was evidently a caretaker of sorts. He brought her a bucket to use for a toilet, and though he emptied it at regular intervals, it still often sat for some time. This, intermingled with Fluffy and the smell of her own unwashed body, suffused the stale air with an almost ignitable stench.

Carrie had mixed feelings about his visits. He would take the bucket and return it cleaned, which was a relief. But then he would stand and plague her with his solemn stare. He never spoke. She didn't know what to make of it. There was no lust in his eyes or anger. Only inconsolable sadness. She dared to speak to him once, asking him what he wanted, but she got no reply.

He brought her food as well: two peanut butter and jelly sandwiches, wrapped in cellophane. These came at what she began to assume were twenty-four-hour intervals, and this was how she began to mark her days. She saw no more ham and cheese—evidently, that had been an inaugural treat. She wondered where she got the fixings—he sure as hell wasn't strolling into Giant Eagle on a Sunday afternoon, though if he went to Walmart after midnight, he probably wouldn't raise much of an eyebrow. The thought almost made her laugh. Almost. But not quite.

Zane came to stare at her, too, and these were the most frightening times, for she could see he was waging some inner battle, fighting for control. She would retreat to the back of her cage, repeating, "Don't hurt me," like an incantation, one she didn't think would work for much longer.

On one of these visits, he showed up with a milk crate. He motioned for her to sit, and when she refused to come near him, he uttered a sharp bark that almost made her faint.

"Sit," he commanded.

"I'm—I'm afraid you'll hurt me."

He shook his head impatiently. "I won't hurt you, Carrie. Not like you hurt me. Sit."

Reluctantly, she edged close to him and then watched as he folded himself down on the straw. He studied her, his eyes glowing like traffic lights on the blackest of nights.

"I thought you might like to look at my things," he said.

"I'd like to go home."

He grunted and pulled the box closer. "Here. I think you'll know some of these."

The box was full of books. Books and VHS tapes and magazines. Mildly curious, she rummaged through them. A lot of them were how-to books on electricity and basic carpentry, but several were novels: A Clockwork Orange; Lolita; The Road.

He pulled out a tape and handed it to her. She smiled faintly.

"Jaws." She took a deep breath. "I love this movie."

She turned it over and studied the scenes on the back. One was of Quint, played by Robert Shaw. Shaw. She looked up.

"Oh."

He grunted with satisfaction. He put it back and pulled out something else, a children's book this time. She felt a stab of nostalgia.

"Charlotte's Web. Another favorite of mine." She looked at him. "I lost my copy, a long time ago. Where did you get this?"

He made no reply. Instead, he took the book away and handed her a magazine. She grimaced.

"Hustler? That's nice. Where did you get these?" She dropped the magazine and picked up a book, its spine broken in several places. "Meadville Public Library. Our library is peddling porn?"

"They were in boxes of donations by the dumpster behind it. That's where I get most of my things." He picked up the Hustler and held it out to her. "Look at this."

"I don't want to look at it. It's disgusting."

"Look at it."

There was threat in his voice, so she did, turning the pages and feeling his eyes on her. She heard his breathing deepen; a gnawing began in her gut. The pages of the magazine shook.

"Stop looking at me," she said.

"No."

He continued to stare at her for a long time, his eyes darkening. She sat, motionless, her head bowed. The magazine fell from her hands.

Zane got to his feet. She did the same, retreating against the wall. He stepped close to her, his face inches from her own. His eyes became like burning coal; she began to tremble so, her teeth clacked in her head.

"Don't," she whispered. "Please."

He ran his hand up her arm and then down between her breasts. "I'm not hurting you, Carrie. I know what hurt is. This does not hurt you."

"It hurts in a place deep inside. You're hurting my soul."

He pushed her shirt up. "No. This is love. I love you, Carrie. I always have. You love me. You will."

She felt his alien mouth on her. Her mind shut down, like a series of switches being turned off. Zane dragged her down. She turned her face to the wall as he pulled off her pants, and then his tongue snaked inside her like an eel. She squeezed her eyes shut and thought of Andy, Andy who would never see her again, and even if he did, would never want her again, because she was nothing. She was less than nothing.

⬚

Afterward, she lay alone in the straw, naked and indifferent. Emily tried to draw her out, but Carrie remained mute. Then she whistled a warning.

"Look out Carrie."

Shaw appeared. He unlocked her cage and entered, carrying a pail and a cloth. Steam rose languidly from the rim.

"Come here, Carrie."

She felt dim surprise. *So you* can *speak.* This revelation brought her little comfort, for even though he wasn't Zane, he was still one of *them.* She began to tremble anew, and gathered her shirt up, covering herself.

"No. Please. No more."

He looked at her sternly and pointed to the ground at his feet. "Come here."

Hopeless, she abandoned her clothes and scooted to him. He knelt before her and dipped the cloth in the bucket, which she saw was filled with warm water. He wrung it out and then began to wash her. He washed her face first, bathing away her tears, then her arms, her breasts, and belly. He took special care between her legs and then washed them too, right down to each toe. Then he helped her dress.

"You are all better now," he said.

She stared at him numbly. "Yes. All better."

"I have to go away for a while, but I will be back. You will miss me?"

"Yes," she said. "I'll miss you."

He unlocked the door. She roused herself briefly and cried out.

"Will you please get rid of that goddamned cat?"

He paused. "Do you remember, then?"

"Yes," she lied, desperate. "Yes, I remember, now please take it away. I can't stand it anymore."

He left her then, taking the foul carcass with him. She rolled onto her side, pulling the old blanket he'd given her up to her chin, though it did little to warm her. She was cold, so very cold.

Emily spoke to her, her voice soft. "Carrie. Are you all right?"

"No. No, I'm not. Zane raped me. Just like you said he would."

There was a pause. "I'm sorry."

Carrie didn't acknowledge this. "Who are these two?" she asked, instead. "Are they related somehow?"

"Zane is Shaw's half-brother," Emily said. "I think he's like an alter ego. A bad one. They seem to struggle with one another. I think

Shaw's in charge of this place, but Zane wants to run things. Zane is crazy—those awful, red eyes. Lately, it seems like he's getting the upper hand."

"Are they the only ones?"

"I don't think so." Emily paused. "I think there's places like this all over this hill."

"I can't believe this is happening," Carrie said. "How have they lived up here, and no one has ever known about them?"

"But you have known. You grew up with the stories, just like I did, right?"

"Yes, but no one I've known has ever actually seen them. Until now," she added. "Lucky us."

She sat up and put her head in her hands, her elbows on her knees. "When I was a kid, my brother told me about this couple that drove up on Round Top to make out. The guy got out of the car for some reason—I don't remember why—maybe he had to pee. Anyway, the girl waited and waited, but he never came back. Then she heard these scratching sounds coming from the roof of the car. She got out, and there was her lover, hanging upside down from a tree limb. He'd been gutted. His fingers were scraping the roof."

"Then what happened?"

"I don't know," Carrie said, lifting her head. "He never would finish the story. I always assumed the pig people got her."

"I heard there was a leper colony up here, and the lepers bred with a bunch of wild hogs. But that doesn't seem true, now that I'm here. I don't know what the truth is."

Carrie got unsteadily to her feet and walked over to the rough-hewn boards that made up the right wall of her pen. She pressed her hands against the old wood.

"Are you right on the other side?" she asked. There was a light rustling sound, and then a gentle rapping on the wall. Carrie closed her eyes and knocked back.

"Yes," Emily said, her voice closer. "I'm right here, Carrie. Can you feel me?"

Tears spilled down Carrie's cheeks, and she pressed her whole body against the wood. "No. I can't feel anything, Emily. How can you still feel anything?"

There was a long pause from the other side of the wood. "I haven't been until you came. I'd lost my hope, until the first time we talked. Remember? You said no one had found me yet. As long as we're alive, there's hope. Think of Andy. How he misses you."

Andy. Carrie began to cry softly, grinding her face into the old wood until splinters gouged her cheek. Even if she did make it out, she wouldn't be able to look at him. She closed her eyes and saw her future, a short one perhaps: Zane on top of her, those scalding eyes boring into her as *he* bored into her, over and over, day after day, engulfing her with his malignant stare. Sensing, at last, her barrenness. And then—and then, what? How would he finish her? Snap her neck? Rip her throat open with his tusks?

She remembered the hourglasses she'd imagined over people's heads, and saw her own now, the sand at the bottom a glittering pile of white.

17 **ANDY CAME BACK TO ROUND TOP** that same night, as he said he would. He walked the road, a flashlight in one hand and his father's .357 he'd pilfered from his dresser drawer, bought years ago for home defense and long forgotten, in the other. He'd never fired the thing in his life and wondered if he even could. Nevertheless, the weight of it in his hand was a comfort.

The trip yielded nothing. He came back every night afterward, determined, stalking the woods, fear shimmying up his spine at every snap of a branch. He came in the daylight too, trying to coax Carrie out of the ground, out of the very air. He knocked on the doors of the farmhouses, but Reggie had been right. No one answered.

Reggie came with him some days, talking a blue streak the whole time. Andy listened sometimes, sometimes not. The young man's voice grew to be as comforting as the gun, though Andy left it in the truck on the day trips. Reggie would have nothing to do with firearms for any reason whatsoever. They offended his cat.

A week passed, then two. The police were making little headway, and as far as Andy could tell, seemed to have given up, but only after grilling him hard about his relationship with Carrie. How long had he known her, how serious were they, were there any other men she might be involved with. On and on. Of course, they easily dug up the death of his son and his divorce, two things that didn't help him. As Detective Ross read aloud the coroner's report on Billy's death, Andy could feel their estimation of him slipping; Evan Clark seemed to look at him with disdain.

"I guess I don't blame your wife for leaving you," he'd said. "Showing such carelessness with your only child."

Ross had shushed him, but not with much energy. He'd looked at Andy long and hard until Andy had felt himself shrinking in his chair. It seemed his poor son would haunt him forever, and as he sat there, he could almost hear his boy whispering to him. *Why daddy, why? Why didn't you hold me tighter?* It was excruciating, and though he knew he deserved every ounce of it, it was still killing him.

Andy asked about Chris. Was he getting the same third degree? Ross had shrugged.

"He's not a suspect, and neither are you, Andy. Not at this point, anyway. You're not even persons of interest. But yes, we talked to Chris. He did, after all, admit to striking his sister. It just happens you two are the last known people to see Carrie before she went missing. We must vet you pretty hard. Neither of you appears to have much motive unless you count the wrinkle of those two big checks."

The checks. Where were the goddamned insurance checks? Andy had wanted to go into the house to look for them, but it was still a crime scene. It remained locked up tight, swaddled in yellow police tape. The media had come and gone, reporting rabidly on Carrie's disappearance at first, tying it in with the other disappearances that had occurred in the area. Andy became an unwitting, minor celebrity of sorts—somehow, they found out he'd been seeing Carrie, and hounded him briefly for interviews. He'd even been contacted by several of the national news shows and recoiled at the thought of being one of those poor, grim people who found themselves unexpectedly, and horrifyingly in the spotlight.

When he wasn't on Round Top, he holed up in his room, conducting half-hearted searches on the internet about pig DNA and stats on the successful recovery of kidnap victims. Neither was very productive.

He decided to make one last night visit to Round Top. Carrie had now been gone for three weeks. He was losing hope. Maybe he was wrong. Maybe she wasn't here. Whoever had taken her had vanished into thin air. Halloween had come and gone, and the thought of Carrie lying in some shallow grave beneath the leaf litter, her body slowly absorbed by the cold, unforgiving ground was more than he could bear. Worse, perhaps, chained to some wall, being systematically raped by some hulking man-beast. One more look. One last time.

He drove up the uneven road at around seven and parked the truck at the edge of the woods on the north side of the tower field. Beyond these woods, the road started back down toward town and passed the run-down farms. Andy started to take the flashlight but left it on impulse; the evening was clear with a three-quarter moon. He donned a wool cap and gloves, for the weather had turned November cold, and checked the pistol in the dome light. Then he got out and started walking.

He wasn't sure what he was looking for on these trips, other than the miracle of Carrie walking lost, but unharmed, toward him. He'd imagined coming upon some hideous mutant and confronting it. Would it even be able to speak? What if it attacked him? Could he kill it? He wondered at the consequences of such an act, right down to the legalities. Would it be murder? Or animal cruelty?

Then he would shake these thoughts off as ridiculous scenarios that were easier to believe when Reggie was running his mouth. Still, in the cold night, amid the stark trunks of trees casting looming shadows all about and the wind whistling through their clattering branches, even the most outlandish propositions seemed plausible.

He stopped for a moment to catch his breath, watching it plume before him. The woods were dead quiet except for the wind and the creaking trees. There was no snow on the ground, and his footsteps had been loud in comparison to the sudden quiet. A faint rustling interrupted it; his whole body stiffened, for the sound had come from directly behind him. Something hard pressed between his shoulder blades.

"You stand real still there, young fella," said a man's voice. "Ease that pistol down on the ground and then turn around."

Andy did as he was told, his heart in his throat. A man of about seventy stood leveling a side by side double-barrel shotgun at him. The wind caught his white hair and lifted it like a sail.

"What's your name, son?"

"Andy. Andy Korn. I don't mean any harm."

The old man gestured at the .357. "You're asking for it, roaming around in my woods with that thing. What are you doing up here every night? I been watching you."

"I'm looking for my girlfriend. She's gone missing, for about three weeks now. I have a hunch she's up here somewhere. Have you seen anything suspicious?"

"Other than you? No." He lowered the shotgun a bit. "What makes you think she's up here?"

Andy hesitated. "A guy I know thinks there's, well, people up here that kidnap women. A strange kind of people."

The old man shouldered the gun and gave him a look of weary contempt. "Pig people, I guess. Am I right? And I bet you got it from that crazy kid with the cat. Right again?"

"Well, yeah. Not just him—I grew up hearing stories about them. I always figured it was an old wives' tale."

"That's because it is. The only pig person up here on Round Top is me. I'm Earl Buckles, fourth generation hog farmer. If you buy your bacon at Marley's Meat Market on Chestnut Street, you're eating my pigs."

"I have had it," Andy admitted. "It's very good."

"Damn right it is." Earl gave him a once over. "Fetch up that hand cannon there and come on down to the house. I was just about to put some coffee on when I saw your lights. I'll tell you more about your pig people."

Andy left the truck where it was and followed Earl the couple hundred yards to his house. It looked like hell on the outside but was cozy and well-kept inside, the décor running on a nineteen fifties timeline. Earl turned up the heat on a percolator set atop the stove and then motioned for Andy to have a seat at his kitchen table. Andy set his father's pistol down carefully and took off his coat.

"I knocked on your door a couple of weeks ago," Andy said. "You didn't answer."

Earl brought two chipped mugs to the table and grunted. "I might've been out back with the pigs. Or maybe I just ignored it. I don't cotton to visitors much. How do you take your coffee?"

"With cream, if you've got it."

Earl went to the yellowed and battered fridge and retrieved an open can of evaporated milk and set it next to Andy's mug. Then he sat down. The smell of brewing coffee soon permeated the air.

"So you lost your girl," Earl prompted.

Andy nodded. "Someone took her from her house on October fifteenth. The front door was busted in."

"Any hoofprints?"

Andy smiled thinly. "I don't think so."

Earl chuckled. "Don't feel bad, son. That story does have some truth to it. All stories do, I reckon. The good ones, anyway. My people come from the old country—Romania. My great granddaddy's name was Isaac Buchelenov. Changed it to Buckles at Ellis Island. He brought some pigs with him—how, I don't know, most immigrants couldn't bring an extra pair of shoes, let alone a herd of hogs—but he did it, along with his wife Helga. They were some of the first to settle here. He liked this high ground—maybe it reminded him of home, I dunno.

"Those pigs were half wild when he brought 'em over, but I guess they about went feral up here. He was the only farmer here at the time, so he just let 'em roam free. When wintertime came, he'd call them in and fatten them up until spring. Then he'd cull a few for market, breed some, and turn 'em loose again. For years, that's how it went."

The percolator began to quiver and steam. Earl got up and poured them each a cup. Andy gave his a liberal dose of the canned milk and sipped. It was strong and good.

"They had themselves a daughter," Earl continued. "Named her Soula."

"Soula? That's an interesting name."

Earl shrugged. "Soula was an interesting girl. Not quite right, I guess. What you'd call ADHD nowadays, or bi-polar. Schizophrenic, maybe. Back then they called it soft in the head. She was wilder than them pigs, though. Liked to run down the path naked in the broad daylight. Isaac couldn't keep her from eating the whitewash off the side of the house."

"This house?" Andy asked.

"Yep. Anyway, Soula took to them pigs. One, in particular, a big boar. Helga went hunting for her at dinnertime one evening and found her rutting with it out behind the barn."

"Holy shit," Andy said.

"Helga wasn't given to cussing but I bet she said something similar," Earl said. "When old Isaac found out, he kicked Soula out of the house. This is where things get a little iffy: the way Isaac told my granddaddy and on down the line, is she took up with that big boar in the woods. And there's where you get your pig people."

"Do you believe that?"

"Do I believe a poor crazy young girl got her kicks laying one of her daddy's hogs? Sure—I ain't a monk—I've seen pictures of women who've probly got high school diplomas doing God-awful things with every animal imaginable. Do I believe she got knocked up and started a new race of people? I've bred hogs my whole life and know a thing or two about genetics. It ain't a close enough match to make a baby."

"I read scientists are making progress in pig heart transplants," Andy said. "With a little more genetic engineering, it'll be possible one day for humans to be able to accept pig hearts."

"Soula Buckles wasn't no genetic engineer," Earl said. "She couldn't even tie her shoes."

"Still," Andy said, and then fell silent.

Earl leaned across the table and looked at him shrewdly. "You *want* to believe it, don't you? You'd rather believe that than think your girl was raped and murdered and left in some dumpster. Which is what we see on the news dang near every day. I got rid of my damned television. Turned it into a planter."

"Thinking she's being raped by some pig person isn't exactly sugar-coating it," Andy countered. "I guess I'd rather believe in the pig people story because at least I've got some hope she's alive."

"And damaged," Earl said. "Twas me, I'd rather she was dead."

Andy swirled the remains of his coffee, kicking up grounds. "Were you ever married?"

Earl nodded. "Lost my wife to the cancer fifteen years ago. She suffered aplenty. We were both glad when she finally went. It cut the grief some to know she wasn't suffering anymore."

"You think she was glad. You don't know. Maybe for your sake, she was glad."

"There are certain things you have to believe to survive," Earl said. "It may be a story, but if it helps, then what's the harm in it?"

"Like pig people," Andy said.

Earl shrugged. "I see your point. All I'm saying is you've wasted a lot of time roaming these woods. But, whatever helps."

Andy donned his coat and picked up the pistol. "Thank you for the coffee and the story. I better get on home."

Earl walked him out. "Luck to you, son. If I see your lights again, I won't pay no mind. Stop back, if you like. Don't forget to buy your pork at Marley's."

Andy smiled and left. He walked back to the truck and headed home. Earl Buckles' lewd horror story had brought him no comfort. He thought of that strange girl roaming the woods, living off mast and fornicating with her boar pig. Bearing strange little mutants, huddled in hollowed-out logs and abandoned fox dens. A twisted tale the likes of Bram Stoker would delight in. He himself was beginning to feel like a character in one of those tales, and he did not care for it.

A deer darted out in front of him, not close, but he nearly drove his feet through the floorboards. He pulled into his parents' driveway with a huge sigh of hollow relief.

His father was sitting in the kitchen, eating a bowl of ice cream. "Where've you been?"

Andy peeled off his coat and hung it on the back of a chair. "Out," he said. "Just out."

"Out with that piece, I bet," his father said, grinning lasciviously. "At least you're getting some kind of job."

Andy was too weary for the jab to smart much. "No, I wasn't. I was out walking in the woods. Up on Radio Tower Hill."

He took the pistol out and set it on the table and then sat down. "I borrowed this."

Bill Korn looked at the gun. "I forgot I had it. You out hunting pig people?"

"You know that story?"

"Of course I do. Everybody does. I even saw one, one time."

Andy looked at his father suspiciously. "Really?"

He held up his hand. "Swear to God. Me and Chuck Keller were up there rabbit hunting, oh, this was back when you were still in diapers. It was getting late in the day—we were headed back to our cars when this great big thing came out of the trees and stood watching us. He had these great big tusks and a dick that was a foot long if it was an inch. Balls the size of melons, I tell you. Then this other one came out—a she-pig. You should have seen the size of her titties—four sets of them, running right up her middle. I said to old Chuck, 'Now there's quadruple the fun!' Lord, did he laugh—"

"Very funny, dad," Andy said amid his father's cackling laughter. He stood, and then glanced at the pistol. His father saw the look, and his smile turned mean.

"Love to, wouldn't you?" he said.

Andy met his father's gaze. "No. I'd like to think I'm better than that, even if you don't."

He picked up the pistol and returned it to his father's bureau. Then he went to bed.

CARRIE HAD DECIDED TO DIE.

She'd made this decision shortly after the last time Zane had used her. It had become an unspeakable routine; with each visit, he seemed to want something else, something more. Sex was somehow not enough; it was as if he wanted to drive life into her, and if not, then her death was the only alternative. These were not thoughts he voiced, and yet she sensed them, tangible as chaff drifting by her on a breeze. She'd come to realize death was inevitable, and the only hope she had left was to make one of her choosing, not his.

The next time Shaw came to bathe her and bring her sandwiches, she pointedly threw them in her waste bucket. He noted this with mild curiosity.

"What," he said.

"I don't want those."

"Then you'll go hungry," he said, unmoved.

She took her water bottle and emptied it out on the ground. "I don't want that, either."

These demonstrations served only to amuse him. "You will, Carrie. Thirst is a powerful motivator."

She shook her head. "You don't get it. I quit. You won't protect me. You don't. Or can't."

"But I do," he said, his brow wrinkling. "I take care of you. I protect you."

She barked laughter, a hollow, desperate sound. "My God, if this is protecting me, what's the alternative look like?"

He studied her a moment, and then picked up the bucket. "Deep down, I think you know."

She didn't know, and with this ominous insinuation, her last shred of hope slipped from her like a dried-up skin. She lost her fear of death. Even if she did get out, Zane would likely find her and kill her. Andy wouldn't be able to help, and she would even be putting him in harm's way, for Zane would kill him to get to her. She turned away from the stale sandwiches, which was no hardship, and she refused to drink. At first, Shaw didn't seem concerned, underestimating her, but when she continued to turn away from the water he offered, it raised a flag.

"What's wrong, Carrie?" he asked, and she would've laughed if she hadn't been so tired. *What's wrong,* she thought. *What's wrong?* "If you don't drink, you'll die."

She met this with silence, and understanding dawned slowly on his face. He became immediately frantic and grabbed her face and tried to pry her mouth open, urging her to drink. She kept her jaws tightly clenched, and he gave up after a while, though he left her bruised.

The weaker she got, the more frantic Shaw became, pacing restlessly back and forth, pleading with her, sometimes yelling at her. He hit her several times in a desperate attempt to rouse her, but the blows had no effect. She'd gone blank.

At the top of her third day without water, Shaw left but soon returned with something in his hands. She watched him weakly, her tongue stuck to the roof of her mouth like a desiccated worm.

The thing in his hand was a handkerchief. He blindfolded her with it. In darkness now, she felt him lift her onto his shoulder. She was carried a short way and then felt herself ascending. Cold air struck her, stunning in its freshness. She stirred in his arms, revived by it. Snowflakes melted on her cheek. She tilted her face up and held out her tongue; the drops of wetness were like bright points of light. Each one flipped a switch deep inside her; she began to gulp and thrash. She felt him move more quickly, trotting over the rough ground.

Shaw set her down, and she nearly fell. He put something to her lips. Plastic. He tipped it into her mouth and she sucked at the water with sudden greed, a lifeline in a bottle. He took it away.

"No. Not too much. Slow." He pushed the blindfold off and rested his hands on her shoulders. She looked around. It was full dark. They were at the edge of a wood, and there was a light dusting of snow on the ground. She saw the blinking lights of the towers off to her right and knew for certain what she had suspected since this nightmare had begun. She was at the top of Radio Tower Hill. Round Top.

His eyes were bright even in the dark, but sad, too. Beautiful blue eyes caught in that tormented face. He pressed his lips to her forehead.

"You have to live, Carrie," he said, looking at her. "Even if it means letting you go. I hate this, but you're leaving me no choice. There will be another time. I'll find another way."

He stepped away from her. "The road goes right into town. You know that. Take the water bottle. I love you, Carrie. *Run.*"

Carrie stood, transfixed by the portent in his eyes. A gust of wind nearly toppled her, bringing with it bone-clattering terror. She turned and ran.

She slipped immediately and fell to her knees. Cold mud soaked into her pants. She got up and staggered on, Shaw's promise nipping at her heels.

Then she ceased to think about it at all, for the snow was coming harder, stinging her eyes. She was barefoot; soon her feet were numb. She had to stop every few steps, her breath coming in ragged, tearing gasps. She sipped at the water, retching once, before stumbling on. She wanted badly to stop, casting longing looks at the darkened houses she passed on her way down. Two things kept her moving: one, the fear that Shaw would change his mind and run her down like a wounded animal. The other was Andy.

After what seemed like hours, she saw the passing headlights of a car on Cussewago Road. She began to cry, a thin keening wail in her throat, no louder than a mouse squeak. She turned toward town, hobbling over the icy pavement on frozen feet. There were few cars; the ones that did go by passed her without even slowing.

Finally, the flashing lights of a plow truck appeared. It slowed, and the driver peered out at her gravely. He came to a full stop and climbed out of his cab.

"Lord, honey, are you all right?"

"I'm Carrie Owens," she said, barely above a whisper. "I've been missing for a long time. Please help me."

She collapsed then. The water bottle slipped from her fingers; she felt the warm hands of the driver as he gathered her up, heard his voice but didn't understand his words. The world capsized. She fainted.

※

She next opened her eyes to dazzling brightness, a world of white; antiseptic smells, low murmurings, and somewhere, the sound of a laugh track. She blinked against the light and saw a nurse standing at her bedside, adjusting an IV. She looked down at her and smiled.

"Well. Hello there, sweetie. I'm Nurse Anne. How are you feeling?"

"Cold," Carrie said, her voice a croak. "So cold. And thirsty."

Nurse Anne clucked her tongue. "I bet you are. I'll get you some more warm blankets."

She held Carrie's head while she sipped tepid water through a straw. "The IV will help you rehydrate. Do you think you could eat something? Some Jell-O maybe?"

"Andy," she said. "I have to see Andy."

"Is he your boyfriend? I'm sure the police will call whoever you want. There's two of them waiting to talk to you. I'll get your blankets and let them know you're awake."

The nurse left and was soon replaced by two plainclothesmen. Both were large and good-looking and offered her friendly smiles. One of them pulled up a chair next to her bed. The other remained at the curtained entrance of her ER bed.

"Hi there," said the one at her bedside. "My name is Detective Mike Ross. This is my partner, Evan Clark. Can you tell me what your name is?"

"Carrie Owens. I live on Belmont Drive. I was kidnapped on October fifteenth from my home. Has anyone called Andy?"

"He's in the waiting room." Ross nodded to his partner, who disappeared at once. "The doctors wanted to stabilize you first before we brought him in."

He smiled tightly. "You've been through a lot, I can tell. Can you tell me what happened? Who took you, Carrie?"

Just then the nurse reappeared, followed by the ER doctor. Carrie accepted the new blankets gratefully, for she couldn't stop shivering. The cold seemed to have sunk deep into her bones. The doctor was about her age; she recognized him from work—she'd done a car title for him about five months ago. Dewey was his name. He offered her a benign smile.

"Hello—Carrie, is it? How are you feeling?"

"Better with the blankets. Thank you. Still thirsty."

"Oh, I'm sure. You're dehydrated, but we'll fix that. Take small sips of water. When was the last time you had any water before tonight?"

"I don't know. Two, three days, maybe?"

"And what about food?"

She shook her head. "None for . . . for days. I quit eating. Just peanut butter and jelly sandwiches twice a day before that."

Looks were exchanged all around. "P B and J," Ross said. "You were fed nothing but peanut butter and jelly sandwiches for three weeks?"

"That's all the longer I've been gone?" Carrie let her head fall back against the pillow. "It feels like a year. I was kept in a pen like an animal. There's another woman up on Round Top. You have to get her out. Her name is Emily Dawson."

"Who has her, Carrie?" Detective Ross asked.

"Shaw and Zane," she said, looking at him. "They're pig people."

A long beat of silence ensued, which was soon interrupted by a commotion beyond the curtains. A man's voice, Ross's partner Evan most likely, admonished someone to take it easy, man, take it easy, and then Andy was there, parting the curtain, a frantic look about him. Then he saw her.

"Oh my God," he said. "Carrie."

She broke down at the sight of him; the IV was evidently working, for tears leaked from her eyes. He pushed past everyone and sat on the bed beside her, scooping her into his arms. She sobbed against his chest, great wracking sobs, and he held her, his shoulders shaking with his own tears. He sat back and held her face.

"Are you hurt? What did they do to you?"

She shook her head, unable to talk at first. "I'll be all right, Andy. I didn't think I'd ever see you again. I wanted to die. I tried to die, but he let me go."

He rocked her, crooning softly. She was aware of the people around them and dismissed them. All she wanted was to feel him, to know he was real, and that *she* was real, too, once again.

At last, he sat back, wiping his eyes, which were raw and wounded, yet shining with relief. "God, you're so cold. You're shivering."

Ross cleared his throat. He looked at the small crowd. "Can we have some space here, folks? Doctor, do you have anything further for now?"

Doctor Dewey shrugged. "No. I'd like to keep her overnight for observation and get more fluids into her. We'll get you admitted, Carrie, but I suspect you can go home in the morning."

He touched her foot. "Welcome back."

The doctor and the nurse left. Ross turned back to her. "I know you two would like some alone time, but Carrie, I need to ask you a few questions. Are you up to it?"

"Yes."

"Okay. Two men took you. Their names are Shaw and Zane? Do you know their last names?"

"No. They don't have last names that I know of."

"All right. And when you say they're pig people, what exactly do you mean by that?"

Carrie sat up slowly. She didn't want to tell them any of it; already the looks on the detectives' faces were of wary disbelief. And then there was Andy. He was watching her intensely, searching her eyes for the truth, for the harm that had been done to her. She feared his judgment, that he would look at her and see damaged goods at best; at worst, an unhinged lunatic.

"I mean, they look like half-pig, half-man. They are very large and covered with bristly hair. Zane is an albino. He is very bad. He would kill me if he could. He was the one who took me. Shaw was my—my caretaker. He washed me. He was the one who let me go."

"So they look like animals," Clark said, speaking for the first time. "And they clearly act like pigs. But they're men, correct? Dirty, hairy men, but just men. Is that what you mean?"

She looked at each of them in turn. "I don't know what I mean. I don't want you to think I'm crazy."

"I want you to tell us the truth," Detective Ross said. "You indicated they're holding another woman. Is this true?"

She looked at Andy. He touched her face. "It's okay, Carrie. Tell them. I'll believe you, no matter what you say."

"According to Emily," she said slowly, "they are a hybrid of humans and pigs. They're trying to improve their bloodline because they want to be whole human. They want to come into the light and walk among us. They capture women and impregnate them. Zane told me there were others, but I never saw them. I never actually saw Emily—I just talked to her through the wall. Emily said Zane raped her almost every day."

The men were silent for a time, and Carrie knew the question that hung in the air. She knew it from the many nights she'd sat with a rape victim in this very emergency room and dreaded it. The awkwardness of it, and the finality of its labeling. Answer yes, and you are this from now on. You are a victim, and if you're lucky, you'll be a survivor. It was a dubious honor Carrie despised.

"Andy, would you consider stepping out for a bit?" Ross asked.

"No," Andy said, his voice edged with steel. "I wouldn't."

"It's all right," Carrie said. "I know what you're going to ask. Was I raped."

"Yes," Ross said quietly. "Were you raped by either of these individuals?"

"No," Carrie said. "I was not."

Relief flooded Andy's face, and Carrie was glad. He held her and she started to cry again, as much for the loss of her truth as for the salvation of her identity. At least for what she thought it was.

Detective Ross took a deep breath. "I'd like the doctor to perform a rape kit on you anyway. Do I have your permission to request that?"

Carrie glanced at Andy. "No. I don't need a kit done on me. I just told you, I wasn't raped."

Detective Ross bit his lip. "Yes, you did. But sometimes, when a person experiences trauma like this, they can forget things. If there's any evidence of anything, we need to collect it now. As a rape counselor, you should know that."

"Yes, I do know that," Carrie said forcefully. "I've seen them done, and I don't want one. I don't need one."

"Can we maybe not argue about it, detective?" Andy said, his voice strained.

Ross sat looking at her, and Carrie tried not to squirm under his gaze. "All right," he said at length. "No rape kit. If you change your mind during the night, call a nurse. I'd like to talk to you again tomorrow when you're feeling better. Call me in the morning and we'll set up a time to come down to the barracks. I'd like to get you with a sketch artist and go over every detail of your ordeal. Okay?"

"Yes," Carrie said. "That's fine."

Ross took her hand and gave it a squeeze. "We're all very glad to have you back. We'll get them, kiddo. Don't you worry. Is there anyone else you would like us to call? Your brother, perhaps?"

Carrie had been smiling at Detective Ross. It left her face like a shadow. "No," she said. "I'll call him in the morning. No sense worrying him. He'll drive out here like a madman and kill himself or somebody else."

"All right." Ross tipped an imaginary hat. "See you tomorrow."

The detectives left. Carrie was moved to a hospital room. A nurse brought her some Jell-O, which Carrie ate with relish and then asked for a cheeseburger. The nurse laughed and said she'd see what she could do. It was three o'clock in the morning.

Andy crawled in bed with her. It was a tight fit, but she didn't care. She wanted him close to her. She was finally warm.

"I must smell awful," she said. "I'm sorry."

"You smell great," he murmured, his nose against her neck. "You're here."

He sat up. "I looked for you, Carrie. I looked every day. I knew you were up there—I just couldn't find you. I'm so sorry."

She said nothing, instead drawing him more tightly against her. She let herself drift, exhaustion overtaking her as shock released its hold. Dreamless sleep swallowed her, and her last thought was that she was safe.

For the moment.

 **LATER THAT MORNING, AS DAWN CREPT** through the hospital window, Andy woke to find Carrie gone. He panicked for a second until he heard the shower running. He rolled onto his back, wincing at the stiffness in his joints from sleeping in a bed meant for one. There was a light tap at the door, and a nurse poked her head in.

"Good morning, sunshine," she said, smiling. "I brought Carrie some scrubs so she doesn't have to put those nasty clothes back on. And here's the breakfast menu—she can have something to eat while she waits for her doctor to make his rounds. He shouldn't be long, but you know how that goes."

"Right," Andy said. "Thank you. You've all been very kind."

The nurse, a woman in her mid-fifties, shook her head. "A lot of us know Miss Carrie from her work with The Women's Place. Such a shame this happened to her. I'm sure she never expected to be on the other side of it."

"She wasn't raped," Andy said. "She would've said so, I'm sure."

The nurse looked at him sadly. "I hope that's true. But a lot of women don't want to face it—at least not at first. My niece was raped by a school counselor, and it was a year before she told anyone."

She handed Andy the scrubs. "I'm sorry. I shouldn't be worrying you like this. You've got enough to fuss about. Bring this menu up to the station and I'll see that the kitchen gets it."

Andy heard the water shut off in the bathroom. He waited a few minutes and then rapped lightly on the door.

"Carrie. The nurse brought some clothes and a menu."

Carrie opened the door, wrapped in a towel. Free of grime and cast in the harsh light of the fluorescents, he saw how badly marked her face was. There were red abrasions around her mouth, and each cheek was colored with a yellowing bruise. Anger of a kind he'd never felt before flooded him. His whole body quivered with it. She saw this, and her face knitted with bewilderment.

"I'm sorry," he said. "It's just—your poor face. I want to kill somebody."

He handed her the clothes and then rubbed his hand over the back of his neck. "Pick out your breakfast. I'll take it to the nurse while you get dressed."

She filled out the menu with trembling hands. A tear fell on the page before she could hand it back to him. She looked up at him with desperate eyes.

"I'm never going to stop crying."

He touched her cheek. "We'll get through this, Carrie. I promise."

He took the menu to the nurse. When he came back, Carrie was dressed and stood looking out the window at the winter scene below. A good four inches of snow had fallen during the night. Now, the sun was out, casting the world in brilliant sparkling white.

"I have to call my brother," she said.

Chris. Andy had been dreading this. "Do you want me to do it?"

Relief flooded her face. "Would you?"

"I don't relish the thought, but yeah, I'll do it." He hesitated. "Look, Carrie, I—I don't know if this is the right time, but we won't have much later today, and when he gets here we won't have any at all. I need to talk to you about Chris."

She stiffened. "What about him?"

He pulled her over to the bed and sat her down. "The night you went missing, I called him to see if you were with him somewhere."

"I wasn't."

He looked at her. "I know. When he got to the house, the police were already there, and he—well, he was pretty hard on me. Your insurance checks are missing, Carrie. Chris tried to insinuate to the police that I took them, and even had something to do with your disappearance."

Carrie stared at him uncomprehendingly. Then her shoulders slumped. "The million dollars is gone? I don't have any health insurance right now. Jesus, cancel the eggs."

"We can get a stop payment on the checks if they don't turn up, don't worry about that. I'm sure they'll reissue them. I hope, anyway. The point is, he really has it in for me. The police grilled me pretty hard when otherwise I don't think they would have."

Carrie was silent for a time, picking listlessly at the edge of the hospital sheet. "Chris has always been protective of me. To a fault. He's always been critical of my boyfriends—not that I've had many. Even Ben—he almost didn't come to our wedding."

She looked at him. "I'm sorry he put you through that. It wasn't fair."

He took a deep breath. "Maybe I shouldn't have told you. But I wanted you to know about the checks before he got a chance to imply that I took them. I didn't."

"I would never think you did," she said. "Call him. Tell him I'm sleeping. I don't think I want to talk to him right now."

Andy went down to the lounge to make the call. Chris answered his cell on the third ring with a cautious hello.

"Chris, it's Andy. I have some great news. Carrie's been found."

There was a beat of silence. "How is she?"

"She seems fine. Dehydrated, mostly. She's here in the hospital— they kept her overnight for observation, but she can go home this morning, I think. The police have talked to her, and we're supposed to go to the station later today for a full account."

"What did she tell them? What happened?"

"Apparently two men were holding her. Her and another woman. She says they're some kind of pig men. It's kind of a fucked-up situation."

Another beat of silence. "*What?*"

"It's not good, Chris, but the police are working on it. Are you in Baltimore?"

"Where else would I be? I can be there in five hours. Is Carrie asking for me?"

Andy hesitated. "She asked me to call you. She's sleeping right now."

"Oh. Okay. Well shit—this is great news. Thank God. Thank you, Andy—thanks for calling me."

Andy ended the call and stood looking at his phone. Then he went back to Carrie's room where he found her tucking into a vast pile of scrambled eggs, toast, coffee, and a double ration of bacon. A doctor stood at her bedside, flipping through her chart. He glanced up and offered Andy his hand.

"Hi. I'm Carrie's family doctor, Jack Fleming. You must be Andy."

Andy nodded. "Nice to meet you. How is she?"

Doctor Fleming smiled. "Oh, she's fine. Tough as nails, this one. You can take her home as soon as she's finished stoking a coronary. Two servings of bacon? Really?"

"I've got a vendetta against pigs," Carrie said around a mouthful of eggs. "Anyway, you shouldn't serve it if it's so bad for me. What kind of a hospital is this?"

Doctor Fleming cocked an eyebrow at Andy. "Good luck, my friend. Carrie, I want you in my office next week for a follow-up, okay?"

He looked at Andy. "There's kind of a media frenzy out front. It doesn't take long for them to find out about stuff like this. Unless you want to be on every morning show on television, I suggest you sneak out the back."

"Shit," Andy said. "I didn't think about that."

"Give me the keys to your vehicle and I'll have hospital security bring it around to the loading area. Then they can escort you out."

"You mean, like Good Morning America and stuff?" Carrie asked.

Doctor Fleming smiled. "Hell of a way to get on TV, Carrie. Save a litter of puppies or something next time."

Carrie thanked him, and he left. She looked at Andy. "Did you get him? Chris, I mean?"

"Yeah. He's on his way."

"How did he sound?"

"Freaked out, at first. Like he was afraid of what I was going to say. Once it sank in, he was okay."

Carrie made no reply to this. Andy went to the bathroom, suddenly overwhelmed by the urge to pee. When he came out, Carrie had pushed her plate away.

"Do you want the rest of this? My eyes are bigger than my stomach, I guess."

Andy finished it, realizing he was famished. Even hospital eggs tasted good. A nurse came in with Carrie's release papers, and after some brief hugs from all the nurses, Carrie was ready to go home. Andy gave her his coat and carried her to his truck, for all she had on her feet was a pair of hospital socks. They escaped the attention of the reporters, for the moment at least.

They drove through town, Carrie looking pensively out the window. When they got to the house, she stirred and sat up. A tattered piece of police tape fluttered in the wind, come loose from its moorings at the wrecked front door. Andy's truck laid fresh tracks in the unbroken snow as he pulled up to the garage.

"There's a keypad on the wall next to the garage door," Carrie said. "The code is 5050 and then the pound sign."

Andy got out and punched it in. The door rumbled upon its tracks, squealing in protest. Andy carried her inside and set her on her feet next to her car. She patted it fondly and then headed inside, Andy at her heels. She stood in the kitchen, her hand uncertainly over her mouth, looking agitated. He touched her shoulder.

"You okay?"

"It's really cold in here," she said.

"We can fix that." He found the thermostat and kicked it up to seventy. After a moment, the furnace thrummed to life. Carrie went from room to room, looking in each one—Andy wasn't sure why at first, but then it came to him: she was looking for monsters. She opened all the closets, pushing coats out of the way, and he watched sadly as she even looked under all the beds. Apparently satisfied, she went back into the master bedroom and shut the door. Andy waited awkwardly, unsure of what she was doing. She reappeared moments later in a pair of fleece pants and a sweatshirt. She walked past him to Ben's office and began pulling out drawers.

"I put those checks right here," she said. "In this top drawer. I know I did. Son of a bitch."

"Would the—the men who took you. Would they have taken the checks?"

Carrie shook her head. "No. They weren't after money."

He winced at the emphasis she put on the word money. No. They'd been after something else entirely.

"Why don't we try to relax for a while. We've got maybe four hours before your brother gets here, and we have to go to the police station. You were supposed to call them."

"That's right. I forgot. Where's my phone? And my purse?"

"I think the police have your phone. I don't know about your purse. I wasn't allowed in the house after it was labeled a crime scene."

"Was Chris?"

"I don't know. I don't think they let anybody into a crime scene. Does he have a key?"

"I gave him a copy when Ben died."

Andy looked at her curiously. "Why?"

She shrugged. "So he could have unlimited access to my life. To help me, if I needed it. I don't know, he asked for one—I gave it to him."

She looked at him sharply. "Do you want one?"

Andy held up his hands. "It's not a contest, Carrie. I don't need one."

She rubbed her hands slowly over her face. "I'm sorry. I'm just nervous about seeing him. I don't know how he'll be. Somehow this is going to end up being my fault."

Andy stared at her. "If he says anything like that, I'll knock his teeth down his throat, I swear to God."

She smiled grimly. "Can I borrow your phone?"

She called Detective Ross and set up a time for two o'clock that afternoon. They went to the living room and turned on the TV. Andy flipped the channel to the Today Show, which was entering its second hour. After about twenty minutes, an update on Carrie came on. She leaned forward, lips parted.

Savannah Guthrie turned the coverage over to Gabe Gutierrez, who was standing in front of the state police barracks.

"What's the latest, Gabe?"

"Good morning again, Savannah. We've just learned that Carrie Owens, missing since October 15th, has been released from

Meadville Medical Center and is reported to be recovering at home with family members. Police are asking the media to respect their privacy during this difficult time, which we are doing. Detective Mike Ross, heading up the investigation, has stated there will be a press conference at four pm this afternoon with an update on their investigation, which is ongoing. Savannah, back to you."

"Wow," Andy said. "It's so surreal."

"I hope I don't have to talk to anyone."

"You won't unless you want to."

"I don't." She looked at him. "I'm so tired. I'd like to lie down for a bit. Sleep some more. Are you all right?"

"I'm okay. It's been a long night. Today will be long, too."

She rose and offered her hand. "Come with me, then? Unless—unless you don't want to."

"I want to." He took her hand and stood. "Nothing's changed, Carrie. I love you. You're the same to me. You're exactly the same."

Her face crumpled, and she leaned against him. "I want to believe that. It can't be true, though. It never is."

He tilted her face up and gently kissed her wounded mouth. "Come on. Let's go to bed."

She crawled under the covers and pulled them up to her chin. He stretched on top of them, fully clothed. Something didn't seem right about taking his pants off, though he would've been more comfortable. She noted this with a pained expression.

"I just don't want to be pulling my pants on when your brother gets here," he offered as some explanation, which was not untrue, exactly.

Carrie fell into a deep sleep almost immediately. Andy dozed fitfully and was awakened some hours later by the sound of a car door slamming. He rose quickly and met Chris just as he was mounting the porch steps. His look was immediately disapproving.

"I figured you'd be here," he said. "Where is she?"

"In the bedroom, asleep," Andy said. "Let her be. You can look in on her, but she needs to rest. She's got a long afternoon ahead of her."

"You think you're in charge, here?"

"Maybe you could cut me some slack, Chris," Andy said quietly.

Chris scowled. "And maybe you can get out of my way."

He pushed past Andy and went to the bedroom. He stood in the doorway a minute, and then made as if to lunge at Carrie. Andy moved to stop him, but Chris pulled up at the last minute. He stood over her, a strange look on his face Andy couldn't read. His throat worked, and his hands clenched and unclenched into fists.

"Chris."

Chris started, as if in a trance. He looked at Andy and then gave a curt nod. He followed him into the kitchen.

"What's the story," he asked. "What's this about pig people?"

"I know how it sounds. They're part pig, part man. They kidnap women and breed with them to become more human."

Chris had found an unopened quart of orange juice in the fridge and drank straight from the carton. "That's crazy talk."

"I was thinking it would be good if she saw a therapist. I have a friend—"

"She doesn't need a therapist," Chris said. "She just needs time. She's been through an ordeal. She's coming home with me. She needs to get away from here."

Andy tried to maintain some control in his voice. "I don't think that's a good idea."

"Of course you don't. You just want her here so you can keep fucking her."

"That's not true. I love her."

Chris snorted and put the juice away. "Sure you do. You're just like all the rest of them. She's beautiful, she's got a hot body, and money, too, now. It all boils down to the same thing. The bottom line is, I'm the one who takes care of my sister. No one else."

"That's unbelievably unfair." Andy struggled to control himself. "You can't just take her away. She won't go."

"Sure she will. Carrie always does what I tell her."

"What's going on?"

Carrie stood in the doorway, her hands balled at her sides. Chris's face changed, softening. He went to her.

"Hey, you." He wrapped his arms around her, kissing her temple, her cheek. Andy saw that Carrie's hands remained at her sides for a long time. Then slowly, she reached up and put them lightly on his shoulders. Her body was ramrod straight.

"You're okay," Chris murmured. "Everything's going to be all right. I'm here."

He stepped back and took her in. "You look great. No harm done at all."

"No," Carrie said faintly. "Not a bit."

Chris turned to look at Andy. "You can go, now. We're fine."

Andy looked at Carrie. She seemed dazed, her eyes clouded over, a puzzled look on her face. "Carrie?"

She shook her head as if to clear it. "What? No. I don't want Andy to go. Don't, Chris."

"He doesn't need to be here," Chris said, his face hardening. "I've got you."

"Yes, he does," Carrie said. "I want him here. I love him."

Chris looked at her for a long time, his mouth contorting, and then pulled something from inside his jacket. "Here's your checks, Carrie. I had them for safe-keeping. I didn't want them to fall into the wrong hands."

Andy felt hot blood crawl up his cheeks. "You son of a bitch."

Carrie took the checks. She swayed on her feet and reached out with her free hand to steady herself against the wall. "I'd like you to go now, Chris. I'm very tired. Thank you for keeping these."

For a moment, Chris just stood there, his hands clenching into fists. "All right," he said finally. "I'll go. For now. You get some rest. I called the police station. They said you're to be down there at two. I'll meet you there. Then I'll take you out to a nice dinner. I have plans for us, Carrie. We have a lot to talk about."

He kissed her on each cheek and then threw Andy a smoldering look. "I'll see you all later."

After Chris left, Carrie sat down at the kitchen table. She held the checks limply in one hand. "I want to leave a little early so we can stop at the bank and deposit these fucking things. All right?"

"I think that's a good idea," Andy said shakily. "Something about your brother isn't quite right."

Carrie stared helplessly out the window at the dazzling day. "I know."

 **CARRIE CHANGED INTO A SWEATER AND** a pair of jeans for the trip to the police station. She tried to put on some make-up to hide the bruises, but it only seemed to exacerbate them, so she washed it off.

Andy took a shower but had to make do with the same clothes from the day before.

They went to the bank, and Carrie deposited the checks. The teller immediately offered the services of their financial advisor. Carrie politely declined.

"I already have one," she said, looking at Andy.

They drove to the barracks in relative silence. "What day is this?" Carrie asked suddenly.

"It's Wednesday," Andy said. "The ninth. Of November."

She sighed. "Almost Thanksgiving. My first without Ben. The first of many, I guess."

"Will I do?"

She shook her head. "I didn't mean it that way. Of course, you'll do. You're more than enough. I just, I don't know, I haven't thought about him much. So much has happened."

She studied his profile. "The holidays must be tough for you, too."

He nodded. "They are. Especially Christmas. You know, with a little boy. It's such a big deal to them. Now it just feels hollow."

"Will your mom make a turkey?"

"God, I hope not. She'll burn the house down."

Carrie laughed. "I could cook if you want. I make a pretty mean bird."

He was silent for a minute. "I don't want you to work on a meal and then have to sit there and listen to my father criticize every crumb."

She was glad he felt that way, for she couldn't imagine anything worse than cooking for Bill Korn and listening to Andy's mom ask about her dead grandson.

"Okay," she said. "Are you going to boycott them completely? That seems kind of harsh."

He shrugged. "I'll think of something. What about your brother? He seems hell-bent on taking you to Baltimore."

Carrie turned to face the window. "Chris can lump it. I'm not going anywhere."

Andy started to say something, but Carrie cut him off. "Holy shit," she said. "Look at the circus."

They were nearing the state police barracks. The place was surrounded by media vehicles of all descriptions. Carrie could see both local and national correspondents bustling about, testing mics and touching up their hair. She found Detective Ross in the melee. He spotted Andy's truck and made his way to it through the throng.

Andy rolled down his window. "Where should we go?"

"There's really no way around them," he said and nodded to Carrie. "It'll be all right. The uniforms will clear a path. I'll be on one side and Andy will be on the other. They'll try to throw questions at you. Just keep your head down and ignore them."

Andy parked the truck and they got out. There was a small group of townspeople with signs that read, Welcome Home Carrie! They cheered when they saw her.

"How nice," Carrie said, touched, and then Andy and Mike had her by the arms and hustled her through the crowd. She ducked her head against the volley of questions, feeling like she was the criminal.

"Carrie! Who took you?"

"Is it true about the other woman? Why did they let you go and not her?"

"What about the pig people, Carrie? Are they real?"

Ross shook his head. "They must've gotten a hold of the ER nurse. Dammit."

Then they were inside and he shut the door. Mike's partner, Evan, was waiting to escort them to a conference room. "Your brother is already here."

Andy put his arm around her as they entered. Chris sat at the far end, drumming his fingers on the table. He didn't smile when he saw them. Carrie was struck by how nervous he looked.

Mike sat down, smoothing his tie, and motioned for everyone else to sit. He took out a small tape recorder and set it in front of him.

"Okay. That wasn't too bad. Carrie, what I'd like you to do is tell me everything that happened to you during the event and anything relevant leading up to it. For instance, the night you went missing, I talked to Andy here, and he mentioned you had a conversation with a young man by the name of Reggie Spavine. Andy indicated the conversation might be significant. I'd like to hear about it, and other things of that nature. Are you comfortable doing this in front of Andy and your brother?"

She took Andy's hand underneath the table. She looked at Chris. He was watching intently, his eyes like two globes in his head. He was there, and not there, in a way. Impossible to read. With Andy at her side, she felt no fear.

"I do. It's fine. I did have a conversation with Reggie, the night Paula Davis and her baby came to the shelter. After the ambulance left, I was sitting on the front step, and he came by on his bike— that wasn't unusual, we saw him a lot—and he told me I needed to watch out because they were watching me. They wanted me because I have good genes. I thought he was talking about my pants—you know—jeans—but he wasn't. He was referring to my genetics."

"Did he specify who 'they' were?"

"He referred to them as The People. He didn't say pig people, but I thought I knew what he was talking about because of what he said to the newspaper that time. It seemed weird he would bring that up. Because of the way Paula's baby looked."

"It was deformed," Mike said.

"Right. It had a terrible underbite, and little teeth protruding from its lower lip. They looked like tusks, to me."

Carrie stole a glance at Chris. His look had gone from blank to bemused. She went on.

"Anyway, it scared me. The night had been so awful, and on top of that—I got pretty freaked out. I never went back to the shelter to work. From then on, I kept having this feeling I was being watched, and I started seeing things, like prints on my windowsill and shifting shapes in the dark. I started to wonder—hope—that it was my husband's ghost, and not—something else."

Mike nodded. "Yes. Your husband, Ben, was killed in a car accident on . . . September fifteenth, on his way back from Hershey. Correct?"

"Yes, and what else happened that night?" Chris asked tartly.

Carrie squirmed and felt hot blood crawl up her cheeks. She felt Andy's grip on her hand tighten.

"I'd like to respond to that, Mike," he said. Detective Ross nodded the go ahead. Andy looked at Chris.

"I ran into Carrie at The Timberland that night. It was a coincidence. I knew her from some notary work she'd done for me when I moved back here. We had a few drinks and then went to a movie. When we came out—"

"I bet that's not all that happened," Chris spat.

Andy turned to the detective. "All right. Carrie and I got a little friendly in the theater. We both felt guilty about it. It didn't go any further—not until much later. What I want to tell you, what I think is relevant, is that after Carrie left, I saw a man standing at the edge of the parking lot. She doesn't even know about this. He was watching us. I couldn't see his face, but it felt . . . creepy. It scared me. I thought maybe it was somebody Carrie knew."

He bowed his head briefly, and then looked up. "Maybe even her husband, somehow. Ben. Now I think maybe it was somebody else. Maybe one of those pig guys."

There was a pause. Then Chris barked laughter, causing them all to flinch.

Mike cleared his throat. "Thank you, Andy. Carrie, let's get to the night you were abducted. What do you remember?"

"Andy and I had spent the day together, on his boat. Ben had been gone almost two months by then. Andy had been helping me, and we'd gotten to know each other well by then." She looked at him. "I fell in love with him that day. We came back to the house, and Chris was there. We got into a fight. About Andy. And the insurance money Ben had set up for me. Chris was angry that I was letting Andy help me with it. *He* wanted to be the one to help me. Like always. Andy left. Chris and I argued some more. I told him to get out. He left."

Detective Ross leaned across the table and folded his hands together. "Did your brother get physical with you in any way?"

Tears spilled over her cheeks. The room seemed to be closing in on her. She could feel their eyes on her—*his* eyes, drilling into her.

"Chris slapped me. I was getting hysterical. He slapped me, and then I slapped him. It was for my own good, I suppose."

"Has Chris ever gotten physical with you before?"

"Oh, for Christ's sake, where are you going with this?" Chris asked.

Ross's partner, Evan, stood by the door with arms across his thick chest. "Let her answer the question, sir."

Carrie wiped her face with both hands. "No. Nothing like that."

"Can we take a break?" Andy said, his voice shaky.

"No," Carrie said. "I just want to get this over with. I remember I took a shower."

"Was your front door locked, or unlocked?" Ross asked.

"Unlocked."

Chris shook his head. "God, if I've told you once, I've told you a thousand times, lock the fucking door."

Andy exploded out of his chair. "Don't you *dare* make this her fault!"

Chris held up his hands. "You gonna hit me in front of these cops? Go right ahead, corn-hole."

"Why don't you tell the police where the insurance checks were all this time, Chris?" Andy said. He looked at Detective Ross. "Remember how he tried to pin that on me? He had them all along."

Ross looked at Chris. "Is that so?"

"Yeah. I took them for safe-keeping," Chris said. "From gold diggers like him."

"When did you take the checks?" Ross asked.

Chris looked at Carrie. "I came back to apologize. You were in the shower. I saw them on the desk. I was so—so mad you would let him take over like that. So I took them. I shouldn't have. I'm sorry."

He looked at Andy, and his eyes went hard. "I'm not sorry the police gave you a hard time, though. I won't apologize for that."

Carrie felt herself shrinking into the chair. Andy towered over her, his body giving off waves of rage. She put her hands over her head and drew her knees up to her chest.

"Can you both please just stop it?" she said.

"I think that's good advice, guys," Mike said. "Take it easy, both of you. Go on, Carrie."

She straightened. Andy sat back down, his face flushed. He kept his hands in his lap; Carrie saw they were shaking.

"The doorbell rang. I opened the door and—" She paused, finding it suddenly hard to breathe. "There was this *thing* standing there. He was huge. He had the reddest eyes I've ever seen. Tusks. Pure white hair, all over. I found out later his name is Zane."

Tears spilled freely down her cheeks, and she told the rest between hitches and starts. "All I remember is the door crashing in. I tried to run. He caught me. And then I woke up in hell."

"Do you remember anything about where you were taken? How you got there, what it looked like from the outside."

"No. All I saw was inside. It's underground, I know that. They're called The Warrens. All I saw was the pen I was kept in. Emily was in one right next to me. You haven't found her, have you?"

"No," Ross said. "We sent troopers up there the night you were found, and again the next morning. There was about four inches of fresh snow on the ground. We couldn't even see your tracks."

Ross looked at Andy. "We also interviewed several of the farmers who live up there. The latest interview took place just one day before Carrie was found. A Mr. Earl Buckles said he found you wandering around his property the previous night. He said you were carrying a large caliber pistol. He also said he'd seen you up there almost every day since Carrie's disappearance. Is this true, Andy?"

"Yes," Andy said. "I was looking for Carrie. I didn't think anyone else was."

"You underestimate the Pennsylvania State Police," Evan said from the doorway. "We spent a lot of time up there."

"Mr. Buckles didn't mention that," Andy said.

Ross smiled. "Mr. Buckles probably didn't know. We can keep a low profile when we want to. You don't have a firearm registered in your name, Andy. Whose gun is it?"

"It belongs to my father. I took it with me in case I ran into—God only knows what."

"Understandable," Ross said, nodding. "But not exactly advisable, considering you're the boyfriend of a missing woman, which, under typical circumstances, could put you in an unfavorable light. It could make you look suspicious to some people."

"Are you saying I'm a suspect?" Andy asked.

"No, what I'm saying is, I don't want there to be any shadow of a doubt, once we get these guys. Lawyers have a way of using things against people for their own purpose. I don't want that to happen here. Don't get any ideas of vigilante justice, okay?"

Andy put his arm around Carrie. "I have her back, detective. That's all I care about. I mean, I want the bastards caught, don't get me wrong, and I feel horrible for the other woman. But, hell, I don't even like guns."

"All right. Let's move on. Carrie, I have a sketch artist I want you to sit down with. Take your time and do your best to remember what these guys look like. Before that, gentlemen, I'd like to spend some one-on-one with her. You can wait outside, or you can go. I have a press conference slated at the end of this. Would any of you like to speak to the media?"

Both Carrie and Andy shook their heads. Chris spoke up.

"I will. I think somebody from the family should make a statement."

Ross shrugged. "That's up to you. I'm sure the newsies would appreciate anything to give their ratings a boost. Evan, why don't you prep Chris a little? Andy, would you wait outside for a bit? I'd like to talk to Carrie and then get her set up with our sketcher. Then you can all go home."

Andy kissed her cheek. "I'll be right outside."

Chris lingered a moment. "What are you going to ask her about?"

Detective Ross sat back in his chair and studied Chris with amused, narrowed eyes. "I don't think you need to worry about it, Mr. Barrett. Go with Detective Clark."

After Chris left, Ross arched his brow at Carrie. "Some brother you got there."

She smiled wanly. "I know. He's very protective of me. Always has been. I'm sorry."

"No need to apologize." He reached out and shut the tape recorder off. "Carrie, I'd like to ask you a few more things, off the record, at least for now. Is that all right?"

"Depends on what you're going to ask me. I've told you everything I can remember."

He smiled. "I know. But so far, we've had mixed company. Sometimes people's answers change when certain other people aren't around. People who care a lot about them. As I said at the hospital, I understand you were a rape counselor."

"That's right."

"Then you know some rape victims can be very reluctant to admit they were assaulted. I'm finding it hard to believe Emily Dawson was being raped every day and you weren't. My curiosity isn't morbid—I need to know what I can charge these bastards with."

Carrie shifted in her seat. "He didn't because he loves me."

"Who—Zane? Or both of them?"

"Zane—or both, maybe. I don't know. I could tell he wanted to. I told him it would hurt me. He didn't, okay? I mean, would it make you happier if I was raped?"

Ross sat back in his chair. "None of this is making me happy, Carrie."

She saw the way the detective was looking at her and avoided his eyes. "You don't believe me."

He sat forward and laid his hands on the table. "I have to admit, I'm having trouble believing any of it, but this part of it, in particular, isn't ringing true."

She sat a minute, wrestling with what she needed to say next in the face of his disbelief. Shaw's words at the last, before she ran, festered in her, and she knew if she didn't tell someone, she would be putting herself—and Andy, perhaps—in grave danger. But if he didn't believe her, what good would it do?

She took a deep breath. "Detective—Mike—there is something else. Even if you don't believe me, I feel like I have to tell you."

His brow arched. "All right. I'm listening."

"When Shaw let me go, he said he was only doing it because I'd quit eating and drinking. He didn't want me to die. He said he would find another way. Another time."

She swallowed hard. "I don't think this is over."

Ross watched her. "Have you told Andy this?"

"No. I—I don't know if I should. I don't want him to worry."

He nodded, subdued. "Okay. Duly noted. I'll let the township know and have them up their police presence on your street. Tell Andy—he needs to know. For now, let's get you set up with Sergeant Barry, our artist in residence. I want sketches of everything you remember, especially your assailants. Don't leave out any detail."

"Does he use colored pencils?" she asked.

"Not usually, but I'm sure he can. Why?"

Carrie looked down at her hands, which trembled like small animals caught in the shadow of a predator. "For the eyes."

21

ANDY SAT IN THE WAITING AREA just inside the front door of the barracks, watching Chris talk to the media. Detective Ross had come out and given a brief update, fielding questions about the possibility of pig people with a deftness Andy couldn't possibly have mustered.

When Chris took the podium, he latched onto the pig people story with melodramatic zeal. Andy could see both Clark and Ross were getting very agitated; at one point, Mike leaned over and said something to Chris, who shook him off. He went on to champion Carrie, calling her brave and courageous. This, at least, was true.

Detective Ross took the podium away from him, calling an end to the festivities. Andy could hear him saying something to Chris and gesturing to the parking lot. Chris shook his head, looking back at the barracks. Ross pointed sternly to the lot. Chris relented and walked to his car. Ross watched him go, hands on his hips. Then he came back inside.

"That brother of hers is getting on my nerves," he said. "Evan told him specifically not to answer any questions about pig people, and he did the exact opposite. The media will have a field day with it."

"I think he's used to getting his way when it comes to Carrie."

"I guess. He's going to have to answer for taking those checks. And I don't like it that he didn't tell us he went back to the house." Ross motioned for Andy to follow him. He tapped on the conference room door, which was now closed, and stuck his head in. "How we doing?"

He nodded at Andy. "They're ready. Come on."

Andy sat down beside Carrie, who looked worn out. He put his arm around her, and she leaned into him gratefully. Sergeant Barry was just finishing up a few minor details. Then he turned two pieces of paper to face them and sat while everyone looked. Andy looked at them for a long time, his heart thudding.

Detective Ross studied them silently. "Jesus Christ," he said finally.

Barry, who looked barely old enough to be out of high school, nodded. "Pretty freaky, huh?"

Ross touched the rendition of Zane. "It's like looking at the devil. This is the bad one? I mean, the worse of the two?"

"Yes," Carrie said. "Shaw calls him his killer side."

Andy pointed at the one of Shaw. "There's something almost familiar about this one. But that can't be."

He shivered and looked away. The pictures made something outrageous seem suddenly very real. He wanted to go home.

"Are we done, detective? Can we go?"

Ross looked at Carrie. "Anything else?"

"No. I guess not. They're good—you did a nice job, Sergeant Barry. Thank you. Will you be going back up to Round Top, Detective Ross?"

"Oh yeah," Ross said. "For sure. If we get any kind of a thaw, that will help, but I'll go back up with dogs anyway and see what we can find. As long as we've got another missing woman, we won't quit until we find her."

"Where's Chris?"

"I sent him on his way. He did a good job of stirring up the reporters. I should've been more careful. You two have a good night. I'll call you if I have news."

When they got back to the house, Andy half-expected Chris to be waiting in the drive, but he wasn't. They went inside; he looked at the clock on the stove: four-thirty. A long day. Carrie went to the fridge and got a bottle of white wine out and opened it. Andy watched her pour a hefty glass and drink liberally.

"I need to go home for a bit," he said. "To my parents' house. I need to make sure they're okay. But, do you want me to come back, or would you rather be alone?"

She looked stricken. "Why would I not want you to come back? Do you not want to come back?"

"I do," he said. "Of course I do. I want to make sure I'm doing what you want, and not assume, that's all. I don't want to leave, especially if you want me to stay. But I need a few things—some clothes, my toothbrush. I was going to stay the night it all happened. Remember?"

"I know," she said, her voice wobbling. "It seems like a million years ago, doesn't it?"

"It does." He set her wine glass down and wrapped her in his arms. "Will you be okay while I'm gone? I won't be more than an hour, tops."

"Yes. I think I'm just going to drink until I pass out."

He looked at her and smiled, wiping away a single tear that had sprung up and slid down her cheek. "Don't drink too much—that stuff will just dehydrate you again. If anybody comes, don't answer the door."

She looked at him sadly. "Andy, I may never open the damn door again as long as I live. Not without a gun in my hand."

The trip to his parents' house was uneventful. He didn't give them time to irritate him and told them he would be house-sitting for a friend. Then he packed a duffle bag with some clothes and left.

He picked up a pizza, feeling a creepy sense of déjà vu as he approached the house. But the door was firmly closed. He'd texted Carrie when he left the pizza joint, and she opened it immediately—unarmed, he noted with relief. She was, much to his consternation, pretty drunk.

They passed the evening curled on the couch, Carrie drowsing on his shoulder. At nine o' clock he shut the TV off and helped her to bed. She was half-asleep and unmindful of him, shoving her jeans off and pulling her sweater over her head. He watched with mixed feelings as she unhooked her bra and let it fall to the floor. Then she donned a pajama top and got into bed.

He stood uncertainly, and then slowly undressed, down to his boxers and tee shirt. He got under the covers, half-aroused and cursing himself for it. She scooted close to him, and he scooted back, not wanting her to feel his erection. She rolled over and looked at him.

"What's the matter?"

"I—I'm sorry. I'm not sure how to be, Carrie. You've got me a little worked up if you know what I mean, and I don't think that's right, right now. I can't help it. Maybe I should sleep in another room."

Her eyes flashed with sudden hurt. "You think I'm crazy, don't you? You can't stand the thought of touching me, isn't that right?"

"No—you're missing the point. I don't think I *should* be touching you—we just found you yesterday, for Christ's sake. You've had a traumatic experience—I don't think I should be trying to make love to you right now, but my dick doesn't care. I mean, you took your clothes off in front of me, I can't help it."

"So this is my fault?"

He sat up. "Carrie, you're tired, you've gone through stuff I can't even imagine, and you're a little drunk. I'm going to sleep upstairs in one of the spare rooms. If you need anything, come get me. Get some sleep."

"You know best, Andy," she said sarcastically. "You know who you sound like? Chris."

That was the last straw. He got out of bed and climbed the stairs, feeling miserable. He crawled into the cold bed and tried to tell himself things would be better in the morning.

Some small sound woke him in the middle of the night. He opened his eyes and found Carrie getting into bed with him. Moonlight spilled across her face, illuminating the sadness there. He reached for her.

"Come here. God, I'm sorry."

She didn't say anything. Instead, she kissed him, her hands entwining in his hair. He tried to pull away but she wouldn't let him go, her mouth hungry on his lips, his face. He'd taken off his shirt, and she moved lower, kissing his chest and belly.

"Carrie—"

She tugged his boxers off and he gave up, letting pleasure overtake him. Then she was pulling at her own clothes, her eyes feverish. She pulled him on top of her and cried out as he entered her, pulling him in deeper and harder, saying his name over and over, like a chant. Her body became like an oven; sweat poured from her, acrid and slick. She never took her eyes from his, and even as he came, he felt gripped by the torment there.

He collapsed on top of her, letting his breathing slow. They stayed like that for a minute, and then, as suddenly as she'd wanted him, she was pushing out from under him. He watched as she went to the window and flung it open; cold air poured in. She stood, taking in great gulps of it, her hands braced on the icy sill.

He went to her, noting the goosebumps pebbling her flesh, her nipples drawn tight and hard. Her breath plumed before her. He put a hand in the small of her back and gently closed the window. She bowed her head.

"You said I'm the same to you. You're wrong. I can never be the same. We barely knew each other before this started. How can I be the same to you if you never knew who I was?"

"Maybe it doesn't matter," he said. "What matters is you, now. I love you now just as much as I could love any version of you. Give us time, Carrie."

She looked up, at their reflections and beyond, into the night. "Chris texted me. He's going home. He promised he would see me soon."

She shivered suddenly and turned to him. "Do you believe me, Andy? About Zane? And Shaw? About them being pig people?"

He hesitated. Her eyes searched his frantically as if her very existence depended on his answer. He opened his mouth, not exactly sure what might come out.

"I believe whatever you want me to believe. I think it's incredible, but not crazy. Does that make sense?"

"That's not the same as believing." She took his hands. "You need to believe me because I'm not sure this is the end of it. I'm afraid they might get me again."

He took her firmly by the shoulders. "That's not going to happen. They'll have to come through me to do it. And a whole lot of cops."

He pulled her close, and then guided her to the bed, drawing the covers over them. He spooned her with his body, running his hand the length of her, warming her. With the warmth came tears; her body shook beneath his touch.

"Carrie. Listen to me a minute. I know you said you weren't raped, but I can't help feeling you're not telling me the truth, pig people be damned. If you don't want to talk to me about it, or anything else that happened, that's okay. I wish you would, but I get it if you can't. But would you consider talking to someone else about it? No matter what happened, I think you should."

"Detective Ross doesn't believe me either. About being raped. Why don't you believe me?"

He half-rolled away and stared at the ceiling. "Something in my gut. I just feel like you're holding something back. Maybe it's something I've seen in myself. When Billy died, I should have gone to talk to someone, and I didn't. It was a mistake."

He turned back to her; though she wasn't facing him, he sensed she was listening. "My buddy Jason is a psychiatrist. His wife is really nice. I think you two would hit it off. Would you be willing to have them over for dinner some night? You could meet Jay—he's a great guy—and maybe it wouldn't seem like such a big deal to go see him."

She was silent for a long time and then blew her nose. She rolled over on her back. "All right. Let's do that. But I think you should put your money where your mouth is and see somebody, too."

He kissed her. "Consider it done."

The next morning, he called Jason. He waited until Carrie was in the shower.

"Man, I've been wanting to call you," Jason said. "It's been all over the news. How is she?"

"As good as can be expected," Andy said. "She needs to talk about what happened with somebody, and I was hoping it could be you. Would that be a problem? A conflict of interest or something, because we're friends?"

"No. Whatever she tells me is strictly confidential, and I take that very seriously. Whatever she wants to tell you about our sessions, if we have any, is up to her. But you won't get word one out of me."

"Okay. I suggested she meet you first—kind of break the ice. How about you and Cassandra come over this Friday for dinner?"

"If you think it's necessary, sure, we can catch up and she can see that I don't bite. If she feels comfortable with me, then we can go from there."

Andy cleared his throat. "She did have one condition: she wants me to see someone, too. Can you make an appointment for me, too?"

There was a pause on the other end of the line. "You should probably go to someone else. You'll get a fresh perspective. And, you might take things a little more seriously."

Andy shook his head. "No. I don't want a fresh perspective. I want yours. You know my story—I don't want to tell anybody else. What, you think I don't listen to you?"

Jason had a good laugh. "I know you don't. But, what the hell. Understand the parameters have changed, though. You're my patient, not my friend. You'll be in my office, paying my fee. Which is quite expensive, by the way."

"Oh," Andy said, a bit taken aback. "I have to pay you?"

Jason had another good laugh. "It's called accountability. People tend to make a little more effort when their wallet's involved. How about this afternoon, say four-ish? That way, if I hit a nerve, it'll be close to cocktail hour."

"Today?" Andy said, pained.

"No better time than, say, two years ago, my friend. And, this way, she'll see you're serious."

Andy couldn't help but notice how happy Jason sounded. Gleeful, even. "I'm glad you're enjoying this."

"I am. See you at four."

When the hour arrived, Andy knew Jason was right; it didn't feel the same. He'd known Jason's receptionist for years and had been waved into his office by her many times as Jason's friend, not his patient. He couldn't help but feel she looked at him differently as she ushered him in this time.

Jason greeted him wearing a lab coat and a pair of fake glasses with the nose and mustache attached. On his head was the classic doctor headlamp.

"Ah, ze crazy person is here," he said in a terrible German accent. "Come, zit on ze couch, and we vill talk about ze mudder and ze penis. Then you vill cry and give me big pile of money. Yah?"

"So much for taking things seriously," Andy said, though he did feel better. "Is this how you greet all your new patients?"

"Nuh—only ze vurst cases." He took off the get-up and shed the coat. He motioned for Andy to sit. "There's the couch or the chair. Take your pick. The couch is good if you need to curl into the fetal position."

Andy opted for the chair. "I'm surprised you could see me on such short notice. Clients wising up, are they?"

"I had Kate move some folks around. So, what's going on? How are you holding up with this situation?"

Andy leaned forward, his elbows on his thighs. "I don't know. I'm worried about her, obviously. I can't help but feel like she's lying to me about being raped."

"Are you upset about the lie? Or the rape?"

Andy looked at him, mystified. "Both, I guess. I don't want her to lie to me, and I sure as hell don't want her to have been raped."

"And what if both end up being true? How will you feel?"

Andy chewed his lower lip. "Mad as hell. I mean, Christ, this whole thing is so messed up. We're not talking about your garden variety rapist here—we're talking about something out of a horror movie."

"Do you believe her?"

"I don't know what to believe. I don't want to believe it. For a while, I did because it was theoretical at the time. Now, it seems real. You asked me how I'm handling it, and I guess the answer is, not well. When I saw the pictures the sketch artist drew, all I could think of was one of those things on top of her and I—I couldn't even look at her."

"If it ends up being true, will you still be able to love her?"

Andy searched the room as if the answer was written on the walls, or hidden among Jason's many books. "I'd like to think I'm better than that," he said finally. "But I am my father's son."

"What does that mean?"

Andy looked at him. "It means I don't know. What if I can't look at her the same way? I want to, I've told her nothing has changed. But, I don't know. I know I should let it go. I can't control the lie or the rape."

"That's right, Andy," Jason said. "But you can control you. You are your father's son, but you aren't him. I've known your dad almost as long as you have. I don't know why he is the way he is. I suspect he had a miserable childhood, and, like most miserable people, he wants everyone to be just as miserable as he is. You've made some mistakes, and you've paid for them dearly. The biggest one is letting him win."

Andy sat and felt an old anger rise in him. "I remember when I was in grade school, the other kids used to tease me about my name. Remember? Kornhole, Candy Andy—all that shit. I went home and told him I hated my name, that the other kids made fun of me. He gave me this satisfied look like he planned it or something. And then he laughed at me. That's when I knew he didn't love me. He's never loved anything—probably not even my mother."

"But you do," Jason said quietly. "You have a lot of love in you. Right?"

"Yeah. Yeah, I do. But I loved Melinda, too. Look how that turned out. I'm scared he's right. Everything I touch turns to shit. Melinda left me. My son is dead. And Carrie? Jesus."

"That's him talking, Andy. Look—bad shit happens. You can control it to some degree, but bad shit still happens. Your job is to admit it. And when the bad shit does go down, come at it swinging— from your heart. Maybe you're right—maybe your dad doesn't love anything or anyone. I think he's got a prune for a heart. But that doesn't make you unlovable. It just makes him an asshole. Once you love yourself, it's a lot easier to not put conditions on others. It'll make it possible to love Carrie, regardless of what happened."

Andy shook his head. "I don't know how I can love myself after what I did. What I didn't do. You've talked about accountability. Isn't it right I take the blame for my son's death?"

Jason shook his head. "Accountability and blame are like half-brothers. Let's try this: You made a mistake. There are two directions you can go, and they look a lot alike, but they're completely different.

Blame is one, but it's a box. Self-flagellation. Accountability is freedom. Understanding. Compassion. And empowerment. You can know you made a mistake and still be worthy of love. You're human. You're flawed. And that's okay. Welcome to the rest of us."

Andy gestured helplessly. "I don't know how to make that shift."

Jason's smile was like a beam of light. "It's work, Andy. You're taking your first step. You're doing it right now, my friend. Right now."

**FRIDAY CAME, AND CARRIE'S** nervousness escalated. Not so much because of Jason's occupation and the purpose of the dinner, though that was bad enough. It was Jason's wife Carrie was more afraid of.

"She's really nice," Andy had said when she confessed this fear. "Very down to earth. She's an herbalist. She owns that store downtown: Make It Green. Do you know it?"

"I've never been in. Great—she owns her own business and he's a doctor. They sound like a power couple."

Andy laughed. "Not really. Jason's a big dork. You'll see."

"I'm just not very social. Never have been. All the friends Ben and I had started having kids, and we sort of drifted away from them. I haven't cooked for anybody in years."

He kissed her. "You cook for me. You're great at it. I haven't had indigestion once."

Sweet, but it hadn't done much to allay her fears. She'd decided on a garden lasagna—Andy had said Cassandra was a vegetarian. It was simple, yet elegant. Almost impossible to screw up. Wine, bread, and a salad would round out the meal, with a chocolate hazelnut torte for dessert.

Andy helped her as much as he could, which generally meant staying out of the way. He had essentially moved in with her. They hadn't had a formal discussion about it, but more and more of his stuff kept showing up. This was fine with her—the only person who might object was Chris, but she hadn't heard from him since he'd gone back to Baltimore. This was also fine with her.

Though Andy continued to share her bed, they hadn't made love again. She was afraid to broach the subject with him and was careful to come to bed in a full set of pajamas. The last time had been hard. She'd wanted it, but for the wrong reasons. She welcomed his affection, but the act itself was too much for her. He'd been right after all, and she tried not to let this irritate her.

The doorbell signaled their guests' arrival. Carrie smiled bravely as Andy opened the door.

"Hey, you two. Welcome. Come in—let me take your coats. Jason, Cassandra, this is Carrie."

"Nice to meet you," Carrie said warmly, but her heart was sinking. Cassandra wasn't just pretty—she was a knockout. Long, blonde hair fell across her shoulders in a thick wave, and the red cashmere sweater and knit pants accentuated a lovely figure. Jason was good-looking in a bookish sort of way. She couldn't help but feel he was already analyzing her. She felt herself shriveling.

"My, what a beautiful home you have," Casandra said, shaking Carrie's hand. "Such a big yard. We live on a postage stamp."

Carrie looked around at the house she'd cherished for years and thought it suddenly looked like a hut. "Thank you. It needs some updating."

"Nonsense," Jason scoffed. "It's great. You're finally moving up in the world, Andy. Congratulations."

"And it *smells* wonderful," Cassandra exclaimed. "Something yummy is cooking."

"It's just vegetable lasagna," Carrie said. "Andy mentioned you're a vegetarian."

"I am. How thoughtful. We brought you some wine."

Carrie took the bottles, a red and a white. They looked expensive. "Shall we open them, or do you want to wait for dinner?"

"Oh, let's open the Pinot Gris. It's very crisp. I hope you like it."

It could be Mad Dog 20/20 and I'd like it, Carrie thought. They moved into the kitchen, where Carrie popped the cork on the wine and the boys applied themselves to bourbon. Carrie took a long, careful sip. It was indeed delicious.

"I'm glad you like it," Cassandra said, and then gave Carrie a direct look. "I'm just going to get this out of the way now, and then we can move on. I've heard about your ordeal, of course. I am so, so sorry."

"Thank you," Carrie said. She liked it that Cassandra didn't beat around the bush. "It's been pretty exhausting, and weird, with all the media coverage."

"Have they been hounding you? I always feel so bad for families that've had a tragedy and the media puts them on display. Some of them like it, I suppose."

"Actually, they've been very respectful. Though I haven't left the house and I don't answer the phone, so they haven't had much opportunity."

"That's smart of you." Cassandra smiled at her, revealing perfect white teeth. "So you and Andy are making a nice couple, yes?"

Carrie glanced at him. He and Jason were engaged in a lively discussion about football. She smiled, pleased to watch him interact with someone other than her brother or a police officer. He looked relaxed and happy.

"Yes. I think we do make a nice couple. I lost my husband a few months ago. I suppose some people would think it's too soon for me to see someone else. It just sort of happened."

"Those people don't have to lie in bed alone at night, wondering at every sound, or clean out the gutters by themselves, hoping they don't fall and the mailman finds them a week later because of the smell." Cassandra raised her glass. "To hell with those people."

Carrie touched glasses with her, suddenly warm and flushed with feeling. "Yes. To hell with them."

The evening progressed, and as it did, Carrie felt more relaxed and happier than she had in weeks. The conversation at the dinner table was comfortable, and Carrie was amazed at how easy it was. She liked Jason right away, and the friendly way he looked at her. It all felt wonderfully normal, and she knew she had Andy to thank for it. She squeezed his hand under the table and he squeezed it right back.

After dinner, Andy asked Cassandra if she would help him find something on the internet, a contrivance, Carrie suspected. Jason offered to build a fire in the fireplace if Carrie would assist.

She helped him ball up newspaper and stuff it into the hearth. "Andy tells me you're a psychiatrist," she offered awkwardly.

"I am, in fact. I have a degree in head shrinking from Stanford. I know all the best jokes."

"Andy said he felt better after he saw you the other day. He said it was hard but good. He's going to see you again, I guess."

Jason stacked wood on top of the paper. "Psychotherapy is like digging out a splinter. You have to go through some pain before the healing can start."

"He thinks I should come see you."

Jason lit a match and held it to the paper. He looked at her. "What do you think?"

"I could see talking to you. It wouldn't hurt, would it?"

Jason smiled. "It's like that splinter. Only for a little bit. The reward is worth it."

"All right," she said. "When?"

"How about Monday morning? Nine o'clock. I cleared a spot for you, just in case."

She took a deep breath, feeling as though she was stepping off a cliff.

"Monday it is."

Jason didn't pull the German psychiatrist routine with Carrie. Andy had told her about it, and she'd had a good laugh, but it would've diminished it somehow if he'd greeted her that way. He must have sensed this, and she was grateful for it.

His office was warm and professional, without anything that might resemble props to her; forced efforts to make her comfortable. She smiled at the couch and chose it, sitting in the middle of it with her legs crossed. He offered her bottled water.

"What would you like to talk about today, Carrie?" he asked, without preamble.

"I—I'm not sure," she said, feeling awkward. "Should I tell you about my parents?"

He laughed. "I am required by law to talk about your parents, it's true. But really, only if you want to. Do they live locally?"

"No. I mean, they used to. My parents are both dead."

"I'm sorry."

Carrie shrugged. "It's okay. They were killed in a car accident. My brother was with them. They were coming back from picking Chris up from the airport. He was coming home from college for spring break. They hit a March snowstorm and went off the road. Chris walked away with a broken arm and some cuts, but they were both killed. He was lucky."

"I guess so. Where were you at the time?"

"At home."

"Why didn't you go?"

She looked down at her hands. "I just didn't feel like it. And anyway, Chris called the night before and said not to bother. He'd be home soon enough. It's a good thing I didn't, I guess. I might've been killed, too, or hurt."

"True. Do you feel bad about that?"

"No. I don't. I mean, I'm not glad my parents died, but we never had a strong relationship." She rolled her eyes. "God, this is starting to sound like a real therapy session."

He smiled. "It sure is. Go on."

"Daddy was a big drinker. That's what caused the accident—he was drunk. My mom drank, too, but not like him. He would get hammered every night. My mom would, like, shrink into herself by the end of the night. She never confronted him about it."

"Was he violent?"

She shifted in her seat. "No. One time. Almost. They got into an argument about money or something. It was bad. I was ten or eleven. I got in between them. Dumb, huh? I tried to tell dad he shouldn't talk about money when he'd been drinking, and he got—"

She paused. She suddenly felt very hot and took a long swallow of water. Her heart was pounding, and she had that feeling of falling again. Jason waited, watching her calmly.

"He got this look in his eyes. Like I'd just spit on him or something. It was like he was seeing me in a different way. I don't think he realized I understood he was a drinker. I was judging him. He took hold of me by my shoulders, and I knew—I *knew* he was going to throw me across the kitchen. It's a sickening feeling, knowing you're about to be hurt really, really bad. Have you ever felt it?"

Jason took a deep breath. "No, Carrie. Not like that."

She nodded. "I was terrified. My mother was screaming, 'Don't you hurt that child!' And then Chris was there. He just snatched me away. He pulled me out of the house and we ran into the woods. We spent the night out there."

"No one came to look for you?"

"We heard my mother calling, but she quit after a while. She didn't try very hard. Chris made us a bed of pine needles and we stayed out all night. He—"

She stopped. Her throat had dried up, but she didn't have the wherewithal to lift the water to her lips. Her vision blurred, and she blinked hard to clear it.

"Carrie? He what? What did Chris do then?"

"Nothing." She looked at Jason and shook her head. "He held me, that's all."

Jason sat for a moment. She felt uncomfortable in his silence as if she was a Halloween pumpkin and he was reaching inside to pull out all her slimy bits. She wanted to leave, and yet felt frozen in place.

"What kind of a brother is Chris?" Jason asked.

"Typical big brother, I guess. He's five years older than me. He's very protective. He watches me—watches *over* me, I mean. He jokes that I'm like a house plant—I need a lot of care and watering."

"How does that make you feel?"

"Like nothing. I mean, I don't think about it one way or another. It means nothing *to* me. I'm sorry, I feel nervous for some reason."

"It's okay. You're doing fine."

"I'm not even supposed to exist, according to my mother. I was, you know, an accident. Unplanned. I guess they only wanted one. Mom used to call me her 'oops.' The best little mistake she ever made."

"She said that to you?"

"Yes. Chris hated it. He said she was jealous of our relationship."

"What kind of relationship did you have?"

She shrugged. "He's my brother. You know. We'd mess around. He'd play this game—The Gobbler—where he'd be under a blanket and he'd, you know, make these gobbling noises, and he'd try to get me. He would corner me and drag me under the blanket. Like he was eating me. And sometimes he would tickle me—you know how brothers are—we'd be sitting on the couch watching Jaws—it's my favorite movie—and he would get the blanket and tickle me at all the scary parts. And sometimes he would tell me he needed for me to pretend I was his girlfriend and he would kiss me and tell me it was because he needed the practice."

"Carrie? Do you need a Kleenex?"

"Why? What do you mean?"

"Because you're crying, Carrie. Do you not realize you're crying?"

She swiped at her face, and her hand came away soaked. She felt so confused. Her head was filled with white noise, and she couldn't fucking *see*. God, why couldn't she see?

"I—I—I'm having trouble—my eyes are burning. I don't know what's wrong with me."

Jason was leaning forward in his chair, and he was looking at her with gentle concern. "Carrie. When you and Chris were on the couch watching the movie under the blanket, how did he tickle you?"

Carrie's nose was running—everything was running. She felt as though she was unraveling, like a mad piece of string in a cartoon. Unraveling to the end, where she would fly away into nothingness.

"He—he would put his hands on my sides. My tummy. He put his fingers in me. *On* me. I couldn't breathe. God, it was so hot. No air."

"Carrie, did you hear what you just said? You said your brother put his fingers in you. He put them inside your vagina?"

Something inside her cracked. She felt it. It was like her head was an egg, and Jason had rapped it against a sharp edge. Memories came spilling out, like little black insects, scuttling out on a putrescent wave.

"Oh God," she said. "Oh, my God."

"It's okay, Carrie. You're safe. You're all right. Remember the splinter—this is the hard part, the pain part, but once you get this out, the healing can start. That night in the woods—the night your dad almost hurt you. What happened?"

Carrie could hardly talk. There was a huge knot in her throat as if something was trying to keep her silent. She swallowed hard, and then the words came, tearing out of her as if her very lungs were trying to break free.

"He held me. He told me there was no one for him but me. He loved me. He would always keep me safe. But I knew it wasn't true. Because sometimes, when he would make me his practice girlfriend, if I didn't want to play, he would threaten to hurt Petey. Our cat. One time, I still wouldn't give in. I told him it was gross. The next day I found Petey nailed to the garage door. I never refused him again.

"That night, I was so scared. So confused. He was lying behind me. Spooning me. He kissed my neck and started touching me. He rolled me onto my back. And he—he—"

She looked up at Jason, and the words came out like bitter bile: "He *fucked* me. My brother fucked me. He said he would never hurt me, but he did. He made me bleed."

The words hung in the air. Carrie felt like she might rattle apart—her whole body shook, and sweat stood on her cheeks, yet her hands and feet were ice cold. She stared at Jason, and even as the truth whirled around her like a dervish, her head continued to shake, as if in some reflexive denial. Yet her body knew, her skin, her very cells remembered what she did not. Until now.

Jason continued to meet her gaze, without a trace even of surprise, let alone anything else. How could he be so calm?

"What's happening to me?" she asked.

"Did you remember any of this before today, Carrie?" he asked.

"No," she said. "How can that be?"

"You've worked at The Women's Place as I recall. You must know about repressed memory. Sometimes, when something traumatic happens to us, we can totally block out the memory of it. It's the mind's way of protecting itself. The memories often leak through in subtle ways—fear or discomfort in being touched without permission or a feeling of being watched all the time. Not liking sex, or, in some cases, promiscuity. Can you relate to any of that?"

"Some of it, to some extent. I've never considered myself to be a very sexual person—I never liked it all that much. I never questioned why—I thought it was just me. I know Ben—my late husband—was frustrated sometimes, but he dealt with it. With Andy, it's been different. The first time we made love felt great. But then everything happened, and I feel like I'm back in that place again."

She put her face in her hands and rubbed it slowly. "The last time we did it, I wanted to do it to feel normal. I didn't, though. And I haven't wanted to since."

She looked up at Jason, stricken. "How am I going to go home today and face him? How can I tell him this? He'll wish he never laid eyes on me. Not that I blame him."

"I've known Andy for a long time. He's a strong guy. You don't have to tell him anything until you're ready. This is all new information to you, too. Don't feel you have to rush. We have lots to talk about, Carrie."

"I thought we were going to talk about pig people today," she said. "God."

Jason smiled. "We'll get to them another day. I'd like to schedule you for the day after tomorrow, okay? If you feel like you're collapsing around this in the meantime, I want you to call me. This is intense stuff, not to be taken lightly."

She wiped her face and blew her nose. "Just when you think the worst has happened to you, something even worse happens."

She looked at Jason sadly. "My whole life has been a lie."

23 WHEN CARRIE WALKED THROUGH THE door from her session, Andy started to ask her how it went, but the words died on his lips. Shell-shocked was the phrase that came to mind. Her eyes were raw and red-rimmed, and they were the saddest he'd ever seen. She looked at him once, and then wouldn't look again.

"Carrie," he said, and reached for her.

She held up her hand. "Don't. I can't talk to you right now. I just can't. I need to lie down for a while."

That had been two days ago. On Wednesday at ten o'clock, Jason had called, looking for her. She wouldn't talk to him.

"She needs to come in," he said. "How bad is she?"

"Bad," Andy said. "She won't talk to me. She won't even get out of bed. I don't think she's eaten anything since Sunday night. I know you can't tell me what you talked about, but what the hell did you two talk about?"

"Yeah. Right. She's got to come in. It's got to be her choice, though—you can't drag her. It's important she make this decision herself."

"I'm pretty scared, Jay. What do I do?"

"Love her," he said simply. "Love the hell out of her. Ask her permission to hold her. Don't startle her. Don't get impatient with her."

"Jesus, Jay."

"I know," he said grimly. "I will say this much: it's serious shit, Andy. Kid gloves, okay?"

So he did these things, but by Friday he'd reached his limit. Her silence was maddening; she ate next to nothing, and when she wasn't in bed she sat on the couch and stared at the TV, not seeing it. Many times, she locked herself in the bathroom; he could hear her sobbing as he leaned against the door. He started spending a lot of time outside, for the weather had flipped back to spring-like. Most of the snow had melted, and a balmy breeze tickled his face as he put up Christmas lights he'd found in the attic.

His phone sounded as he was coming down the ladder. A chill went through him as he looked at the number on the screen.

"Andy. Detective Ross. Is Carrie available? I've been trying her cell, but she doesn't pick up or call back."

"Um, yeah. She's been a little under the weather. Hold on."

Andy hurried into the living room, where Carrie was staring at an episode of Friends. She looked up at him slowly, her eyes vacant. He held the phone out to her.

"It's Detective Ross."

She took it, and he reluctantly stepped back to give her some privacy. She put the phone to her ear.

"Hello?"

She listened for a long time. "All right. Yes. I can come down now. Okay. Bye."

He took the phone back. "What is it?"

For the first time in a week, a little life came back into her eyes. "They've had a break in the case. The weather. He said they've found some things of great significance and he needs me to come down right away."

"I'll drive," he said, and then stopped. "I mean, is it all right if I come with you?"

"Yes." She stirred and ran her hand over her hair. "Oh yes. I definitely want you there. Should I take a shower?"

"A quick one," he suggested. She hadn't taken one in days, and as much as he loved her, she smelled like an old gym bag. "You'll feel better."

Forty minutes later, they arrived at the barracks. Ross and Clark were waiting for them in the main conference room. When he saw Mike Ross's face, he knew something was wrong. Mike directed him to sit at the end of the table and for Carrie to sit across from him so that she was alone. Detective Clark leaned against the wall by the door, looking solemn. Andy sat down, feeling like a patient about to receive a cancer diagnosis.

Carrie had gotten somewhat animated on the drive over, but as she sat before the detectives, she grew quiet again, and her eyes flicked back and forth between the two men. She glanced at Andy a few times, and he tried to smile encouragingly. He didn't like it that Ross had seated them apart.

"I understand you're not feeling well, Carrie. I'm sorry to hear that. Thank you for coming down. As I said on the phone, this break in the weather has been productive for our investigation. We went back up to Radio Tower Hill on Wednesday with two bloodhounds we borrowed from Allegheny County. They picked up on the remains of some scattered human feces. We began a tightening search radius based on its location and stumbled—literally, Evan tripped over it—on a ventilation pipe sticking out of the ground about four inches. We located a trap door hidden in the grass. It opened on this."

He pulled a picture from a folder and pushed it in front of Carrie. Andy leaned forward to look. The picture showed a small room, lit by a police spotlight. In it was a cage, maybe eight by ten, made of woven wire fencing and old boards. Straw littered the floor. Outside the cage was a small desk and chair.

"That's it," Carrie said excitedly. "That's where I was kept. Except—"

She paused, frowning. "It's too small. Where's the rest of it? Did you find Emily?"

"No, Carrie. It's just the one room. There was no one else there."

"I don't understand. It's a huge place—I didn't see it, but I could sense it. Shaw called it The Warrens. A series of tunnels—Emily said it was an old aqueduct maybe."

Ross ignored this, instead setting a milk crate on the table. "We also found this, among other things. Do you recognize these things?"

He set out a series of items, each encased in sealed plastic bags. A copy of Charlotte's Web; a VHS tape of Jaws; books that looked like the how-to variety. Andy saw Carrie redden as Ross laid out a big stack of skin magazines: Hustler, Playboy, Penthouse. His own skin began to crawl, and sweat sprang to his forehead.

"Yes," Carrie said. "These are Zane's. He showed them to me."

"He did, did he," Ross said. "This Zane person."

"Yes. It was kind of creepy. Jaws is my favorite movie, and I had a copy of Charlotte's Web as a kid. I asked him where he got it, but he wouldn't tell me."

Ross leaned across the table. His face was watchful, intent, and very grave. "We found lots of fingerprints on these items. Some partials, some complete. We haven't run them all down yet, but two are of special interest. One set is yours. The other, and the one that appears most frequently belongs to your brother."

Carrie stared at the detective uncomprehendingly. Andy felt all the spit dry up in his mouth. His jaw unhinged slowly, leaving his tongue cleaved to the roof of his mouth.

"What?" Carrie said finally. "Chris?"

"Something about your brother struck me as a little odd the last time he was here," Ross said. "Detective Clark ran a background check on him when you disappeared, but, frankly, what we found didn't raise any major flags. Until now. Did you know your brother was brought up on a misdemeanor weapons charge in Maryland in 2001? He was pulled over for a traffic violation and was found to be carrying a concealed weapon without a permit. During the course of this, he was fingerprinted."

Carrie looked thoroughly confused. "Chris owns a gun?"

Clark nodded. "A Glock 9 mm. Nice piece."

Ross laid his hands on the table. "Your brother's prints weren't just on these items here. They were all over that room. The desk. The chair. The lock on the cage door. The trap door."

He reached into the folder and began setting out a bunch of photographs. "I had a hunch. These are pictures of the women who've been abducted over the last fifteen years. This is a picture of you. Do you notice anything about them?"

Andy stood so he could see better. The pictures were all candid shots, missing women smiling for the camera. At first, he didn't notice anything. But then a pattern began to appear, like some awful puzzle slowly coming together, and his eyes widened with dawning horror.

All the women were slender and very pretty. They all had brown eyes and long, medium brown hair. Andy looked at them, and then at the picture of Carrie. He looked at Carrie and sank back into his seat.

"Oh my God," he said.

Carrie looked at each of their faces and then at the pictures, her face growing more and more panicked. "What?" she asked. "What is it?"

"Look closely, Carrie," Detective Ross said. "They all look like you. Andy sees it. I see it. Evan sees it."

Carrie shook her head. "No. I don't. I don't see anything."

"There's a forensics team up on that hill right now. They've been there since yesterday. They established a perimeter around that hole in the ground. They've found two graves already. One was fresh—a few months old. The woman's identity is preliminary, but we're pretty sure it's Emily Dawson."

Carrie shook her head. "But—that can't be. I just talked to Emily. It has to be someone else."

Detective Ross continued to look at her soberly. "I suspect we'll find eight more graves like hers. Carrie, do you have any idea where your brother might be?"

"He—he texted me a few days ago. He said he was going home. He said he would see me soon."

"Home where?"

"Maryland. Baltimore. That's where he lives. You know that."

Ross and Clark exchanged glances. "Carrie," Ross said, "your brother hasn't lived in Baltimore for ten years. Well, I should say, not at the address on his license. But we checked tax records and things of that nature, and have found no evidence he's lived in that state since his wife died."

"*What?*" Carrie stared at him. "Rachel? Rachel isn't dead. I mean, I haven't seen her since their wedding, but that's because Chris said she doesn't like me. She—"

Carrie sucked her breath in as Ross produced one more picture and a newspaper clipping from his dreadful folder.

"This is Rachel's obituary. She died in a car accident. Her car went off the road for no known reason. The crash was listed as suspicious but ultimately ruled accidental because the investigators could find no evidence to the contrary. But the officer I talked to said he didn't like it. Something about it felt wrong. She was on a back road she had no routine business on—she wasn't on her way to work, or to the store. There were no skid marks—she just left the road and struck a tree. The car caught on fire. They had to identify her by her dental records."

"Christ," Andy said.

"I asked the officer if they ever considered Chris as a suspect, and he said no, there was no way to connect him. But he also said he didn't like Chris—had a funny feeling about him."

He pushed the picture toward Carrie. "You probably never thought much about what Rachel looked like, but in the context of these other women, look at her. She looks a lot like them. Like you."

Ross took out another, final piece of paper, this one a photocopy. He pushed the pictures of the women aside and set it down directly in front of Carrie.

"This is a copy of your brother's Maryland driver's license." He pointed to the name. "Christopher Zane Barrett."

Carrie recoiled from it as if stung. "No. Oh, no." She looked up at Detective Ross. "No."

"You said that albino pig man was Shaw's killer side. His name was Zane, isn't that right? Did you not make the connection, Carrie? Or did you not want to?"

Carrie put her hands to the sides of her head and pushed her chair back. Her face had gone ashen except for two hot points of red on each cheek. She looked around the room as if she'd never seen any of them before.

"I can't do this anymore," she said and stood. "Oh, no, I can't. This—no. No."

She turned and stumbled into the chair. It tipped over with a sharp bang. Her legs tangled in it and before anyone could catch her, she went down in a dead faint. Andy rushed to her and turned her over.

"Carrie." He shook her gently but got no response. He looked up at Ross, who stood over them with a look of deep concern. "I think I should call her doctor. He's a psychiatrist."

"I think that's a great idea," Ross said. "Let's put her in my office for now. I have a couch in there."

Andy picked her up and put her on Mike Ross's ugly green couch. Then he called Jason's office, and after a bit of wrangling with Kate, his receptionist got Jason on the phone.

"Okay," he said when Andy filled him in. "I can be there in ten minutes. You two are going to be my only clients if this keeps up."

He hung up before Andy could apologize or protest. He looked at Carrie, who was still out. "How long does a faint usually last?"

"I don't know," Ross said. He held her wrist. "Her pulse is good— rapid, but good, and she's breathing all right. I'll give her some smelling salts if she doesn't come around pretty soon."

"I don't understand any of this. Why is she making this stuff up?"

"I don't think she is," Ross said. "Not on purpose, anyway. It's a good thing you've got a shrink on the way."

Not long after, Jason walked in. Detective Ross was about to give Carrie a dose of salts. He paused long enough to shake Jason's hand and then cracked the packet under Carrie's nose. She jerked and opened her eyes. She saw Jason and her face crumpled.

"That's the same face my wife makes when she wakes up in the morning and sees me," Jason said, smiling kindly. He looked at Andy and the detectives. "Would you give us a few minutes, guys?"

Ross took Andy back to the conference room and left him there. He waited, his face in his hands, for what seemed like hours. The pictures, still scattered across the table, stared up at him mutely. He picked through them, fraught with disbelief.

After about a half-hour, everyone filed back in the room and resumed their original seats. Jason sat down next to Carrie. He gave her shoulder a quick, reassuring rub. To Andy, she looked as if her world had come completely apart. Which it had, he supposed. He was about to find out just how much.

Jason leaned over and whispered something in her ear. She nodded and lifted her eyes to Detective Ross. Andy wanted badly for her to look at him, but she wouldn't, or couldn't.

"Earlier this week, I went to see Jason so he could help me process what happened to me on Round Top. We never got there.

We discovered I have what he calls repressed memories of my childhood. Things I had blocked out because they were so terrible. I didn't remember—or didn't choose to remember—that my brother Chris had abused me for years."

She stopped, her throat working. It seemed she had to physically wrench the words out. "Sexually. He would make me look at those magazines with him, and he would—he would masturbate while he watched me flip the pages. He did all the horrible things you read about. He threatened me if I wouldn't cooperate. He killed my cat. The first time he had sex with me, I was ten."

Carrie began to cry. Her whole body shook; Jason put a hand on her shoulder. Andy sat, his heart pounding so hard he thought it might burst from his chest. A dull roar began in his head, nearly drowning her out as if anything could. Every word was like an ice pick in his brain.

"The night I was taken, I truly thought there was a monster at my door. I don't know how I saw what I saw. It seemed so real. But it couldn't be." She touched the color copy of the license. "It was Chris who took me. He put me in that room."

Detective Ross folded his hands and leaned across the table. "Did your brother rape you in that room, Carrie?"

She began to cry harder and hid her face in her hands. She nodded.

"How many times? Once? Twice?"

She nodded amid wracking sobs and kept nodding. Ross slumped back in his chair.

"Too many to count?"

She nodded one last time. She combed her fingers through her hair and held her head, her chest hitching. She turned her eyes to Andy finally, and he saw the terrible truth there.

His stomach lurched. He shot out of his chair and bolted from the room. He pushed his way through the barracks and button-hooked around the side of the building in time to vomit into a dirty patch of snow.

He gripped the concrete wall and did it again until there was nothing left. A hand fell on his shoulder. He jumped. It was Evan.

"Take it easy, man." He pulled out a handkerchief and gave it to Andy. "You okay?"

Andy wiped his mouth and leaned against the wall. "I don't know if I can go back in there."

"Sure you can. You gotta be at least half as brave as she is. She's been through hell. She needs you. And right now, she thinks you ran out on her. We're gonna stop at the men's room, you're going to splash some water on your face, rinse your mouth out, and then we're going back in there and finish this."

Andy felt a flash of anger. "I want to kill him."

Evan smiled. "I know. But don't. Let me and Mike take care of him. You're no good to her sitting in a jail cell, and he ain't worth it. We'll take care of him, and you'll take care of her. Because you love her, right?"

Andy let his head fall back against the concrete. "I do," he said. "God help me, but I do."

**24** **CARRIE SAT IN HER CHAIR WITH** her legs drawn up against her chest, her chin resting on her knees. *It's over*, she thought. *He's gone.*

She didn't blame him. If the tables were turned and she had to sit and listen to the madness spewing from her mouth, she would have bolted, too. She would give anything to get away from herself. She was poisoned, tainted. Certifiable. Nuts.

But then the door opened and he came back in and sat down next to her. He was pale, and he looked like someone had round-housed him in the face with an encyclopedia, but he was there. He put his hand on the back of her neck and pressed his face to the other side of her knees so their foreheads touched.

"I love you," he said quietly. "No matter what."

It broke her open inside. She felt something give way, like the tide before a tsunami pulls out and then rushes back in, a wave of feeling so profound it would have knocked her over had she not been sitting. She couldn't speak; instead, she smiled and gave a single nod. He kissed the tip of her nose and then sat back. Detective Ross looked at him.

"You going to make it?"

Andy took a deep breath. "Yes. I believe so."

Ross nodded. "Carrie's doctor was just explaining what sort of phenomena we're dealing with, here. Jason, would you mind recapping for Andy?"

"Sure." Jason leaned forward so he could see Andy. "Repressed memories are very common among sexual abuse victims. The creation of a substitute reality is a little rarer, but not unheard of. A person who is experiencing significant trauma can trick themselves into believing something else is happening to them. The horror of the circumstance still often bleeds through, but at least the victim is in control. In Carrie's case, she created the pig people. Monsters, yes, but easier to take than the reality of being kidnapped and assaulted by her own brother."

"I get that," Andy said, looking at her. "I wanted to believe in them, too. Somehow, it was better than the thought of you lying dead in a shallow grave. At least I could believe you were alive."

"Why pig people?" Ross asked. "Why not vampires, or trolls?"

Carrie glanced at Jason. "I've heard the pig people story my whole life—a lot of people have. But I grew up with them. It was one of the threats Chris used to scare me into submission. 'If you don't let me do this, the pig people will come in the night and get you.' And the night Paula Davis had her baby at the shelter—that poor, deformed baby. Reggie Spavine came and said they were going to get me. He wasn't trying to be mean, but it was a creepy coincidence."

"It fueled the fire for what was to come," Jason added.

"Creepy indeed," Ross said. He paused. "So, just to be clear, for the record, there are no pig people, right?"

"No," Carrie said sadly. "Just one. My brother."

She shook her head. "It *is* hard for me to let some of it go, though. I mean, I swear I talked to Emily."

"The mind is one powerful muscle," Jason said. "Your imagination was in overdrive. You've been experiencing a form of PTSD for years and didn't know it. Witnessing Paula Davis's death—watching her kick her baby to death—that was traumatic in its own right. I think what we have here is a perfect storm for the creation of an alternate reality. Your mind was merely trying to protect itself."

"Was Paula one of the women? She told me she was being held against her will. Did Chris have her?"

"No," Ross said. "That was another odd little coincidence."

"Synchronicity," Andy murmured.

Ross glanced at him. "Synchronicity. Whatever. The township police were conducting a separate investigation on that situation. Paula Davis lived on Radio Tower Hill with her father. Evidently, he had been keeping Paula in the basement for years. The baby you're referring to was his, which would explain its substantial deformities."

Carrie shook her head. "My brother had no connection with Paula. You're sure?"

"At this point, we cannot make any connection between the two. And Carrie, I saw a picture of Paula Davis's baby. Frankly, it didn't look like a pig to me at all. It had a severely cleft palate, and several of its digits were fused. But a pig? Not to me."

"I think you're still getting your realities mixed up, Carrie," Jason offered. "Shaw and Zane are not real. Paula's baby is only relevant in that it helped your mind create a false reality. The pig people story had been embedded in your mind for years. It was prepped to see what it wanted. The baby was just a sad coincidence. Or, as Andy has posited, synchronicity. Carl Jung would be thrilled."

"What is that?" Ross asked. "Synchronicity."

"The dictionary definition is the coincidental occurrence of events that seem related but can't be explained by science," Jason explained. "Something like that. It's also a great album by The Police."

Carrie sat amid the men, feeling small and very much at their mercy. They all knew more about her than she did. Except for Andy. She stole a glance at him. He looked just as shaken as she felt.

"What else do I have to look forward to, Jason?" she asked.

"Your mind will start to backfill," Jason said. "Like with your repressed memories. I bet you've remembered a lot more since we talked."

"Unfortunately, yes," Carrie said. She took Andy's hand. "I'm sorry. I shut you out. You had no idea what was happening."

"It's okay," he said, smoothing her fingers. "I hope you don't again. If nothing else, I want you to feel like you can talk to me."

Ross cleared his throat, and Carrie thought she detected a little impatience. "I'd like to get back to Chris if we could. I'm going to put out an APB on him and classify him as armed and extremely dangerous. Minimally, he'll be charged with kidnapping and rape in your case, Carrie, and once I get a DNA sample from him, we'll try to connect him with the deaths of these other women. That won't be easy—some of them have been missing for a long time—but forensics might be able to find a pubic hair or his skin under their nails."

Carrie felt herself imploding. "I can't believe he killed all those women. Because of me?"

"Don't make this your fault, Carrie," Jason warned. "It's not. Your brother is a sick man. Somewhere along the line, he developed an obsession with you. That's his fault—not yours."

"Jason is right," Ross said. "I see too much of this stuff in this business—it is *never* the victim's fault. Ever. That's just one more way he has of abusing you. Don't give it to him."

"So where is the son of a bitch?" Andy said.

"We suspect Chris has established residence here in the area," Evan said. "He hasn't applied for a Pennsylvania driver's license, that much we know. He could be renting a property under a different name or squatting somewhere—maybe in a hunting camp. But I doubt it. I think he'd want something permanent, someplace where he'd have relatively easy access to that hole in the ground on Round Top. This is a rural area—there's lots of places to disappear if you need to."

Ross looked at Carrie. "I did a little checking up on your whole family while I was looking at Chris. Your parents died in a car accident, correct?"

Carrie felt suddenly uneasy. "Yes."

"According to the report, your father's blood alcohol level was twice the legal limit. They were killed, but Chris walked away relatively unscathed. He was twenty at the time. You would have been fifteen."

"Yes," Carrie said. "I had to go live with my grandmother until I went to college."

She paused. Detective Ross was watching her. Andy was watching her, too, his brow knitted with apprehension. "You said Rachel died in a car accident. So did Ben. What are you saying?"

"I think there's a pattern, there, yes," Ross said quietly. "And I think, until we find your brother, you two should stay off the road as much as possible. I'm going to put two uniforms at your home. Are you staying there, Andy?"

"Yeah. I have been. I'm not going anywhere."

"Good. It'll be easier to monitor you."

Carrie shook her head. "No. I don't want anyone else putting themselves at risk on my account. I don't want the officers."

Ross looked at Evan, mystified. "Am I not being clear? Carrie, all evidence is pointing to the possibility—the probability—that your brother has killed thirteen people: nine women, your parents, his own wife, and your husband. If that's true, I guarantee that *that* guy—" he pointed at Andy, "is next on the list. He told you himself—Shaw told you—he'd find another way. Another time."

"You really don't have any say in the matter," Evan said. "Protecting the citizens of this state is our job. Thanks for the thought, but don't worry about it."

Carrie met this with silence. She felt exhausted by everything that had transpired, and it wasn't ending. Everywhere she looked, there was a new horror ready to rear up in her face—another kind of mean jack-in-the-box. The death of her parents seemed remote, and she had never really known Rachel. But Ben—poor sweet Ben, whose only misdeed had been to fall in love with her. It broke her heart, and though she'd cried enough tears for a lifetime already that day, she began to cry again.

"Why would he kill Ben?" she asked, though she knew the answer. Jason offered as much.

"He doesn't like anyone else having you," he said. "That's why Andy is in so much danger."

"Why did he let me go, then? He should've kept me."

"I suspect your brother is conflicted," Jason said. "He knows his feelings for you are wrong, and yet he can't help it. I think those other women served as surrogates. He picked them because they looked like you. But they weren't the real thing. He kept trying, unfortunately, and as he became more unsatisfied, he killed them. I suppose you could even say they saved you, in a way."

"Oh, God," Carrie said. "Please don't say that."

Jason shrugged. "He probably saw he was hurting you. His love for you is real—in a weird way, he wants the best for you. That's why he let you go."

"I wanted to die," Carrie said. "I stopped eating and drinking. It infuriated him. He tried to force food down my throat. He begged me to eat. Then he hit me. Nothing worked. He knew he was going to lose me. He wants to control everything about me. How I live. And how I die."

There was a beat of silence. Detective Ross cleared his throat again.

"All right. I'm going to put a statement out to the media. Clear up this pig people business so they can get off that and maybe help us find Chris. He's probably ditched his Maryland license plate and swapped it with a plate he stole off someone's car here. I'll run a check and see if any plates have been reported stolen in the last few days. If he's been to Round Top lately, he knows we've found his little love nest—sorry Carrie—which means he's on high alert. This will be a new feeling for him. He's flown under the radar for years."

"That's right," Evan said. "He could be pretty scared right now. He might leave the state. Or he might be getting ready to make one final move."

Jason put a hand on Carrie's arm. "How are you doing, kiddo?"

"Shitty," she said, and then laughed shrilly. "Embarrassed, of all things. I can't believe this is happening. It's too much."

She looked miserably at Andy. "If anything happens to you, I'll kill myself."

"That's not an option," Andy said. "Nothing is going to happen to me."

"That's right," Ross said. "Behave yourselves and stay home. Let us do our jobs. You'll both be fine. Two troopers are waiting to escort you home."

Andy stood. "Can we stop at the store on the way home? If we're going to be there for a while, we may need to stock up on a few things. Cigarettes and booze, mainly."

Ross chuckled. "Your sense of humor is still intact. That's good. You'll need it."

His smile faded. "Seriously, though. If you see Chris, do not engage him. Especially you, Andy. I know you'd like to punch his ticket but don't. Don't even think about your dad's pistol. Just call 911. Let us handle it."

"I won't do anything," Andy said. "I'm no vigilante. I would like one punch, though. One good, hard punch."

Mike and Evan exchanged a knowing glance. "We'll see what we can do."

Carrie got unsteadily to her feet and shook the detectives' hands. "I'm sorry about all this," she said. "I know you say it's not my fault, but I can't help feeling it is."

"I'm sorry I had to unload all of that on you," Ross said, looking genuinely apologetic. "It's the worst part of this job."

"And you have to do it all the time," Carrie said. "I don't know how you stand it."

Ross smiled thinly but made no reply. He ushered them out to the waiting troopers and bade them goodbye. "We'll be in touch."

Jason gave both Carrie and Andy long hard hugs. "Be safe, you guys. Call me if you need anything. You know, if you run out of the booze and cigarettes. Or, if you need to talk."

They thanked him and then got into Andy's truck. He drove them to the grocery store, the troopers following closely.

"Do you want anything special?" he asked. "Do you want to come in with me or stay here?"

"I'll stay here," she said listlessly. "I don't care. Get whatever you want. Do you need money?"

"No, I've got it." He paused, looking at her. "Remember what I said back there, Carrie. I love you, no matter what. I'm not afraid."

She wiped her eyes. "I guess you better be. You've got a fucking target on your back, thanks to me. I don't know how you can love me after what you've heard today. This is shit—nothing but shit. It's my life—and now it's yours. My brother's a lunatic and I'm bat shit crazy. Hallucinating pig people—alternate realities. An imaginary dead woman. And let's not forget the incest—oh my, no, that's the juicy part! Too bad I repressed it for so long—I could've been having this much fun a lot sooner."

"I wish you'd look at me."

She found she couldn't. Beyond him, she could see the troopers watching them intently. "Those policemen are wondering what the hell we're doing."

"Let them wonder. Look at me. Carrie, do you love me?"

With great effort, she met his gaze. Andy, with his sad gray eyes, full of hope and worry. His kind, generous hands. Andy, with his lost little boy and his broken heart. There was only one answer to that question.

"Yes, Andy," she said, her voice trembling. "I absolutely do."

His eyes shone. "Okay. That's all that matters to me. Wait here. I'm going to get some food, and then we're going home. We'll have a nice dinner, watch TV, and wait for this to be over. Then we'll get on with our lives."

He kissed her hands and got out, waving briefly at the troopers before trotting across the lot to the store. She leaned against the window and looked out on the strangely warm November day, a week before Thanksgiving. She should've told him to get a turkey—who knew how long they'd be holed up in her house, like fugitives. Not that it mattered. She wasn't feeling particularly thankful at the moment.

She was terrified.

 **A HALF-HOUR LATER, ANDY TURNED** down the drive to the house. As they pulled up to the garage, he saw something on one of the doors. He heard Carrie suck her breath in and looked at her. Her eyes were wide and staring, her hands clapped to her face. As he watched, she dragged her nails down her cheeks, leaving red wheals. A low moan began in the back of her throat.

"Carrie? *Carrie*? What is it?"

"Oh God," she whispered. "It's the third cat. It was him. He left a dead cat at Bert's. And he hung one on the door of my cage. Zane—Chris—asked me if I remembered, but I didn't. He was sending me a message. He was talking about Petey."

She looked at him hopelessly. "He's been here, Andy. Chris has been here."

The troopers backed in beside them and got out. Andy and Carrie got out, and they all approached the door. It was indeed a cat, an orange tabby this time. It hung limply on a nail driven through its chest. Andy put his arm around Carrie, as much for his own comfort as hers. The sight of the animal, dead as dead could be, brought the reality of what was happening home more than anything else had.

Both troopers were scowling deeply. One of them, Sergeant Pearson, according to his nameplate, stepped up for a closer look. "What does this mean?"

"It means my brother has been here," Carrie said. "He killed my cat when we were kids. As punishment for not—cooperating."

The troopers looked at one another and then drew their guns in tandem.

"Give me your key," Pearson said. "Wait here."

They walked around the house, checking the doors, and then went in, guns still drawn. They emerged about ten minutes later, announcing the all clear.

"Does the suspect have access to this house?" Sergeant Pearson asked. "A key of his own?"

"Yes," Carrie said wearily. "He does."

Pearson's partner, Adams, checked his watch. "We can have a locksmith out here and change the locks."

"This late on a Friday afternoon?" Andy asked.

He snorted. "For something like this? Oh yeah. You bet. We have a guy we use all the time. I'll call him. In the meantime, you guys relax as best you can. We'll be outside."

"Do you want some coffee or anything?" Carrie offered.

Pearson shrugged. "Nah. We're good. Maybe tomorrow. I hear the weather's supposed to get bad again. There's a big storm coming across Lake Erie. We're supposed to get almost a foot by Sunday."

Andy looked at the sky, which showed no sign of an impending storm. It was a fine clear blue. "Hard to believe, now."

The troopers went back to their car. Andy watched them through the window, joshing each other back and forth. They seemed to carry their duty lightly. He remembered standing in the yard, talking to Chris the night Carrie went missing. He had been there, moments before evidently, and taken his sister and put her in a hole in the ground, and then come back here and accused Andy of that very wrong-doing, or something similar.

"You ballsy, fucked up son of a bitch," he murmured, his breath fogging the glass.

He turned to find Carrie watching him. He went to her and wrapped his arms around her. She felt so frail. He bent and kissed her.

"How about I make us a big pot of spaghetti? We can have bread and some wine. I picked up a cake for dessert. I'm starving—aren't you?"

"I'm not hungry," she said, muffled against his chest. "Maybe in a little while. It's early. I would like a drink—I was thinking more along the lines of a big shot of whiskey."

He smiled and stroked her hair. "That does sound good. Go sit on the couch and I'll bring it to you."

"Will you please get rid of the cat? I can't stand it that it's still out there." She shook her head helplessly. "God, why did he have to do that? Poor things. They didn't deserve to die."

"It's pretty vicious," Andy agreed. "They can add animal cruelty to the list of things they read off while they're strapping him in the fucking chair. I'll take care of it."

The evening passed without incident. The locksmith came and had the locks changed on all four doors in about an hour. Andy immediately felt better, but Carrie seemed to get more and more depressed. She barely picked at her food; he wanted to say something but held his tongue. Around nine o'clock she brushed her teeth and went to bed. Andy followed suit, exhausted. He looked out the window at the patrol car and wondered how those two would be able to stay awake all night, and supposed it was not their first stakeout. He drew the blinds.

He stripped down to his boxers and crawled into bed next to her. To his surprise, she kissed him and slid her hand down into his shorts.

"Are you sure, Carrie?"

"I want you," she said. "I need you to make me feel good."

He was tired, but not that tired. "That's not going to be easy with two state troopers in the driveway, but I'll do my best."

But halfway through, he couldn't finish. An image rose unbidden in his mind, an image of Chris on top of her, doing this to her, and his erection folded like a luffing sail. He rolled away from her, embarrassed.

"I'm sorry. I can't do this. I got this image of Chris. Please don't get upset—it has nothing to do with you."

It did no good. She pulled the sheet over her and rolled onto her side, away from him. "It's all right," she said, her voice barely audible. "Forget it. I don't blame you. I wouldn't want me either."

He sighed. This ground was all too familiar. "I do want you. I'm just really tired, and I don't know why I thought of him. It's all so ugly, Carrie."

"You ran away from me today," she said. "I bet you wish you'd kept going."

He put his hand on her shoulder. "I ran out of there because I had to be sick. Hearing what he did to you literally made me sick. Where were your parents during all of this? And why would Chris kill them?"

She rolled onto her back and stared at the ceiling. "My mother knew. She walked in on us one night. Chris had started coming to my room, at first just to sit and watch me sleep. I'd wake up sometimes and find him sitting there. After a while, he got bolder and started getting into bed with me. Mom must've gotten suspicious because one night she just came into my room. She freaked out. She pulled Chris off me and grabbed a magazine—Vogue, I think. A big one. She started beating me with it."

"*You?*"

Carrie's face twisted. "She screamed and called me a whore and beat me with that rolled-up magazine like a dog. Chris just stood there, watching, and the whole time she was beating me, he never lost his erection. When she finished, she just walked out. She never said a word to him—she just gave him this hurt look."

Andy closed his eyes and remembered the picture the sketch artist had drawn. Two sides of a man, both malignant in their way, a monster created out of a savaged mind, yet very real. Prurient, foul, and cruel, but real.

"After she left, Chris got back in bed with me and picked up where he'd left off. Afterwards, he told me he would fix this. He was sorry she beat me, and he would fix it."

"But he let her beat you."

"Yes. She and Chris had a special relationship—that's what he told me. Then again, he told me she was jealous of our relationship, so who knows. Maybe he was playing us against each other. I don't think they did what he was doing to me, but I don't know for sure."

"Jesus, Carrie. Where was your dad in all this?"

"He was a drinker. I doubt he had any idea any of it was going on."

"Do you think Chris killed them?"

"Yeah. Yeah, I do."

"And you didn't remember any of this until you talked to Jason. How did he trigger it all?"

"He asked the right questions, I guess. No one's ever asked me about my brother. I don't even know how we got onto the subject. I thought we were going to talk about the pig people. Which, I guess we did after all."

He shook his head. "I'm so mad right now, Carrie, I feel like I could fly apart."

She touched him. "Don't be. There's nothing you can do about it."

"I know," he said. "That's the worst part."

The next morning, the storm Sergeant Pearson had predicted arrived with a vengeance. The temperature dropped twenty degrees during the night, and a stiff westerly wind had snow on it. A fresh set of troopers arrived, a pair of Smiths. They were older, and not overly friendly, perhaps not thrilled about sitting in their car all day in the middle of a snowstorm. Andy didn't blame them.

The day passed in slow motion; Andy felt tension piling up in him as deep as the snow on the walkway. By four he was restlessly staring out at the darkening yard, debating on whether to call Detective Ross. He had no reason to—he just wanted to talk to someone with authority.

At five his phone rang. He didn't recognize the number.

"Andy, this is Don Pritchard. I'm with the Vernon Volunteer Fire Department. Are your parents William and Judy Korn?"

A chill shot through him. "Yes. What's happened? Are they all right?"

"They're fine. A little smoke inhalation. They've had a fire at their home, I'm afraid. A pretty destructive one. Can you come back over here?"

Andy paused. "I'm sorry, what? I haven't been there today. What do you mean?"

Pritchard cleared his throat awkwardly. "I'm sorry, your mother said you were here earlier today. Talking about insurance, I believe is what she said."

Andy sighed impatiently. "My mother gets confused easily. She has dementia. Of course, I'll be right there."

"Great. They're at the neighbors' house. A Mr. and Mrs. Jack Kline."

"I know them. I'll be there in ten minutes."

"Make it fifteen, son. The roads are bad."

He ended the call and went to the living room where Carrie was staring at the TV. He sat down and put his hand on her knee. She looked at him with hollow eyes.

"I have to go out for a bit," he said. "There's been a fire at my folks' place."

Her eyes widened. "Are they okay?"

"I think so, but it sounds like the house is bad. I'm gonna go over and make sure they have a place to stay and stuff. I won't be gone for more than an hour."

"I don't think you should go," she said, her brow creased with worry.

"I have to, Carrie. They're my parents. Besides, Chris isn't going to run a Ford F150 off the road with a Prius. I'll be all right."

Once outside, he got the troopers' attention. Smith Number One rolled down his window.

"I have to leave for a while," Andy said. "My parents' house caught on fire."

"We heard that on the scanner. You want us to call a car?"

Andy hesitated. "They're ten minutes away. I really don't think you need to."

"You're not supposed to leave the house, sir," Smith Number Two said politely.

"They're very old. I have to. I'll be right back, and I won't go anywhere else."

Smith Number One gave a curt nod. "We'll let Detective Ross know."

"That's fine," Andy said, wondering if that was supposed to be some sort of threat. "Carrie's inside. Thank you."

The drive to his parents' house was slippery and nerve-wracking. He had to park down the street because of the firetrucks, and walked back, his breath pluming. He saw at once the house was a total loss. There was a big, smoking hole in the roof, and the upstairs windows were blown out, the siding charred and black. The house hadn't been worth much, to begin with; he assumed there wouldn't be much to salvage.

A fireman directed him to the neighbors' house. His mom and dad sat at the Prines' kitchen table, each with an oxygen mask up to their face. His dad looked tired and old; his mother, confused as ever.

"Why, hello, dear. I'm afraid your room got burned up."

"That's okay, mom. You and dad are all right?"

"It's that awful smoke," his mother said, coughing delicately. She nodded at Mrs. Kline. "If Peggy hadn't been doing her dishes and seen it coming from the upstairs window, we might both be dead. I had no idea anything was happening at all. And your father certainly didn't know—they're having a Matlock marathon on TBS."

"Mom, a fireman said you told him I was here earlier today. I wasn't, though. Was there someone else in the house?"

Judy Korn frowned in puzzlement. "He was such a nice man— he wanted to sell us some homeowner's insurance. Isn't that a coincidence? I was a little nervous at first, but he seemed harmless. He took a tour of the house and then said he'd be in touch. It wasn't a half-hour later that Peggy was banging on our door."

"Dad, did you see anybody in the house?"

Bill Korn scowled. "There wasn't anybody else there. I surely know when somebody's in my house—I notice *you* haven't been."

"I've been staying with a friend," Andy said, not wanting to get into it.

His father saw through that. "That minx from the TV. The pig woman. Spouting foolishness—probably hoping to get her own reality show."

"I hope that young man comes back," Judy said, sucking on her oxygen. "He had the nicest blue eyes."

Andy froze. "Blue eyes? Was his name Chris?"

Judy shook her head vaguely. "No. I think he said it was Andy. Maybe that's why I thought it was you. I get so mixed up sometimes."

"I have to go." Andy looked at the Klines. "Can they stay with you for tonight, at least? Until I make other arrangements?"

Peggy Kline offered him a sympathetic smile. "Of course. As long as they need to."

Andy trotted down the street to his truck, slipping on the icy pavement. He turned around in someone's drive, dialing his phone as he went. Carrie's phone rang and rang, and then went to her message.

"Goddamn it. Carrie—call me. I think Chris might be on his way to the house. Get with the troopers. I'm on my way."

He ended that call, trying to drive and dial at the same time. Detective Ross's number went straight to voicemail.

"Fuck." He waited for the tone. "Detective Ross, this is Andy Korn. I think Chris is making a move on the house. I've called Carrie. I had to leave because someone set my parents' house on fire. I think it was Chris. Please call me."

He put the phone aside and concentrated on driving. It was full dark now and snow had begun to fall in earnest. For the first time since this started, Andy was scared. If it had been Chris in his parents' house, that spoke of a profound level of psychotic planning. He knew he would have to create a situation serious enough to get Andy away from Carrie. But why? There were police at the house— if Chris didn't know that yet, he would find out soon enough.

"Because he's not after Carrie," he said aloud, his heart pounding. "Not yet. He's after you."

A car pulled up behind Andy, its lights filling his rearview mirror. Fear shot through him as it pulled around him in a swirl of snow and passed him, disappearing harmlessly into the dark, its taillights winking out of sight. Andy relaxed his grip on the wheel.

His phone began to ring. Detective Ross. He grabbed it and thumbed the answer tab, taking his eyes off the road for a second. When he looked back up, taillights, bright red in the white-out, filled his view. He jumped on the brakes, too hard. The truck's rear end swung out in a slow fishtail and then swung back. The right rear tire caught the thick snow on the shoulder. The truck flipped.

Andy's world went end over end. The airbag went off, hitting him in the face. Dimly, he could hear Mike Ross calling his name. The truck rolled several times down an embankment, where it came to rest on the driver's side.

He sat for a minute in the sudden silence, too stunned to move. Then he began to assess himself, flexing his fingers, moving each limb. Nothing seemed to be broken, except maybe his nose. It gushed blood, staining the airbag and his shirt. He unbuckled his seatbelt and looked for his phone; unable to find it, he clamored over the passenger seat to the door. It yielded to his push with a sharp squeal of dented metal.

He climbed out, cutting his hands on broken glass, and dropped to the ground, where he clung to the underside of his truck, his body trembling with shock. He heard a small swooshing noise and looked up. A figure was coming down the snowy embankment, but it brought him no comfort. It was Chris. He had a gun in his hand.

Andy decided his best bet was to keep the truck between them. He'd never make it up to the road, and if he ran off into the night, Chris would track him until he collapsed from exhaustion. They were surrounded by nothing but woods. If he could keep him at bay long enough, perhaps a passing motorist would see Chris's Prius and his tracks going off the road.

He heard Chris's footsteps come to a halt and saw his breath pluming on the other side of the truck. He muttered a curse.

"Where are you, corn-holer? You were supposed to die in the crash, dummy. I guess they really do build these things Ford tough. I see your tracks. I see your bleeding. Be a man and come on out. Let's end this."

Andy kept silent. He was sure Chris could hear his heart, it was thrumming so hard. He crept to the truck's nose, keeping low. It was hard to stand—his body wanted to lie down, and his head swam. He probably had a concussion.

"I guess you know by now how much I love Carrie," Chris said. "I see the police have been to Round Top. So much for the pig people story. She made that up to protect me, did you know that?"

"That's a lie, Chris," Andy said, unable to keep silent. "She's got PTSD, from all the shit you did to her. Couldn't you get a woman the regular way?"

Chris laughed. "You've seen the roster by now, I imagine. I can get any woman I want. But I want her. I've always wanted her. I guess we're alike in that regard, aren't we?"

"I am nothing like you, you fucking psychopath."

Chris laughed. "Psychopath. Ouch. Speaking of loonies, your mother is a real piece of work. Did they make it out of the house, or did I cook them?"

"They're fine," Andy said, struggling to control himself. "You didn't have to involve them."

"How else was I supposed to get you out of the house? Anyway, I did them a favor. They should be in a home. I know we're in agreement on that."

Andy said nothing. He continued to creep around the truck, marking Chris by his voice. He needed to keep him talking.

"Why couldn't you just be a brother to Carrie? What happened?"

There was a pause from the other side of the truck. "For years I was. Then one day, she asked me about the birds and the bees. She said mom wouldn't tell her. She was only ten—she hadn't even started to get her boobs yet—but I thought, what the hell. It was fun, telling her. It made me feel important. Then I asked her if she'd like me to show her. She didn't want to, at first. That night in the woods I finally wore her down."

"You raped her."

"Semantics. I don't know why I love her like I do. She's special. So fragile. I don't think mom cared about her like she cared about me. Dad was too busy drowning his sorrows. I had to love her. No one else would."

Andy sensed Chris had stopped, absorbed by his own tale. He eased around the bed of the truck, and there he was, his back to Andy. He broke for him.

Chris must have heard the rush at the last second, for he turned, catching Andy as he crashed into him. They went to the ground. Andy reared up and punched him in the face. The wreck had thrown Andy's balance off, though, and he toppled over from the force of his own blow. Chris still had the gun. He stood, and pointed it at him.

Andy got slowly to his feet. There was no arguing or bargaining with those eyes. They were as cold and flat as a squid's. He thought of Carrie and the unfairness of it all. How little time they'd had.

"I guess this is it, Andy," Chris said. "I'll tell her you tried."

"Please don't hurt her, Chris."

"I would never hurt her," he said and pulled the trigger.

The bullet took Andy in the breast. The force of it knocked him backward, and he fell and kept falling. There seemed to be no bottom anymore, and he spun into a world of white. His last thoughts were twofold: the first of his son, and how things were finally coming full circle. The last was a small piece of gratitude. At least he'd gotten his punch.

Then, lights out.

**CARRIE WAS IN THE BATHROOM WHEN** her phone rang. She never heard it, and she didn't bother to check it when she came out because she had checked it right before she went in. She went back to the living room and sat on the couch, the TV on low. The clock on the wall said it was close to seven. Andy had been gone for almost an hour.

She thought back to the night before and their failed attempt at love-making. Foolish, to think anything would ever be normal again. Nothing had ever been normal, to begin with. She was one of those horror stories she herself had described to trainees at The Women's Place. No wonder she'd been drawn to the work there. She'd lived it and hadn't known it. No one had—not even Ben. Now Ben was dead, because of her, and she knew the guilt for that would never go away, like Andy's guilt over his little boy.

Faintly, Carrie heard a noise that sounded like two pops in rapid succession. She sat up, unease creeping into her belly. She waited. Then she heard the garage door rumbling up. Andy was home.

She went into the kitchen, a greeting on her lips. It dried up in her throat like she'd taken a big dose of alum. Zane stood in the mudroom, his massive shoulders filling the small space. His eyes seemed to be lit from within, like a red-eyed jack-o-lantern. She shook her head and blinked, and it was Chris, of course, it was. Him, all along.

He grinned at her. "Hey, sis!"

She bolted for the door. He caught her as she clawed at the new deadbolt, blinded by her own hair. He hauled her back, lifting her off her feet, and she began to scream.

"You changed the locks, but not the keypad code for the garage," he said, grunting with effort as she struggled. "Details, Carrie. Details. I was always better at them than you."

He pulled a gun from his pocket and rapped her smartly on the head with it. It didn't knock her out, but it did knock her for a loop. She sagged in his arms. He laid her gently on the floor.

"That's it, there we go."

Her vision blurred. She kicked weakly at him. He pulled her hands behind her and she heard the muffled *zing* of a zip tie. Then he duct-taped her ankles together and hoisted her into his arms. He took her into the garage and stuffed her into the backseat of her own car.

"We'll have to take yours," he explained. "I parked the Prius at the end of the road so I could cut through the woods."

"Cops," she said thickly.

"Exactly. I couldn't very well drive up the driveway. I'm sure they were expecting me." He tucked her feet in and shut the door. He got into the driver's seat and started the Honda. "It was like shooting fish in a barrel. The first one was asleep—never knew what hit him. The second guy was so surprised I bet he didn't even have time to piss himself."

"Andy will be home soon," she said. "He'll know you took me."

Chris backed out of the garage and started down the drive. "No, he won't. Andy is dead, Carrie."

It was as if he had reached into her chest and ripped her heart out. The pain was terrible—literal, physical pain. She squeezed her eyes shut against it until tears slid down the sides of her face.

"No," she said, and it came out a sob. "Chris, why did you do that?"

"You know why. He was in the way, just like all the rest of them. I was so happy when I finally had a chance to get rid of Ben. God, I had to wait and wait for the right opportunity. Remember when I texted you and asked where you were? It was perfect that you were at a bar because I wanted to have a celebratory drink with you. Of course, you wouldn't know we were celebrating, but I would. And then to find you in the parking lot, making out with yet another guy! I couldn't believe it. God, I was so *pissed*.

"I stood there and watched you. After you left, I know Andy saw me. It took everything I had not to kill him right there. But I knew that would be a mistake. He drove off like a little coward anyway. He knew he'd made you into a whore."

"Did you run him off the road?"

"Yeah. But he didn't die in the wreck like the others. I had to shoot him. He died well—didn't beg or anything. I gave him an A for effort. But it's not the way I wanted it—I was hoping to make it look like an accident, like the others. Not that it matters—things have gone too far now. Wouldn't you agree?"

Carrie stared at the car's ceiling. Tears tracked down her face. God, it hurt so bad. "You just left him? Dead, by the side of the road, like a—a deer? Left him, dead in the snow?"

Chris's voice was brittle and annoyed. "Get over it, Carrie. You didn't really love him. You couldn't."

"Yes, I did," Carrie said. "I loved him so much."

With some effort, she sat up. She looked at Chris's reflection in the rearview mirror. He met her gaze. She had a brother in there somewhere, but he was not in evidence at the moment. She did not know the man who looked back at her.

"Did you kill mom and dad?"

"Fuck, yeah, I killed them. I told you I'd fix them. *Her.* It was pretty easy, actually. We stopped for lunch after they picked me up at the airport. Getting dad plastered was no trick. Then I just kept distracting him, and he finally drifted off the road. Of course, I didn't know if they would die—it was kind of a gamble, which made it more fun. I might've gotten myself killed, too. It was a chance I was willing to take for you, babe.

"And look how it worked out," he said happily. "After that, I did some research on how to run people off the road. It's not hard, and a great way to fly under the radar."

She looked away. "Where are we going? Back to Round Top?"

"No," he scoffed. "The police are all over that hill. They're finding all kinds of treasures, although this storm is probably putting the kibosh on the fun for now. I'm taking you to my little cabin in the woods. I bought the place after Rachel died."

"You killed her, too, you mean."

He shrugged. "Semantics. The cops will find it eventually, but it'll be over by then."

"You killed all those women, didn't you? Because they looked like me? Why, Chris?"

There was a long pause. "Because I couldn't have you. I tried to stop wanting you, really I did. Being a brother to you was never enough. But I did try. Those women were cheap imitations, at best. Once you've had the real thing, there's no going back."

"Like going from first class back to coach."

He laughed, delighted. "Exactly! You're my first class. That's why I married Rachel. She was my first attempt. She was a lot like you—funny, smart, hot. But, like I said. Not you."

Carrie looked out the window. They were on some back road, lined with trees interrupted by the occasional house. She had no idea where she was and didn't bother asking. What was the point? Andy was gone. A big hole had opened right through the middle of her. She wished Chris would kill her and be done with it. She said as much.

He looked at her for a long time. "I don't know what I'm going to do yet. I don't want it to come to that, Carrie. But—it's getting so hard. I shouldn't've let you go. But you were dying. I didn't want to lose you that way. I thought if I let you go I could buy us more time. Think up a plan."

He smiled at her. "And you helped. You remembered the pig people. I always loved that story. That's why I picked Round Top. Spooky, up there. And very creative, on your part. It's just one more way we're on the same wavelength."

"Thanks."

"Sure. I'd like to be able to stay up here—it's a nice place, I know you'll like it—but I doubt it will work. Even though it's deeded in Rachel's name—her maiden name—the cops will figure that out. I bought it for her before we got married. I had a feeling I might need it."

"Why didn't you bring me and the others here to begin with? You didn't need the pig people story. You didn't even know I was living it."

"Never shit where you sleep," he said, and then laughed long and hard.

He turned her car right, down a long drive. Faint tracks were outlined beneath the new fall of snow, and he followed them to a small house. Under any other circumstances, it would have struck her as quaint. Now, it looked like her final resting place. A monument to falsehoods.

He gathered her up and toted her to the front door, which he unlocked, balancing her carefully. The inside was sparse: a kitchenette and small living area that contained a yard sale sofa and a television with a DVD player.

"Do we get cable out here?" she asked.

"No, it's not hooked up. I just watch movies, or read."

He took her straight back to the bedroom, where she suspected she would be spending most of her time, what was left of it. He deposited her on the bed, facing the wall, and cut her bonds. She rolled over, rubbing her wrists, and swung her legs over the side and sat up. He shed his coat and sat down on the bed beside her.

"What do you think?" he asked.

"About what?" she said dully.

"The place—do you like it?"

"Oh. Sure. It's great."

"I knew you'd like it." He put his hand on her thigh. "How about you get undressed?"

"How about you go fuck yourself."

He sighed and reached into his coat pocket and pulled out the Glock. "Don't make me threaten you, Carrie," he said. "I hate it when you make me do that."

Anger began to fill her, like water flowing beneath the door of a flooding room, spreading in a smooth, ominous wave. She stood and turned to face him. She stripped, high color in her cheeks.

He watched, a strange light in his eyes; she saw his breathing deepen. He put his hands on her hips, the metal of the gun cold against her skin, and pulled her to him. He pressed his face into the flat of her belly.

"Remember when we spent summer vacation in Myrtle Beach? You wore that little black bikini? I took pictures of you running around on the beach in that thing. I still have them. You were thirteen, I think. Rachel caught me using them one day. Going down memory lane, you might say. She flipped out—called me all sorts of terrible names: pedophile, child molester. She threatened to call the police—to call you, even. But I couldn't let her do that. I know what a poor memory you have—I didn't want her to upset you."

"So you killed her. To protect me, like always."

He looked up at her. "That's right. Here. Lie down."

He moved so she could lie down on the bed. He laid the pistol on the bedside table and peeled his clothes off, never taking his eyes off her. She held his gaze, willing herself not to look at the gun. He climbed on top of her. Her body went rigid, her skin crawling with goosebumps.

"It's just us now," he said, stroking her cheek. "Whatever happens, we'll do it together."

He kissed her, but her mouth maintained a grim, hard line. He looked at her, frowning.

"Come on, Carrie. Stop being difficult."

He tried again, and this time, she opened her mouth to accept him. He slid his tongue in, probing deeply until she thought she might choke. She buried her fingers in his hair and met him, kissing him fiercely.

He broke the kiss, gasping. "Oh yeah. Now we're talking."

His mouth moved down her body, his tongue leaving a slick, like a snail trail. She looked at the gun. Her hand reached out; she could almost touch it. She kept her eyes on Chris, one hand holding his head, the other stretching, reaching. Her fingers grazed the barrel.

She pulled back as Chris raised himself and slid into her. She groaned a desperate sound, and pulled him down on top of her, tightening her legs around him.

"Hold me, Chris."

He wrapped his arms around her, his face against her shoulder. She held him, and she reached. Memories came to her in bright flashes: Chris, teaching her how to ride a bike; Chris, walking her to the school bus; trick or treating; Sunday dinners. Memories of a brother lost somehow, lost to something unnamable, crippling in its cruelty. It had cheated them both.

Her finger hooked the trigger guard and she brought the gun around and held it to her side. She felt his orgasm, filling her with his prurience. He raised up to look at her.

"I love you, Carrie," he said.

"I love you, too, Chris."

Then she shot him.

27

THREE WEEKS LATER, CARRIE SAT IN Jason's office, sipping eggnog, sans bourbon. Outside, light snow was falling. The Christmas season was in full swing, and Carrie was having a hard time with it. Loss bore down on her so heavily that, many days, she could barely get out of bed. Jason said this was perfectly natural.

"You've experienced more trauma in the last few months than most people have in a lifetime. Feeling that loss is part of the grieving process—even for the people you didn't know."

"It stings," she said. "Like a thousand bees. I wake up in the middle of the night sometimes, and I want to crawl out of my own skin. Sometimes I wake up in another room. My dreams are bad. I want to go backwards, but I don't even know how far back I'd go. To my birth? To Chris's? And if I did, what would I change?"

"It's immaterial. There's probably nothing you could have changed anyway. Hindsight is twenty-twenty, right? Your healing isn't in looking back—it's looking forward, at your future, and letting time take care of that sting."

He sipped his own eggnog. "It's been a week since we last talked. Then, when I asked you how you were feeling about Chris, you said you felt nothing. Has that changed?"

She considered. "Yes. I feel sad he was—what he was. Sad I had to kill my own brother. I know if I didn't, he would have killed me, and then himself. I try not to feel guilty. But he was still my brother. I loved him, despite everything. I just don't understand why. How? I'll never understand it."

"I'm sure it had a lot to do with his relationship with your mother."

"What a cliché."

Jason smiled. "And all clichés have a basis in reality. Most perpetrators have been victims themselves. Even if your mom and Chris didn't actually have sex, they obviously had what we call emotional incest, which can be just as damaging, psychologically."

"It didn't come from my mother," Carrie said. "Not all of it. There was a monster inside him. My mother may have nurtured it, but it was always there. A sad little boy with a monster inside him."

"And so perhaps you freed him," Jason said. "Better you than the state. He would've gotten the death penalty, I'm sure."

She shivered. "I have a hearing next week. My lawyer says I don't have anything to worry about—it's procedure. Self-defense, cut and dried."

She paused. "They've found all nine women. Five of them so far had Chris's DNA on them in some shape or form. Some of the families have said they'd like to meet me. I'm scared of that. I'm afraid they blame me."

"I don't think you're responsible for their closure to such an extent," Jason said. "I'd be wary of that. Maybe after some significant time has passed."

"I was thinking I'd start volunteering at The Women's Place again. I never thought I made much of a counselor, but now I feel like I can make a contribution. Do you think it's a good idea?"

"Not yet, Carrie. Give yourself some space. You have a lot of pain to expunge. Counseling other people and exposing yourself to vicarious traumatization would be dangerous. You have a budding relationship you should be focusing on right now. Concentrate on it, and getting well. In six months or a year, I think volunteering there would be noble."

"I do tend to rush things," she admitted.

Jason smiled. "You do. How are things going in that area, by the way? Your newfound love?"

"Good," she said, musing. "We have our days. Getting to know each other, I guess. Sometimes I feel like I've known him my whole life, and then he surprises me and I feel like I don't know him at all."

Jason laughed. "Sounds about right." He looked at his watch. "I think we're out of time for today. Next week?"

"Yes. Thanks for the nog." She stood, and then impulsively gave Jason a hug. "That's not appropriate, I know, but I don't care. Thank you, for everything. I am feeling better. It's slow, but I'm getting there."

"No harm in a hug," he said. "You take care—tell your fella I said hello."

On the way home, Carrie stopped at the pharmacy to pick up a few things. She drove home through the snow-muted streets, the late-morning traffic light. She pulled into her garage and cut the engine, listening to the cooling ticks. She went inside, kicking off her boots, and padded quietly through the house to the bathroom where she put away toothpaste, shampoo, and another item which she kept wrapped in a separate plastic bag. This she tucked beneath her hair dryer. Then she went into the living room and stopped, smiling at the man napping on the couch. His left arm, wrapped in a sling, lay draped across his chest. There was a freshly healed cut across the bridge of his nose.

She tip-toed over to him and kissed him lightly on the lips. He gave a start and then opened his eyes. He smiled.

"You shouldn't sneak up on an invalid that way," Andy said. "I might pop a stitch."

"You don't have any stitches anymore. Do you want some lunch?"

He sat up, wincing. She pulled his shirt back and looked at the ugly scar where doctors had removed the bullet that had missed his heart by inches and broken his shoulder instead. By the time Detective Ross found him, he'd lost a lot of blood, but Chris hadn't managed to kill him. Carrie got the news at the state police barracks, where she'd driven herself after killing Chris. The news saved her, for she felt she'd crossed over some invisible line, and there was no going back. If Andy truly was dead, she was going to kill herself.

But no, Andy was alive, Ross had said, and asking for her. Ross drove her to the hospital, and she'd wept with such relief at the sight of him. He'd spent two days there and was now on the road to a full recovery.

"Lunch sounds good," he said. He got slowly to his feet, wincing again, and she wondered if he wasn't milking it just a little. That was fine with her.

She made them sandwiches, and they ate at the kitchen table, watching the snow fall. He took a sip of water and then surprised her with a question.

"Would you marry me?"

She looked at him. "You're asking me over egg salad? I mean, are you asking me?"

He wiped his mouth with a napkin. "No. I don't have a ring. I just wondered if you would."

"I don't need a ring, Andy."

He finished the last of his sandwich. "All right," he said and took her hand. "Will you, then? Marry me?"

She looked into his sweet, hopeful eyes, and thought of the thing in the bathroom, wrapped in its plastic bag, and decided it didn't matter. She loved him, no matter what.

"Yes, Andy," she said. "I would love to marry you. I'll even take your silly name."

He raised an eyebrow. "Carrie Korn?"

She considered, and then laughed. "Okay. Maybe not. I'll keep Owens—for Ben if that's all right."

"That's perfectly fine, and the right thing to do." He sat back and looked at her, happiness spreading up his face. "Okay then. This is great. I hope I can make you happy. I'll try like hell."

She kissed him. "You already do. Shall we consummate this momentous occasion?"

He looked at his arm. "You may have to do most of the work."

Now she knew he was milking it. She grinned and took his hand. "It's not work. Come on."

Several days later, Carrie was downtown, doing some Christmas shopping. She was walking across the mall parking lot when she saw a familiar figure. Despite the snow, Reggie Spavine weaved his bike through the parked cars, GT riding on his shoulders. Reggie wore a battered Santa Claus hat and was belting Jingle Bells at the top of his lungs. There was something sardonic in his rendition; shoppers gave him a wide berth, laughing nervously at the spectacle. Carrie walked over to him.

"Hi pretty night lady," he said, slowing his bike and smiling at her. "You have come back from the brink. I saw on the Tim Horton's television that The People set you free. I am curious as to why you were sent back to the light unharmed."

"Not unharmed," Carrie said. "But not ruined. It was my brother who took me, Reggie. Not pig people."

Reggie absorbed this information slowly. "This explains why you were set free. The People would not be so generous."

"He was a sick man. He killed those other women. He was . . . divided. Like Jekyll and Hyde, sort of. You know what I mean?"

"Yes, I understand, and it makes much sense."

"Does it?"

"We are all halves of wholeness: darkness and light. There are even splits within the splits—perhaps your brother could not reconcile these? He longed for perfection, a concept which in itself is flawed. He could not differentiate between the light and the dark. To him, they looked the same."

He looked at Carrie solemnly. "He is dead, isn't he?"

"Yes. I killed him."

A look of terrible sadness passed over Reggie's face. "So much pain, pretty lady. I am truly sorry for you."

"Thank you, Reggie." She studied him. "So, the pig people don't exist. I created an illusion, to protect myself from the truth."

He began to pedal his bike slowly around her, as he'd done on that night a long time ago. "Perhaps you did. You told yourself a story, and the world needs its stories to survive. The story of government, the story of science. The story of God. People enjoy the concept of the true story, when in fact that puts the moron in oxymoron. The irony is, people are being drawn more to the story, and not the truth. When we choose not to see the difference between the two, then we become lost."

"Yes," Carrie said. "I see that. I have lived that. But it was not a conscious choice."

She watched as Reggie carefully lifted GT from his shoulders and set the big cat in the basket of the Schwinn. She reached out and stroked his head.

"You seem to eschew the idea of a good story," she said. "And yet you believe in the pig people? Because, that is a story, Reggie. Why are you creating your own illusion? Or is that the drugs talking?"

He tipped his Santa hat back and eyed her shrewdly. "That is another story people tell themselves to explain what they do not understand. I do not require the false benefit of mind-altering chemicals. I am, as they say, high on life, pretty lady. As to The People, they are real, to me. You have your stories—will you permit me to have mine?"

She met Reggie's dark eyes, black in the flat winter light, and saw pain there, and sadness, and longing. It tweaked her heart; she and Reggie were not so different, perhaps.

"Fair enough, Reggie," she said. "Have a Merry Christmas."

The young man lifted his cat back onto his shoulders. He laughed then, in a way that made her shiver, not from the cold. He pedaled away, still laughing, and plucked the hat from his head and tossed it into a garbage can.

Carrie walked to the mall entrance and turned back to look, but Reggie and his big cat were gone.

That night, Carrie had a dream. In it, she woke at some small sound and crept to the kitchen. There, sitting at the table, was Shaw. He was wet and bedraggled, his clothes torn in several places. One tusk had been broken off. She went over and sat down across from him. She felt no fear.

His blue eyes registered her and livened. He placed his thick hands on the table and reached hesitantly toward her. Then he stopped.

"What are you doing here, Shaw?" she asked.

"I came to see you one last time, Carrie," he said, his voice a low rumble. "Before I go."

"Where will you end up?" she asked. "Do you know?"

"No. I don't. I suspect I won't like it."

She hesitated and then slid her hand across the table to him, touching those wrecked hands. "Maybe only Zane will go. Maybe you can go someplace different."

He looked at her, his blue eyes full of regret. "No. We come as a set. I go where he goes. He won the fight, Carrie. I wasn't strong enough. Now we'll both pay."

Tears slid down her face. "I don't understand. Why couldn't you just love me?"

He looked at his hands, spread on the table. "I did. I loved you, and I protected you as best I could. But I couldn't protect you from the thing that counted most. My killer side."

He fell silent. She watched as a terrible sadness overtook him, and he sagged in the chair. She wept for this poor, amalgamated creature, who didn't know who he was, or what he was, and never would. A creature she had known all her life, and yet somehow, not. A part of her loved him, and always would.

"Thanks for letting me go, Shaw," she said.

He looked up at her. "Thank you for letting *me* go, Carrie."

"I don't think I really let you go. I think I pushed you."

He shrugged. "Semantics."

Two days later, Carrie stopped by Bert's office. She hadn't seen her old boss in months and figured she owed her a visit. She missed her gruff, matronly attentions.

Lola/Jennifer squealed with delight at the sight of her and gave her a big hug. Carrie's replacement, a young blonde, watched them shyly from her workstation. Bert herself came out at the commotion and dragged Carrie back into her office before dispensing her own bear hug.

"Sit," she commanded, clearing a chair of a pile of NASCAR magazines. "You're all over the news, girl. You're a real celebrity."

"A dubious one," Carrie said, smiling wanly. "How's the new girl?"

"She ain't you, but she'll do. How are you?"

"All right. Recovering. Getting lots of therapy. Sometimes I feel like it's all a dream, and I'll wake up, and Chris will call me. But he doesn't. It's better he doesn't. Or can't, I mean."

"It was him, all along?"

"Yeah. All those people—my parents, those women, two policemen, and Ben. And almost Andy."

"And almost you," Bert pointed out. "You know you did the right thing, don't you?"

"I did what I had to do. It doesn't make it any better."

"No, I suppose not." Bert sat back and sighed. "I ain't never killed anybody. Wanted to, but never done it. I don't envy you."

"I never thought I would," Carrie said. "And surely not my own brother."

"You got some big balls, I'll tell you that," Bert said, smiling. "What's next for you?"

Carrie shifted in her seat. "I'm getting married next summer. And we may have some other big decisions to make."

Bert looked at her for a long time, and Carrie felt she was reading her every thought. The big woman's watery blue eyes softened, and she nodded.

"Whatever you decide, I'm sure it will be the right thing," she said. "Don't let anybody make those decisions for you. Those are yours."

Carrie stood and gave Bert another long hug. "Thank you. I'll stop back and see you soon."

Bert gave a curt nod. "You ever decide you want to work again, you come and see me. I'll dropkick that hot little thing right out the back door."

Carrie went home. Andy was nowhere to be seen at first; then she saw the basement door ajar and remembered he'd said something about needing to change the furnace filter. Good. That would give her time.

She went to the bathroom and unwrapped the item from its plastic. She peed, and then stood looking at it, one hand braced on the counter, her heart pounding. A minute passed. She heard footsteps on the basement stairs. She'd not closed the door completely, and Andy rapped on it lightly before poking his head in.

"Hey. You're home. What's that?"

She looked at him, her lower lip quivering. His brow knit with concern.

"Carrie? What is it?"

She held it out to him. "It's a pregnancy test. I'm pregnant, Andy."

She looked down at the little plus sign, and she thought of Paula Davis and her poor, warped baby, and she thought how so much of life boiled down to a fifty-fifty chance that things would go right or wrong. She thought of Chris and the deep divide within him. She thought of Andy and his boy. Her knees gave out, and she reached for him.

And he caught her.

ABOUT THE AUTHOR

Nancy Williams is a graduate of Allegheny College and is a life-long resident of the very real town of Meadville, Pennsylvania. She is the author of four other books: *Hawkmoon, Grace, Blood Truth,* and *Rabid Philanderers, Inc. PIG* is her fifth. She lives in northwestern Pennsylvania with her husband, David and their cat, Chloe.

CPSIA information can be obtained
at www.ICGtesting.com
Printed in the USA
LVHW040036031122
732209LV00003B/421